# NECROMANCERS ON DRUGS

## by Jason Murphy

**Beaumont and Crane**

*Published by Beaumont and Crane, Inc.*

*ISBN-13: 978-1-7359761-4-3*

*Cover design by: Todd Gimbeltaube*

*Printed in the United States of America*

*For the mighty Redfern,
who slept on my feet while I wrote
most of this.*

*See you down the road, Big Guy.*

# CONTENTS

# ACKNOWLEDGEMENTS

*The following bit of weirdness would not have happened without Allison. Thank you, darling.*

*Thanks to Jeff, for helping me discover Clark's role in all of this. I'm in your debt.*

*To Rod – I'm so glad I can depend on you. Thanks for your suggestions. Thanks for your friendship.*

*To Marrit – You're an amazing editor. I am grateful. Let me know if things start to get out of hand, okay?*

# CHAPTER ONE

"Did those tacos give you hot snakes?"

"What?" Zeke asks, arching his eyebrow at me. He takes off his headphones, and I can hear the rapid-fire rage of early punk.

"Those tacos from the gas station. Did they give you diarrhea?"

He's disgusted, like I'm accusing him.

"'Cause you've got diarrhea face," I say.

"The hell are you talking about?"

"You look like you've got to poop. Two to beam down, Scotty. Like there's going to be a problem."

Zeke stares through the windshield, appraising the nursing home like he might have to fight it with his bare hands.

"I don't like nursing homes," he says.

It feels like we're going to be sitting in the parking lot a bit longer, so I prop my feet up on the dash and sip my coffee.

"No one likes nursing homes," I say.

"I have a phobia."

"Really? Why? Did something happen? Did you get locked in one overnight and then the old people shucked off their wrinkly skins and chased you around to suck the marrow from your bones?"

He rolls his eyes. He does that a lot. "It's way too early for you to be this weird."

"Well, what happened?"

"I have a phobia," he says, his words all sharp and pointy.

We sit in silence. When he doesn't put his headphones back on, I ask, "You want to know what my phobia is?"

"Werewolf Guy Fieri?"

"You want to know what my *other* phobia is?"

Zeke reaches down and draws a knife from a sheath on his lower leg. I'm pretty sure he won't stab me. Pretty sure. He looks down the blade, like he's checking the sights on a rifle. It's a nervous tic. "No," he says, "but you're going to tell me anyway."

"Pooping in public."

He sighs. "Man, that's like two poop references in two minutes. Are you okay?"

"You'd think that gas station bathrooms would be the worst, right? But most of them around here are actually pretty clean. The NuCare Pharmacy over on Cannon Drive, though? Jesus Christ. The door doesn't lock. And it looks like a war zone in there. I had to, one time. In there. I don't even know if I could tell you about it."

"Don't."

"But I had to go. I had to. You know? I was out of options. So, you know what I did?"

"Please stop."

"I overcame my phobia. I dealt with it."

He sheathes the knife and shakes his head. "Yeah. I get it. But you're messing with me. I need you to stop."

I take another sip of coffee. He's right. I *am* messing with him, but he's got to get over this. We need this job. The coffers of Occultex Incorporated aren't exactly overflowing with bounty. We're not just broke, we're *super goddamn broke*. Like scrounging for money under the couch cushions and taking frequent trips to the pawn shop broke. It turns out you can burn through thirty grand pretty quickly. Don't get me wrong, the money from the job at the Oswald Academy went to good use. Kind of.

Okay. So, I freaked out a little bit. Maybe kind of sort of had a nervous breakdown. It was a tiny one, I think, but after fighting the undead and demon children and casting spells, I started to think that maybe reality was bullshit and nothing mattered, so why not buy things that make me happy? There was a mania to it. New Chuck Taylors. Then some *more* new Chuck Taylors, but a different color. A nice couch. Some art for the walls. The new TV barely fits into the living room. I bought a bunch of books on the occult. Not the kind of things you can grab off Amazon, but the weird stuff. Leather tomes written by hand and allegedly in blood. I bid for one bound in human skin, but Zeke wouldn't let me pull the trigger on that one. I couldn't afford it, anyway. Flesh books are pretty pricey. It was a spending frenzy, and each time I swiped the debit card, a mad giggle bubbled up inside me, one in the back of my brain.

Why not? Nothing matters. Ha.

And I laughed some more.

When he was done mourning them, Zeke had to replace all the weapons he lost in the fire. He got a custom katana forged by some guy in Okinawa who professed to be an old wizard. There were some really shiny nunchucks, a bunch of throwing stars, a dagger that was allegedly used by a witch hunter, a bone-handled machete with ancient runes of protection scrimshawed into the pommel, and a new red bag to put it all in. He wasn't having any sort of breakdown. He's just bad with money and likes stabby things.

We'd blown through the cash. My justification was that I was afraid that all the lawsuits after the undead bloodbath would tie up our funds. But the Lazlo twins just paid everyone off—victims, lawyers, and I suspect, some police. The blame conveniently fell on John Elder, the unhinged tour guide of our little ghost-hunting expedition. He had a psychotic break, murdered people, and died in the fire. It was bullshit, of course, but once the juggernaut of money and legal manipulation started rolling, we all had to step out of the way. Hell, even the Oswald Academy itself was razed after most of it burned to the ground. Now it's on its way to becoming an overpriced and definitely haunted subdivision. It's like no one has seen *Poltergeist*.

"We need the money," I remind him.

"I know."

"The Lazlos know something about what happened to my friends. Getting close is the best way to expose them."

"Great plan."

"And they're the only ones hiring us right now."

We tried. We tried to hold down real jobs. It didn't work out. I was at teller at a bank for about two weeks. Then someone recognized me and made a big deal out of it. I was the guy from TV! Let's be honest, even a cursory internet search of my name will take you to some unsavory stuff. Fraud arrests, exposed as a charlatan, *etcetera*. I was let go. Zeke was a bouncer at a bar down on Sixth Street until he hospitalized a patron who wouldn't quit touching his mohawk. To be fair, I totally saw that one coming. I even tried going back to debt collections by phone. It was in an old strip mall between a nail salon and a bail bondsman. That lasted about three days. They don't want you to tell the senior citizens you're preying on that the material world is a lie and that the laws of man are just fictions we believe to avoid thinking about the horrible and dark truths of the universe.

"I know they're the only ones hiring us," Zeke says. "Doesn't mean I have to like it. You and I both know those fools belong in jail. *Under* the jail. They were involved in Elder's shenanigans. And they damn well know what happened to Alan and the rest of your old team. It stings more than a little to compromise my principles just to cash a check. And why can't they ever hire us to like … I don't know … mow their lawn or something?" he asks. "Or at least something cool, like an exorcism or wrestling a Chupacabra."

He's not wrong. The last few months have reduced us to being errand boys for those creepy old weirdos. I just kept getting drawn back. Once I was free of the Oswald Academy, I thought that maybe I'd sell my books and go work at a coffee shop somewhere. I'd never watch another horror movie, never go on another ghost hunt. Just put this nightmare behind me. But it was a scab. I had to pick it. If I kept picking at it, maybe the nightmares would go away. Maybe I'd stop feeling the madness squeeze my throat when I was in the shower or standing in line to get barbeque.

3

The jobs for the Lazlos were benign at first. On the east side of town, they sent us to fetch a pinata covered in blood and offal. I'm trying not to think about it. Two months ago, there was a tarantula in a shoebox. The owner claimed the spider was over a thousand years old and could pick lottery numbers with 80% certainty. He lived in the back of an abandoned McDonald's. Two weeks ago, we peeked inside another package they had us pick up, only to find a severed hand. I stopped being curious after that. They've been stringing me along, promising hints of the truth about the Lighthouse, Alan and my friends, and everything that kickstarted the fecal monsoon that my life has become. But nothing. They know I need the money. I've been trying to keep my enemies close, but I think maybe they're keeping me closer.

Today, the job is an old man. We're busting him out of the Cavendish Assisted Living Facility. As always, the Lazlos were stingy with the details, but Rupert assured me this would be an action-packed morning. He chuckled, elbowed me, and winked, like he and I were sharing a lewd joke.

"Pick old Harvey up, sneak him out the back, and don't let any of those fuddy-duddy nurses see you or boy howdy, there's gonna be trouble!" he said, while his sister, Kitty, just grinned and nodded from her wheelchair.

I've gone from fighting undead horrors at an abandoned school to breaking a geriatric out of a nursing home. Life is awesome.

Zeke sneers at his cat-patterned scrubs.

"Pretty sure those are for women, dude," I tell him.

"Doesn't bother me," he says. "It's the cats. I don't like cats. You know this."

"But they're wearing tiny stethoscopes!"

"I hate you," he says. He takes a deep breath, closes his eyes to focus, and throws open the car door. "Game time."

\*\*\*

We cross the parking lot like gunslingers. Very nervous gunslingers. Our car sticks out among the pearl-white vans and modest sedans. The gleaming vans all say "Cavendish Assisted Living" on the side and are parked in rows, soldiers awaiting orders. Our Civic has some sort of weird leprosy on the hood, more than a few dents, and a Big Boys sticker Zeke slapped onto the bumper. Zeke himself isn't exactly inconspicuous either. I asked him to wear a hat to cover his mohawk, but he looked at me like I'd asked him to stop being black for a few minutes.

Suddenly, I'm very afraid that this is going to end up with us in jail. I worry about that a lot these days. I'd rather go back to fighting ghosts.

Nursing homes all look the same, with soft gray bricks and just enough foliage so that it doesn't look like a prison or a hospital. Tucked away in South Austin, this three-story building is indistinguishable from the extended-stay hotels that flank it.

"Game time," I say in a gravelly voice. "It's game tiiiiiime."

"Now's not the time, bro," Zeke mutters as we make our way up to the tasteful topiary lining the front walk.

"No, because it's *game time*," I say, chuckling. "When did you start saying that?"

"Just now," he says.

"Game time! It's cool. Maybe I need something badass to say before we start a job, like *let's rock!* Or maybe *go time*. That's a good one. *Go time. Go* time and *game* time."

"Don't be nervous, Clark. We got this."

"I'm not nervous."

"Yeah," he says. "Yeah, you are. You get all annoying like this when you're nervous."

"You're nervous, too!" I say, but looking at him, you wouldn't know it. Even in nursing scrubs, the kind with little cats dressed like doctors, Zeke looks languid and cool, like nothing can bother him. And if something *tries* to bother him, it might regret it. He moves with easy grace, sliding through the world.

"I'm not nervous," he says. "I was nervous, but then I focused my *chi*."

"You focused your chi? Because it's game time?"

"Exactly," he says, and opens the door.

In the lobby, we're hit with cool air and the smell of industrial cleaner masking years of incontinence. I see Zeke swallow his fear. We walk right past the front desk without acknowledging the receptionist. She raises her head to say something, sees our scrubs, and goes back to her computer.

Through the lobby is a modest cafeteria decorated with benign pictures of smiling families that probably came with the frame. It's all walnut tables and mauve carpet. A few people mill about. Some are pushed in wheelchairs. Others read the paper or just stare out the window. To our left, a set of doors leading to the east wing. To our right, the west. Dead-eyed orderlies trudge back and forth, not sparing us a glance. We both notice that unlike our scrubs— mine green and Zeke's feline—theirs are muted blue. Zeke shoots me a worried glance. His eyes spark, and I can feel his *chi* leaking out onto the floor.

"Keep it together," I tell him.

"It's together. It's all together. Where do we go?"

I look at the name written on my hand.

"Harvey Bunson," I tell him. "That's all they gave me."

"Bunson? Like the Muppet?"

"I guess, yeah."

"Where in the hell is he?"

Before I can again tell him that I really don't know, an orderly yells from the other side of the lobby, "Hey, Laura, tell Chad I've got to take Mr. Morgan back to his room. We've had an accident."

He wheels Mr. Morgan around and heads to the west wing. Mr. Morgan is a gnarled old root, hands clutched to his chest, and a gown that slips open to reveal a patchwork of occult tattoos.

Didn't expect that.

I'm not sure who looks more miserable, the orderly, or the withered old man in the chair.

Then I realize it's Zeke. Zeke is the one who looks the *most* miserable. Standing at the intersection of hallways, his eyes are wide and his lips move without making sound.

"Hey. Hey. Game face. Game face!" I tell him in a whisper.

He recovers, swallowing it all down again.

"I'm good," he says. "But if Bunson shits in the car, I'm gonna get out and walk."

"Don't be a dick, man. They can't help it."

"I know! That's why it freaks me out, okay? It's mortality, bro. It's the horrible goddamn future that waits for us all. I can't handle that."

"We've fought the living dead together, but it's a senior citizen that makes you worry about your own mortality?"

"Yes! I'd rather these people jumped out of their diapers and tried to kill me. I would feel a whole lot better for me *and* them. Instead, we're here in this tomb and they're all trapped and waiting to die, and it's breaking my heart, and I really don't ever, ever, ever want to go out like this, you hear me, bro? Fuck this!"

I grab him by the arm and drag him aside. Laura, the girl at the front desk is watching us.

"Hey. I get it," I tell him. "But now's not the time for an existential crisis. Let's find this guy, toss him in the back seat, and haul his ass back to the Lazlos, okay?"

Beads of sweat collect on his forehead. He's already got pit stains, even though it must be 65 degrees in here.

"Okay?" I ask him again. "It's game time, right? Game time!"

"Yeah. Yeah man," he says, and takes a deep breath, trying to shake it off. "I'm good. I'm good."

"Okay," I say, and smile at Laura across the way. I hope she hasn't called security yet. "You want to go sit in the car? Keep it running in case we have to escape? That would be pretty badass, right? Would you feel better if we like beat some people up or something? Set something on fire? 'Cause I'll do that for you. You know I will."

Zeke nods. "I know you will, Clark. I know. But I'm good. Let's just do this, okay? I got it. I'm here. I'm with you."

"Okay," I say and give Laura another *everything is fine* smile. "I'm going to go talk to this lady and see if I can figure out where they're keeping Harvey. You wait here. Focus your *chi*."

Zeke nods, closes his eyes, and tries to control his breathing.

At the desk, Laura summons her customer service smile. "Is everything okay?"

"Asthma. What kind of cleaning products are you using here, Laura? That can't be good for the residents. I might have to file a report."

"Oh!" she says, her smile melting. "Oh, I don't know. I could …"

"Whatever," I say, acting agitated. "Where is Mr. Bunson?"

"Mr. Bunson?"

"Harvey Bunson. He's supposed to be waiting in the lobby, per our instructions."

"Oh. Well ..." she looks to her computer.

"This was fifteen minutes ago, Laura. We're on a schedule," I say and give her an exaggerated sigh. "I can't believe this. Is the administrator here?"

"Well, he … I can call him if you—"

"No. Just tell me where Mr. Bunson is right now. Harvey. Bunson. We'll go get him ourselves if you people can't be trusted to do your jobs."

She types his name into the computer. "Well, he's in the high-risk ward, Mr. …"

"Yeah, I know he's in the high-risk ward, Laura. That's why they sent two of us. You know what could happen if he doesn't make this appointment, right? You understand that?"

"No," she says, wilting under my barrage of bullshit. "What … what could happen?"

"Bad things. Very bad things, Laura. Now, are you going to badge us into the east wing, or are we going to have to stand here until somebody who knows what they're doing shows up?"

"Sir, the high-risk ward is in the *west* wing."

"Great. Are you a tour guide? Or are you going to open the damn door?"

Her mouth flops open and closed. There might be tears.

7

I rub my eyes with my thumb and forefinger. "I'm sorry. That was mean. This ... this is just really stressful. You know how it is, dealing with all this. This stuff. The high-risk stuff."

"Oh. Oh sure. I'll badge you in. I'm so sorry for the inconvenience," she says.

"What room?"

"Umm. 237."

"Because of course it is. Thanks, Laura. You're great. I'll tell Leon how much help you've been," I say as I walk away.

"Who is ... Leon?" she asks.

"Take care, Laura!" I wave over my shoulder and nod for Zeke to hurry his ass up.

As we get to the door, a green light above flashes, and the lock disengages. I smile again back at Laura. She gives a feeble wave as we enter the west wing.

"What the hell is the high-risk ward?" Zeke asks, his voice nearly breaking.

***

The west wing is more institutional than the lobby or cafeteria. Gone are the soothing colors and AM Gold playing over the PA. This is white-on-white. Stark corridors with doctors flanked by nurses and people hooked up to quiet machines in cold rooms.

Zeke and I walk with a purpose, like we belong. Going somewhere off-limits is a lot like shoplifting. If you act like nothing's wrong and you're supposed to be doing what you're doing, no one will question you. Zeke's anxiety is rubbing off on me, however. Nervous sparks crackle up and down my spine as I try not to check the faces of the people we pass in the hall. Are they looking at us? Do they cast suspicious glances at our scrubs or at *Zeke's damned mohawk*?

The worst that could happen is that we get ejected. Maybe the cops get called. It wouldn't be the first time. Back in my ghost-hunting days, I got the cops called on me for trespassing all the time. I'd get a slap on the wrist, and they'd let me go.

This feels different, though. This feels like a Lighthouse. I keep stealing glances at lab coats, looking for the blue logo. The moment we set foot in here, I began looking for it on the walls or emblazoned on a door. A blue lighthouse with an all-seeing eye on top. I look for it everywhere now, like it's lurking around every corner. Even when it's not there, I see it. I dream about it. In my dreams, I'm minding my own business. I'm at the liquor store or the pharmacy, buying candy and toilet paper when the lights dim, and I find that I'm alone. Then the shrieking starts. The sounds come from over the PA system. Mixed within the cacophony are the wails of my friends. I try to run, but I can't find my way out. And the lights keep getting dimmer until it goes dark.

Yeah. It's a real drag.

Next to me, Zeke goes rigid. He grabs my arm, squeezing far too tightly, and pulls me aside.

"What is—?" I start to ask, but then I see it.

Coming down the hall is a group of orderlies. The four of them move slowly, like a funeral procession. Each of them holds a thick, metal chain tethered to an ancient looking woman in a wheelchair. To say that she is old is to say that the sun is warm. If her eyes weren't fluttering, I'd think she was a corpse exhumed from some crypt. Her skin is paper-thin and mapped with infinite lines. Wispy strands of white hair cling to her head. Her spindly wrists are strapped down to the arms of the wheelchair. A fifth orderly, his face ghost-white with fear, pushes her along. Leading the way is a priest in full vestments—the long robes, the aspergillum, and the tufted biretta hat. He stares at the floor, lost in his prayers and sprinkling holy water in his path.

"Ecce Crucem Domini," he says.

"Behold the Cross of the Lord," the orderlies say in unison with quavering voices.

"Fugite partes adversae."

"Be gone all evil powers."

Zeke and I let them pass. I bow my head in prayer, repeating the litany along with them.

Bringing up the rear is a beast of a man, all dressed in purple. Muscles bulge under purple coveralls. His purple hockey mask is decorated with sigils I don't recognize. I didn't expect purple hockey masks, much less enchanted ones. He's carrying a long cattle-prod-looking thing, waiting for something to go down. Zeke's going to want to fight this dude. I just know it.

The moment they round the corner, Zeke and I follow. They inch down the corridor, doctors and nurses all stepping aside. Finally, at the bottom of a ramp, they make their way to the door we need.

High-Risk Patients and Class Three Authorization Only Beyond This Point.

A doughy but armed security guard flashes his badge across the reader, opening a pair of steel doors. The old woman begins to twitch, causing the priest to splash a spray of holy water across her. She writhes in her restraints, and the chains go taut as the orderlies pull as far away from her as possible without letting go.

9

Zeke and I watch as long as we dare before continuing down the hall. Once we're clear, I glance up and down the empty corridor and drag him into a storage closet.

Both of us gasp and try to catch our breaths.

"What in the actual fuck?" I ask.

"Is it weird that I feel better about this whole thing now?"

"How does *that* make you feel better?"

"That was something I can kick in the face. This is my wheelhouse."

"Well now I'm a little freaked out. I thought this was a nursing home!"

Zeke shrugs. His cool returns, cascading over him. "I guess it's a nursing home for evil old hags."

"Yeah. Fine. But what now?" I ask, looking around.

It's a supply closet full of toilet paper, adult diapers, and the like. Part of me was hoping for maybe some pepper spray or a holy shotgun.

"We walk out there and make security dude open the door," Zeke says, like it's the most obvious thing in the world.

"How?"

"I've got like three knives on me right now. It won't be a problem."

"You are not stabbing a security guard."

"Can I kick him?"

"Maybe."

"'Cause I kinda want to kick every damn person in here."

"Yeah, I'm with you on that, but if we can get out of here without committing felony assault, I'd prefer that."

"Man, I just want to know what's up with this Bunson dude."

"What do you mean?"

"I mean, if they're keeping him in the high-risk ward, what's his deal? Are we gonna need a priest just to get him out to the car?" Zeke asks.

"Shit."

He's right. This just got more complicated.

"Listen, I ain't worried about it," Zeke says. "Bunson acts up and starts with some black magic or whatever, I pop him in the mouth. It's cool. But how do you want to get in there?"

I look around the room and see just what we might need. "We're gonna Chewbacca this."

\*\*\*

Zeke's heavier than he looks. He's pretty lean and all muscle, but with him strapped to a hand cart like Hannibal Lecter, it's all I can do to keep from dumping him on the floor. We kept the straps tight to make it convincing and pulled a laundry bag over his head.

I wheel him around the corner and nearly tip him over.

"Dude!" he says with an angry whisper. "Careful."

"I'm trying. I'm not good at this. Just be quiet. Someone will hear you."

"This bag smells like old man ass. I think it might have been a diaper bag."

"We're almost there."

When we get to the ramp, the guard raises his eyebrows.

"Here we go," I whisper to Zeke.

He begins to fight and thrash against his restraints. I can barely steer him down the incline. The guard comes to help.

"What the hell is this?" he asks. "There's not another scheduled transfer on my list."

"Do I look like administration to you?" I ask him.

Zeke begins to growl. That might be a bit much, but it seems to work on the guard.

"Is he not sedated?"

"We shot him up with fifty cc's of ephemerol!"

Zeke wrenches his body hard enough that the cart tilts onto one wheel.

"Damn it!" I say and struggle to keep him from falling to the floor. "Can you just help me out here?"

The guard moves to help me hold him in place.

"No, man. The door. Just get the damned door," I say.

"I just need to check—"

*"Fichas jahakes moon!"* Zeke says in a feral growl.

The guard steps back.

"Oh no," I say. "His gag came out."

"Addrivat! Addrivat!" Zeke says.

The guard fumbles for his badge. "Should I call someone?"

I wrestle with the cart as Zeke continues to spout nonsense through the linen bag. "Just open the damn door before he casts a spell or some shit, okay?"

The sensor buzzes with a swipe of the badge, and we're in. Behind us, the guard quickly closes the doors, and we're in another hallway. More antiseptic white and blinding fluorescents. Zeke quits struggling as I wheel him past more rooms. These doors are reinforced steel with embedded windows of bulletproof glass. Many of them are scuffed and scratched from the inside, and I'm reminded of a lion exhibit I saw once at the Phoenix Zoo. I check to make sure we're not being watched before hurriedly unlashing Zeke.

He jerks the bag off his head and gags as he tosses it to the floor. "The smell's not going away. I'm gonna be living with that for a few days. Barf."

We shove the hand cart and restraints into a corner and continue down the hall. In each of the rooms is a new horror.

A man in a medieval monk's cloak, walking from corner to corner of his otherwise empty cell.

A round woman in a flower-print dress and blue hair, calmly rocking back and forth in an old wooden chair. She could be a grade school teacher or a librarian. Her face is completely smooth. No eyes. No nose. No mouth.

A naked old man, crawling along the wall like a spider.

"Oh holy shit Jesus Christ," I say under my breath.

"Did they say this Bunson dude had to be alive when we drop him off?" Zeke asks.

"It was implied, I think."

"Great."

Room 237 is midway down the hall.

"I don't want to look," I tell Zeke. "You look."

Zeke peeks in. "Just another old dude."

"If he was just another old dude, he wouldn't be in here. And if he was just another old dude, your voice wouldn't be shaking."

Zeke crosses his arms. "I ain't shaking."

"A little. And you've got pit sweats."

"I was exerting myself by pretending to be crazy."

I look him up and down. "Do you need to go wait in the car?"

"No, damn it. I'm good. You're infantilizing me and—"

Another orderly walks by and nods politely at our manufactured smiles.

"Can we just do this and get out of here?" Zeke asks.

The mere implication that he's scared is enough to piss him off. If that's what I need to do to help him keep it together …

"Is he floating or anything?" I ask. "Does he have like snakes for eyes or something? Is it some *Nightbreed* shit? I don't think I can handle any *Nightbreed* shit right now."

Zeke takes another peek. "Nah. He's just watching TV."

Zeke's right. Harvey Bunson is an old guy in a white jumpsuit, reclining on his bed while watching some soap opera on a small TV in the corner of his room. He's balding and leathery, the kind of guy you'd end up sitting next to at a dive bar, the regular who'd maybe been banned two or three times for screaming or pissing in the corner.

"Okay," I say. "Let's grab him and go."

The door won't open. Another badge scanner is embedded in the wall next to it.

Zeke dangles the guard's badge at me. "Boom," he says.

"How the…? You were all tied up."

"Don't doubt me, son," he says and waves the badge over the scanner.

Harvey Bunson glances over his shoulder when we step inside.

"Harvey," I say. "We're with Occultex Incorporated. Time to go."

A grin spreads across Harvey's face, revealing rows of nicotine-stained teeth.

"Hot damn! 'Bout time. I'm ready. Let's go," he says and claps his hands.

"No witchy business," Zeke says. "You cast a spell or turn into a snake or something, I'm gonna put you down. Got it?"

"Yeah," Harvey says, suppressing a laugh. "Yeah, man. Whatever. Let's do this. It's game time!"

Zeke and I flank him, each of us taking an arm. We lead him down the hallway, walking as fast as we dare.

"We can't go the way we came," I say.

"Yeah," Zeke says, steering us the other direction. "Harv? Got any ideas?"

Harvey points. "This way, then hook a left. There's an emergency exit next to the stairs."

We're hustling in that direction when a doctor walks by. I try not to look at him, but from the corner of my eye, I see him turn and stare as we pass. Zeke shoots me a worried glance.

"Keep moving," I whisper.

A few more turns and I see the red bar across the emergency exit door. The old man was right. He's practically bouncing in our grip, his face beaming.

"Would you be cool?" I ask him.

"Yeah. Yeah. I'm just so happy to see you. Happier than a puppy with two peckers."

"Right …" Zeke says.

We pause at the emergency door. "The alarm is gonna go off," I say.

Zeke says, "Just do it. Go around and get the car. Harv and I will keep—"

"Hey!" A voice says. "Hey! Stop!"

The security guard and the doctor come rushing up to us.

"What the hell are you—" the guard starts.

Zeke cuts him off with a piston-kick to the guy's stomach. The guard goes down with a groan that sounds like his soul is escaping. Stunned, the doctor staggers backwards and throws up his hands. Zeke snarls. The guy turns and hauls ass back down the hall, his lab coat flapping behind him.

I shove the door open and the alarm begins to whistle. We're out behind the building, surrounded by stacks of wooden pallets and grimy dumpsters.

"Fresh fuckin' air!" Harvey cackles. "Goddamn sunlight!"

We run as fast as Harvey can keep up, trying to make our way through the alley and to the front lot.

"I guess we should have had an exit strategy," Zeke says.

"I thought we'd just walk in and push some guy in a wheelchair out to the car. Bam. Done," I say.

"Not quite," Zeke says as we round the corner. He nods behind us, where a gang of orderlies spills out of the fire exit. "Want me to?"

"No! Just go. Run!" I say, because all we need is Zeke murdering a bunch of guys with his karate.

We race across the lawn and through the parking lot. Harvey is just able to keep up with his old-man trot. More orderlies emerge from the front doors. They spot us just as we get to the car. We pile inside and I say a little prayer of thanks as the engine starts. I'm never sure it will.

Tires squeal. I whip the Honda around in reverse and nearly clip a white minivan that sits in a row of other white minivans. The engine sputters and coughs before finding its rhythm. We lurch forward and peel out of the lot. The scrub-wearing goons chase after us in the rearview, shouting and shaking their fists.

Harvey rolls down the window and climbs halfway out.

"What the hell are you doing?!" I yell.

He howls with laughter and shoots them the finger. "Suck my saggy balls, you fascist shitbags! Suck 'em!"

***

# CHAPTER TWO

I jerk the wheel right, skidding around a turn. Harvey nearly goes tumbling out the window, but Zeke snatches the back of his jumpsuit and pulls him inside. Harvey laughs and slaps his knee.

"Woo! You boys want to get some blow?"

"What?" I ask.

"I mean, I'm a little strapped for cash right now, but I'll get you back," he says.

"No, Harvey. We don't want to get any blow," I tell him and turn to Zeke. "Does he mean cocaine?"

"We're not out of the woods yet," Zeke says, and looks behind us.

Down the road, a white minivan with the Cavendish logo on the side careens around the corner.

"Great," I say and take the first turn down a tree-shaded street lined with midcentury modern ranch houses. "We've got to get the hell out of here."

But I don't know where we are. I don't know this neighborhood, so I take random turns, doubling back on our path and winding deeper into suburbia.

"You're trying to outrun these bastards in a Civic?" Harvey asks. He's clutching the strap in the back that most people use to hang dry-cleaning.

"I didn't know this was going to be a getaway kind of thing," I say.

I try to head northwest, toward the highway, but I slam on the brakes as we barrel into another *cul-de-sac*. Zeke clutches my arm before I can throw it into reverse. In the rearview, one of the white vans blasts by. We hold our breath for a second more.

"What? Holy shit!" Harvey says. "Bill! Yeah. Yeah … it has been a long time."

He's grinning and nodding his head, looking at the empty seat next to him. For a second, I thought he was on the phone.

"Five goddamn years," he says.

"Yo," Zeke says, interrupting him. "Yo. Now's not the time for some *A Beautiful Mind* meltdown, okay?"

Harvey rolls his eyes and looks at Zeke. "Rude," he says.

"Just sit your ass still and quit babbling," Zeke says.

At Zeke's feet is his new red athletic bag, brimming with nasty weapons. He keeps nudging it with his heel. It's his security blanket. His eyes scan the neighborhood, watching for Cavendish vans, but I can see what's happening. Part of him is taking mental inventory to determine what he might need if we get pulled over. Nightstick? Hatchet? A gladius with Latin etched into the blade?

"Midnight?" Harvey says, and leans over to intently listen to something only he can hear. "Yeah," he says, muttering as if his bookie just gave him a big tip. "Yeah, I can do that. *Fuck* yeah."

Zeke narrows his eyes and shakes his head. "This is some foolishness, Clark."

"I know."

"You know how I feel about foolishness."

"I know," I say and start to turn.

"Wait!" Harvey says.

I brake. At the end of the block, sitting at a stop sign, is another white van. It's waiting. We're at an intersection with the nose poking out from behind a tree and a car parked on the street. I don't think they've seen us. If I gun it, I can zip across before—

"Don't," Harvey says, without even looking.

"Listen," I tell him. "Just shut up for a second, okay? I need to focus."

"Wait," Harvey tells me, looking down at his hands. "Ten more seconds and that van is going to go left."

"What?" I ask him.

"Four ... three ... two ... one ..."

Zeke and I crane our necks to check. The Cavendish van pulls out into the street, turns left, and heads in the opposite direction.

"Okay ..." I say and take one last look up and down the block.

"Nope!" Harvey yells again.

"What then, damn it?!" Zeke asks.

"Two on your left. Hold what you've got," he says, and he tilts his head like he's struggling to hear.

Half a block to the left, a white van pulls into the intersection and stops.

"Wait for it," Harvey says.

Another van comes up behind them. They pull up next to each other, roll down their windows, and the drivers begin to chat. They're exchanging plans with their hands, mapping out the patterns they'll take through the neighborhood as they fan out and hunt for us. After another second, they break off into different directions.

"Okay, go!" Harvey says, and I jam on the gas. "Go! Straight! Go go go!"

We dash across the street just as I catch yet another van prowling into the intersection.

"How many of these assholes are there?" I ask.

Zeke takes a long, hard look at Harvey. "And why send so many people after this guy? Why are you so damned important?"

Harvey waves Zeke off, listens to the empty space next to himself, and says, "Turn here."

I turn left. Another shallow *cul-de-sac.*

"Damn it, Harvey," I say as I brake and start to spin back around.

"No," he says and points to a house straight ahead. "There. Driveway. Pull up there. Right now."

I look at Zeke. Zeke shrugs.

"Hurry!" Harvey says.

I steer the Civic up into the driveway. The blinds are closed. The lights are off. Nothing special about this house, as far as I can tell. It's a mid-mod ranch house with brown brick and some children's toys decorating the lawn.

"Harvey? What—" I start, but Harvey just points straight ahead.

As if he willed it, the garage door rattles upwards. Inside, it's cluttered with plastic storage bins, old shoe boxes, and some unused exercise equipment, but there's just enough room for us to guide the Civic inside. The moment the car is clear, the garage door descends. I kill the engine.

Harvey hops out of the back seat. "Come on," he says with a grin. "They'll be gone soon."

Harvey rubs his hands together and climbs out of the car.

"Why are you getting out?" I ask. I turn to Zeke. "Why is he getting out?"

"Foolishness!" Zeke says and chases after the old man.

Zeke and I follow the noises of Harvey ransacking the house. The place is already in disarray. Unopened mail sits on the kitchen counter. Plates are in the sink. Unfolded laundry fills up an armchair. We catch up to Harvey in the back bedroom, where he's looting the drawers beneath the bed.

"I thought you said it was here," Harvey says, just under his breath.

He's pulling folded T-shirts from the drawer and casting them at his feet, not even looking at them.

"Harvey," I ask. "What the hell is this?"

He ignores me. Zeke stares him down in a look that no one should hope to be on the receiving end of. The red bag is in Zeke's hand. He's itching to open it.

"You sure?" Harvey says. "Quit jerking me around."

"Who the fuck are you talking to?" Zeke asks.

Harvey goes to the other side of the bed and opens those drawers.

"I think we're participating in a burglary," I say to Zeke.

"Certainly looks that way," Zeke says. "Hey, Harvey? Enough of this shit. We didn't drive you around so you could rob people. Now—"

Harvey pops up from the other side of the bed and grins. "Bingo!" he says. In his hand is a Star Wars lunchbox he fished from beneath some lingerie.

"Whose house is this?" Zeke asks.

"No idea," Harvey says as he rifles through the lunchbox.

His eyes light up when he retrieves the baggie of weed. "Boom!" he says, and grins. "Either of you got a lighter?"

Harvey doesn't wait for us to answer. He's found their pipe and a long red barbecue lighter. Sitting on the edge of the bed, he starts to pack the pipe.

"No. Huh-uh. No," Zeke says, and reaches to take it away from him. Harvey pulls back, keeping it just out of Zeke's reach.

"We've still got seven minutes or so before we can go anywhere," Harvey says as he takes his first pull. "Just give me a damn second."

"How do you know this? What's your deal?" I ask him. "Are you clairvoyant or something? Can you see the future?"

"Not me," he says before erupting into a coughing jag. "But they can …"

He waves the pipe at an open space next to him on the bed.

"Who? Ghosts?" Zeke says. "There are dead people following you around, telling you where you can score weed? Like *The Sixth Sense*, but … for weed?"

"Well," Harvey says and shrugs. "Yeah."

I look at Zeke. "This is what my mom meant about not living up to my potential."

"They told me you were coming," Harvey says and takes another hit. "Clark and Zeke, right?"

"They told you? Are we dead?" Zeke asks. "Maybe we died back at the hospital. Or hell, we died at the Oswald Academy and my purgatory is running around doing this stupid bullshit with Clark for all eternity."

"Harvey," I say, turning to him. "Am I Bruce Willis? 'Cause you have to tell me if I'm Bruce Willis."

"Shit no," Harvey says with a laugh. "If you two assholes were dead, you wouldn't be so useless."

"Our Haley Joel Osment is kind of a jerk," I tell Zeke.

"And he smells like old cheese."

"So, you're like Rez," I say to Harvey.

"Who in the hell is that?" he asks.

"Our friend Rez. She can speak to ghosts," I say.

"She can speak to them?" Harvey says. "That's cute."

For a second, I'm transfixed at the markings up and down his arms. They're like prison tattoos, the crude, black lines etched into the skin with some homebrew device. The linework has bled away, leaving the intricate patterns looking like they were caught out in the rain. I half expect to see some white power insignias or other trash scrawled across his knuckles and up his forearms, but instead I find magic symbols. Chaldean Neo-Aramaic writing across his elbow. Verses from the *Tibetan Book of the Dead* on his wrist. A black, Sumerian seal across his bicep.

He glances up at a clock on the wall, stands, and stuffs the baggie of weed into his jumpsuit. "Whoops. Got to go," he says, waving for us. "Come on. Gotta move. Hurry."

We're halfway through the kitchen when we hear the racket of the someone unlocking the front door.

"Oh shit," Harvey says.

"Who is that, Harvey?" Zeke asks.

Harvey frowns and ducks out of sight as he hurries to the garage. "Yeah, that's not good."

"Harvey?" I ask.

"Just get in the car," Harvey says, corralling us down the hall and into the garage.

I run over to the driver's side and scramble for the keys. In the other room, someone is talking on the phone as they come through the front. Harvey dives into the back seat.

"Well, raise the damn door!" Harvey says with an impatient hiss.

"Hold on a second…" the voice in the other room says. "Hello? Jill?"

The garage door starts to rattle upward. I start the engine and get ready to floor it. The three of us watch as the door slowly ascends. In the doorway to the garage, a Whole Foods kind of dad in khakis and a pressed denim shirt pokes his head in. His jaw falls open.

"Go!" Harvey says and cackles.

Zeke watches the door crawl upward. "Almost there …"

"What's going on?" The man in the doorway asks.

I hit the gas. The car lurches backward, and as we fly under the door, I expect to hear the roof scrape across. But we make it. The man stumbling into the garage follows us, his face slack. I steer the car into a wide, sloppy arc, bouncing the back tires over a curb. Harvey is howling with laughter and kicking his feet into the air.

"Woo!" he screams and pats me on the back as we speed away.

"Which way?" I ask him.

"Any way," he says and lights another bowl. "Those Cavendish dicks are gone, so let's just git."

I take my time anyway, easing up to every intersection to look up and down the street. But he's right. No more white vans. After a few more turns, I find an onramp and race onto the highway. We're northbound into the impenetrable Austin traffic.

Harvey keeps smoking. "Ain't you high enough?" Zeke asks, getting irritated.

"Never," Harvey says and stretches his legs out across the seat. "Looks like we're gonna be here a while."

He's right. We're absorbed into the wall of blinking taillights, crawling along so slowly the speedometer doesn't so much as twitch.

"You guys know where we can score some cairn root? Let's get turnt," he says.

"Turnt?" Zeke asks. "Please don't say *turnt.*"

"You've never had cairn root?" Harvey says, leaning forward to talk to us in the front. "Let me borrow your phone. I know a guy. You're gonna love this shit."

I use the steering wheel as a stress ball. "Nah. It's a school night. I try not to do drugs with weird old people on school nights."

"Who'd you say you were with? Chuck didn't send you, did he?"

"Occultex. Occult Technologies, Inc," Zeke says like it's the end of the conversation.

"Never heard of it. This gig ain't what it used to be. Now there's startups and shit."

"We're paranormal investigators," I say. "Kind of. Not really. We … we do … things for—"

"We're fixers," Zeke says. "We get shit done."

I like that. *Fixers.*

"Where we headed, anyway? Private airstrip? Titty bar?" he asks.

"Candle House," I tell him as I try to find a way to navigate us into a faster lane.

Harvey sits up straight. "Candle House?" The spark in his voice flickers and dies. "The Lazlos?"

"Yeah. Just dropping you off. That's all I know," I say.

In the rearview, the blood drains from his face. He sets down the pipe. When he sees that I'm watching, he shakes it off and offers a smile.

"Right on. Right on."

Zeke and I exchange looks as Harvey stares out the window and pretends nothing's wrong.

"So, how do you know Rupert and Kitty?" I ask him.

"Oh," he says and gives a half-hearted shrug. "You know … did some business with them a few times over the years. Nothing much."

"Business?" Zeke asks. "What kind of business?"

"Whatever," he says and smiles again. "It was nothing. Not a big deal. Just whatever they needed."

He's kneading his fingers together and biting his lower lip.

"Were you a Specter Scout when you were a kid?" I ask him.

I've found that there are two types of people in my orbit: those who were Specter Scouts and those who weren't. Most of the people I know in this line of work, this increasingly strange barnyard of oddities and misfits, were in the club. I was. It was like the Cub Scouts, but for weird kids. Did you like ghost hunting? Magic? Or like learning about cryptids like Bigfoot or the Jersey Devil? Then send $5.95 to the Specter Scouts and get up-to-date newsletters about the paranormal exploits of the Lazlos and their friends! Kitty and Rupert would send photos of themselves in adventures all over the world—praying at the steps of a temple in Nepal, sanctifying a forgotten graveyard in the Appalachian foothills, or maybe just smiling for a headshot. Sometimes you'd get a patch for your jacket, a small, signed poster, or a plastic ring that helped "channel your mystical energies." It was the training ground for any weird kid. Maybe one day, if you paid your dues and said your prayers, you, too, would get invited along on an investigation.

Harvey is lost in thought but tries to keep smiling at me like he's paying attention. "Nah," he says. "I was too old for that shit. Too busy, you know. Working and getting laid and ..."

His voice just trails off.

"You doing all right there, Harvey?" Zeke asks.

"Yeah. Yeah, I'm fine. Just ... that was a long time ago, is all." Harvey fidgets in his seat, avoiding eye contact.

Time to dig. "How well do you know them?" I ask him.

He squirms, but doesn't answer. I'm tempted to pull the car over and just ask him flat out.

*Tell me about the Lazlos. What's their deal? Are they crazy? Are they dangerous?* If he's this scared, I need to know why. Zeke could convince him to spill his guts, I'm sure, but that might get a little violent for this early in the morning.

"Harvey, come on. Do you—" I start.

"I gotta take a shit," he says.

"You gotta ... Well, okay," I say.

"You couldn't have gone back at the house?" Zeke asks him.

"Yeah, that would have been great. That guy comes home and I'm sitting on his throne. He woulda shot me. Then what would you tell those Lazlo freaks?" he says, shuffling uncomfortably. "Can you just find a gas station or something? Seriously."

I sigh and check the clock. The deadline is 10 p.m. That's what the Lazlos said as they pawed at me with their spindly fingers and paper-thin skin.

"Just get him on back here for us, Clark," Rupert had said through cracked lips and yellow teeth. "Ol' Kitty, she's hot to make this happen. I tell you what."

Kitty had playfully swatted his leg. "Oh, Brother, you're such a cut-up. I'm sure Clark isn't going to dilly-dally, are you, Clark?"

Their eyes were hungry. They licked their lips at the thought of getting this guy. I resolve to just drop Bunson off and run. 10 p.m. I'm literally going to run out of their house before the weird, geriatric sex party starts. No thank you.

I look to Zeke. He shrugs. "You're the pooping-in-public expert. Pick a bathroom."

I take the next exit off the highway and nod to a Pik-n-Pak on the feeder road. "This place is pretty clean."

The gas station is a small, lonely thing in the shadow of the overpass. It sits in between a self-storage facility and a discount nail salon. The parking lot is empty but for the carcass of a dead grackle.

Harvey jumps out of the back before I'm completely stopped. He stands there for a second, looking around, assessing.

"Watch him," I tell Zeke.

Zeke starts to get out, but Harvey is already walking halfway across the lot.

"Is he … going to poop on the *side* of the building? Where the hell's he going?" Zeke asks.

Harvey stands over the dead bird pasted to the asphalt, cocking his head as he examines it. Its black feathers twitch in the mid-morning breeze. Harvey crouches and starts to pull feathers aside so he can get at the meat.

"Hey!" Zeke says and climbs out. "Hey, don't go messing around in that shit! Are you serious?"

Harvey works his finger through the remains, digging.

"What the hell, man?" Zeke asks, but keeps his distance.

Harvey stands and holds up a gristly length of the bird's spine. He grins. "For luck!" he says.

"Luck? What is wrong with you?" Zeke asks. "Just go wash your damn hands and poop. And then wash again. Okay?"

Harvey nods, pockets the wet and sticky bone along with a fistful of feathers, and heads inside as Zeke holds the door open. Over his shoulder, Zeke throws me a *can-you-believe-this?* look as I watch from the comfort of the car. Inside, Harvey makes his way over to the bathroom while Zeke stands at the magazine rack. I watch the street behind us, looking for patrol cars or white vans. I don't know what would happen if the orderlies from the nursing home caught up to us. Would they just call the police? That was my original assumption. Now, I'm not so sure. Whatever was going on in that high-risk ward was not something they would go to the police about. No, they'd handle it themselves. Maybe Zeke and I would find ourselves in a nice, white room, drugged to the gills for the next thirty years. That's Zeke's nightmare made real, but with the right medication, I think it sounds kind of nice. Comfy clothes? Clean sheets? A soft, opioid haze that takes the edge off your day? Sign me up.

I flip through a comic book I find on the floorboard. *The Specter Society*. Dammit. Why couldn't it have been *Iron Fist* or *Ghost Rider*? No, it had to be this one. I can't even remember how long I've owned this. I think my mom bought it for me after I badgered her during a quick stop at 7-Eleven. It's ancient. For some reason, I've held onto it. The staples are loose, and the pages are torn. Maybe it was sentimental at one time, but now it's just bile in the back of my throat. When I adopted my *Vandermeer the Mystic* persona and acted like a psychic to grift people out of money, I turned to the Specter Society for inspiration. The gang of ghost-fighting heroes stood in action poses on the cover.

Dr. Dexter Challenge! Intrepid explorer and daring leader of the Society.

Ganymede! Enigmatic master of sorcery.

Dr. Void! The gas-mask wearing practitioner of black science.

Morning Glory! The beautiful billionaire industrialist.

The Lazlo Twins! Savants of the occult.

United, can they defeat the sinister PARADOX DEMON?!

My stomach turns. I knew these stories inside and out when I was a kid. Most of my friends were into the Justice League or the X-Men. I hitched my wagon to these weirdos and now here I am. I wonder how many other kids bought into the lie. Maybe comics *will* rot your brain.

Tap tap.

A noise at the window. I look up from my phone, expecting to see Zeke trying to get my attention, but he's still inside. I twist in my seat, now looking for a panhandler, but there's no one there.

Tap tap. Tap tap tap.

Again, on the window. I don't know anything about cars, but maybe it's the engine? There was some weird smoke the other day. I should have that looked at once we make a million dollars and never have to worry about things again.

A stabbing pain flares in my earlobe.

I lurch to the side. My head smacks the window.

Another stabbing pain in my neck. I scream and throw up my arms. The jolts assail me— something biting at me, clawing. An invisible rustling in the air around me. The beating of wings.

"Shit!" I yell, scrambling to open the door. Across the parking lot, the carcass of the grackle is writhing on the pavement. It squirms and flaps a broken wing, like it's trying to get up.

Inside, the invisible thing is all over me. The car fills with the smell of rot and coppery blood. I flail, trying to get it off. It begins to shriek, squawking madly as it pecks at my face. I still can't see it. My fingers push through something ephemeral and cold, but there's nothing to grab onto, nothing to choke. I throw the door open and lunge for the pavement, but the seatbelt jerks me back into place. I unsnap my belt and fall out. Still, it comes, flapping and squawking. I swat at it like I'm on fire and try to shield my eyes.

Suddenly, tendrils of smoke erupt in mid-air. The ghost-thing thrashes in front of me and I can barely make out the shape of the bird. Smoke belches from its mouth and eyes, consuming it. Ghostly feathers flutter down, disappearing into smoke before they hit the ground.

And then it's over. I'm crab-walking away from the car. Thirty feet away, Zeke is standing over the grackle's physical corpse, holding a can of lighter fluid. The bird's earthly remains smolder there in the parking lot.

"You alright?" he asks.

"A bird. A ghost bird. Did I just get my ass kicked by a ghost bird?"

Zeke comes and helps me to my feet.

"How do I look?" I ask. "Did he peck off my nose or something? Are both of my eyes here? I think I have my eyes. You know I have a thing about birds! I once saw an emu take a little girl's eye. Her *eye*, Ezekiel!"

"Okay. Calm down. You got a couple of good bites, but you're alright."

We look through the front glass of the convenience store. Harvey hasn't come out of the bathroom yet.

"Go!" I tell Zeke. "Go! Go!"

We rush inside. The clerk is behind the counter, scowling. "You've got to pay for that lighter fluid, man!"

Zeke tries to open the bathroom door. Locked. He throws himself against it.

"Harvey?" I ask. "Get your ass out here. Summoning a ghost bird on me is a real dick move."

Zeke presses his ear to the door, looks at me, then shakes his head.

"Do it," I tell him.

He steps back and nails the door with a single, ear-splitting kick. It flies open, hanging from one hinge.

"Whoa!" The clerk yells. "I'm calling the police!"

The bathroom is empty. A single toilet and a sink. No window. On the floor is some sort of crude ritualistic symbol. The bird's spine is in the middle, surrounded by ancient sigils writ in blood and sanctified with greasy, black feathers.

I step back out to make sure we didn't miss him, that he's not hiding next to the slushie machine or the Mexican candy. The clerk walks up to us and says, "Guys, the police are on their way. Right now. You can't do this."

He holds the phone out as proof the cops are coming.

"The old man," I ask him. "Where did he go?"

"Hey, this is not my problem ..."

"Did you see him?" Zeke asks. "While I was outside, did he sneak out?"

The clerk sees the weird altar of blood, bone, and feathers, and his eyes go wide.

"I don't ..." he says before taking careful steps backward. "You need to leave. Please leave the store. I'm going to have to ban you. I'm banning you. You're banned. We don't allow devil stuff in here. The store has a strict no-witchcraft policy."

"Is there a back door?" I ask.

"Please leave."

\*\*\*

We're sitting in front of an Arby's. Zeke won't look at me. He's just shaking his head.

"They told you. They *told* you. Don't give him any bones," Zeke says.

"Well, I didn't give him any. He dug them out of that—"

"I saw it, dude. I was there. You should have warned me that the dude shouldn't have access to bones."

"What the hell does that even mean?" I ask. "I mean, when someone says that, what are you supposed to say? I thought maybe they meant human bones. You know—femurs and skulls and stuff."

"Did the Lazlos say 'Don't give him any femurs or skulls?' No, they just said 'Don't give him any bones.' Period. I would have appreciated a heads-up."

"I'm the one who got ghost-birded!" I say, spilling a little bit of my diet soda. "Me! I got my face all pecked like Tippi goddamn Hedren! And I thought you could punch ghosts. What the hell happened to that?"

"I *can* punch ghosts. You know this. You've seen it."

"How can you punch them if you can't see them? You couldn't see all the dudes Harvey was talking to. I thought I could trust you to handle that part of our investigations, but no. I'm just sitting here minding my own business and boom! Ghost bird, going for my damn face!"

"Just call them," Zeke says, taking a desultory bite of his gigantic sandwich.

I sigh and stare at my phone. I don't want to call them. I don't want to hear their raspy Southern drawls or picture their yellow, artificial grins.

"We never talk on the phone," I tell Zeke. "They always send that albino messenger guy with a handwritten note."

"Then write them a letter! I don't care. Just tell them we can't find this guy and we need to know what to do next."

The only number I have for them is an 800 number. It's the general line for their foundation and all I can find on the internet. I dial and after a second, a chime plays, a peaceful sound of harps, and then a voice that sounds like it was recorded on an old answering machine. I recognize it immediately as Kitty Lazlo.

Hello, this is Kitty Lazlo. My brother Rupert and I are just so glad you called. Are you experiencing something in the realm of the paranormal? Do you have night terrors? Cold spots in your home? Unexplained noises or visions? Then you might be under attack by the forces of darkness. Well, I've got good news for you, friend. We can help. My brother and I have over fifty years of experience in protecting and helping people with their encounters with the occult. Press ONE if you're experiencing a spiritual or demonic presence in your home. Press TWO if you've witnessed something in your neighborhood or workplace. Press THREE if you or someone you love currently or have in the past suffered from lycanthropy. Press FOUR if you're a young boy or girl who would like to be a Specter Scout! Otherwise, please stay on the line to speak to a live operator at the Lazlo Foundation. We have occult specialists standing by to help you.

70s AM radio starts to play. I put the phone on speaker and set it on the dashboard. Zeke and I shove roast beef sandwiches into our faces while we stare at it.

Barbara Mandrell gives way to Juice Newton gives way to Eddie Rabbit.

Zeke reaches forward to disconnect the call just as someone appears at the driver's side window. Expecting another bird attack, I yelp and get horsey sauce all over my surgical scrubs.

But it's the Lazlos' albino butler. Hairless, lanky, and always grinning, he's dressed in a cheap, western-cut suit, like he's emceeing the rodeo. His smile could swallow the car. It doesn't flinch as he taps on the glass. I roll the window down. Just a little.

"Hey …" I say.

Through the crack in the window, he slides in an envelope. It's got a wax seal and my name written across it in florid script.

"Are you kidding me right now?" Zeke says, regarding the note like it might bite one of us.

The butler—I still don't know his name—turns without saying a word and with crisp, almost robotic steps, walks away. We stare at him as he makes a beeline—not to a waiting car or even a bus, but like he picked a random direction and committed to it. He walks straight across the parking lot, past a pawn shop, and into an empty field. He just keeps going.

"I don't like that dude," Zeke says.

"Same," I say, tearing into the envelope.

"How in the hell do they do that? How do they know where we are?"

It's something I've tried not to think about too much. They can always find me. For a while, I thought maybe the butler was following me or that maybe they'd slipped some sort of tracking device into my jacket, but none of that adds up. They just seem to know. It's never something I've discussed with them, but they've alluded to it.

"Oh, we know how to find you!" Rupert would say when I would ask for a direct phone number.

"We always do," Kitty would add.

Threats delivered with a smile.

"What's it say?" Zeke asks. "Does it remind you not to give Harvey any bones?"

I sigh, toss the letter into the back seat, and start the car. "We gotta go see them."

*Dearest Clark,*

*Please come see us immediately. It's super-duper important!*

*With love,*

*Kitty and Rupert Lazlo*

***

# CHAPTER THREE

"Nope," Zeke says as I climb out of the car.

"No? What do you mean?"

"I mean 'nope.' That's what I mean. I'll wait in the car."

I turn and look up at the faded neon compound that is Candle House. From a corner hilltop, it looms over the neighborhood. Tall, dead grass and weeds run riot through the lawn, obscuring the filthy windows and the scaling paint. One house is sharp purple. Another, electric aqua. A third, nuclear orange. It's multiple tract houses now tethered together through a network of post-hoc tunnels and chambers. Even after twenty years of disrepair, the Day-Glo colors dominate the block, so bright you can feel the house's presence even when you're not looking.

"You're gonna make me go in by myself?" I ask him.

"Yeah. Unless you think there's gonna be trouble. If things get ugly, I'm there with you. I'm down. You know that. But if you're just getting an ass-chewing? I'll just wait right out here."

"Are you scared of them?"

He gives me his *bitch, please* look. "Listen, I've spent my whole life trying to avoid creepy old white people and it's worked out just fine for me so far. You just dragged me into a whole dang hospital full of them. I've had enough creepy old white people today."

"Fine," I say. "Just don't eat my curly fries."

As I make my way up the walk, something is different. There's a buzz around the compound. Usually, this place has all the energy of a decayed roadside attraction off a forgotten highway, but today, it's alive. The central drive in the courtyard is full of moving trucks, three of them. Men in coveralls hoist large pieces of furniture all draped in dusty sheets. An ornate, ironwood table. A lamp made of stained glass. An old phonograph. The workers hold all the items at arm's length and say nothing. They speak with their eyes, furtive glances that share an undercurrent of fear. A pair of barn doors gape open, threatening to swallow them up. The men move with quick, light steps as they cart things out of the bowels beneath the purple house. They gather around the orifice, gazing into it like they're not sure the last guy that went in is actually going to come back. When he does, carrying the next dusty artifact, they all breathe a sigh of relief. At first, I think the place is getting looted and I'm not sure how I feel about that. They're my only source of income and they *are* elderly, but ... they're super creepy, so maybe they *should* get robbed.

Standing nearby is the butler, monitoring everything. He's wearing different clothes now. The suit is gone. Now it's a pearl-snap shirt embroidered with roses, tucked into a pair of Wranglers that are about three sizes too short for his bony legs. He's a cartoon skeleton in a cowboy hat. When he sees me, he tips his hat and motions to the back door of the lime green house. His grin doesn't falter. The movers keep their distance from both of us.

In the sunroom of the green house sits Kitty Lazlo. Kitty is in a rocking chair, smiling at me as I approach. She's wearing a plaid shirt and a denim skirt with a dancing poodle embroidered onto it.

"Going square dancing?" I ask as I join her.

She laughs, and the rasp of her voice curdles my stomach. "Oh, you little joker. Heavens no. Brother and I haven't been dancing in a coon's age."

She slaps my leg and I laugh along with her. I say, "Okay. Not sure if that's racist."

"What a cut-up you are!" She says again, and I can't look away from the ruby red lipstick slathered too-thick all around her mouth. I wonder if every morning, they have the butler come in and pancake on their stage makeup.

"Brother! Get on in here! Our little friend is here!" she says.

She pins me down with her smile, not speaking as we wait for her brother. I twist under the stare and pretend to be fascinated by the photographs on the wall. As with most of Candle House, it's a shrine to their exploits back when they were big-shot paranormal investigators. One of the photos catches my eye. I've seen it before, a line of people posing, wearing costumes that are weird even for 1976. The Specter Society, all decked out in lab coats or khakis like they were going to wrestle rhinos or make first contact with a lost Amazonian tribe. It's the comic book brought to life. This is the truth behind those old stories, or if not the truth, it was at least the lie made flesh. This was the team, traveling across the globe to investigate bizarre phenomena and do battle with the forces of darkness. If I saw this photo under any other context—if it wasn't placed right here in this damned house—I would think it was just cosplay.

*Sterling Graves, the brilliant astronomer and mathematician*! Broad-chested and steely-eyed, he stares down the camera as if he's trying to break it with the force of his disdain. *Tobias Locke, the Immortal Man!* A spindly wraith, his wrinkled flesh is paper-thin over his angular bones. It's said that he had mastered every esoteric practice from India to Peru. *The Sinister Dr. Void*! What dark scheme is she hatching beneath the gas mask that keeps her alive?!

I find myself whispering the names as I pass over each one, remembering their comic-book exploits. In high school, when the weight of the world saddled me with perpetual disappointment, I cast aside the Specter Society as a sham. It was just pro wrestling, just like everything else that used to bring me joy. It's all fun and flying elbows against evil until you realize that they're just assholes trying to sell you something.

I snap out of my reverie as Rupert appears in the doorway, gaunt and grinning. His jet-black hair piece rests atop a face slathered with makeup so thick I can see it collecting in his wrinkles. He's holding a tray of iced tea.

"Howdy there, Clark!" he says. "It's so durn good to see you!"

He sits next to Kitty on a bench with floral-printed vinyl cushions and starts pouring the drinks.

"Well, Clark," he says, shaking his head, "I'll start this off with a very, very important question. You have to answer me honestly."

Here goes …

"Okay," I say.

"Sweet or unsweet?" He cackles, casting spittle onto my already stained surgical scrubs.

"Oh, no thank you. I'm good," I tell him.

He looks shocked and aghast. "What? But this is Sister's own sun tea!"

"It is," she says, nodding. "It's real, real good."

"Ain't nothing better on a hot day than a glass of iced tea!"

Going into Candle House has always been like descending into Fairyland. Don't eat or drink anything offered, or you might never be able to leave.

"You two are just the best hosts, really, but I'm okay for right now. Might get one for the road, though!" I say with a smile every bit as fake as theirs.

"Well, alright then. That sounds like a plan!" Rupert says and pours himself a big glass.

When he drinks, his own lipstick leaves a thick smear around the rim.

"Now, Clark," Kitty says, taking my hand. "You know what we need to talk about, son."

Her hands are cold and clammy and if I look down, I'm sure I'll see that she's placed a dead frog into my hand. Instead, I purse my lips into my most serious face and nod.

"Yes. Yes. I'm really sorry. I didn't know Mr. Bunson would try to escape. Zeke and I drove around looking for him, but he just vanished," I tell them.

"Oh, he's a slippery one, all right," Rupert says.

"No, I mean he literally vanished. From a locked bathroom," I say.

"Oh yes," Kitty says. "That's what we were afraid of."

She *tsk-tsks* and shakes her head, as though she's disappointed that I accidentally broke one of her dishes or tracked in mud.

"Wait. You knew he could do that?" I ask.

"Oh yes. It was all in the pamphlet we prepared for you," Kitty says. "You did read all of the pamphlet, right?"

"I did. Cover to cover."

I didn't.

"Clark, I apologize, son," Rupert says. "This is something we should have discussed face-to-face. *Mano y mano.* You know what I'm saying?"

"Not ... not exactly?"

"That Harvey," Kitty says, "Lord, he's a dangerous fella."

"Oh? Oh. Dangerous? Like ... how dangerous?"

Kitty just shakes her head. "Mm. Mm. Mmm. It's no good that he's out there running around. No good at all."

"You're gonna have to go get that fella back here, Clark," Rupert says.

"Well, I—"

"No fooling," he says. "There's a reason he was down there in that hospital."

"Yeah, about that—"

"Oh, that old place," Kitty says. "You boys certainly were brave, charging in there like that."

"We were?"

What type of hell did we just dodge?

"Oh yes. Whole lotta dangerous characters in there," Rupert says. "You don't want to go messing around with them. No sir."

Kitty shakes her head. "No sir. Not at all,"

Rupert leans in. "And now one of those dangerous characters is out and about in our fair city, Clark."

"And that's the last thing in the world we wanted," Kitty says.

"The very last thing, Clark."

"But we've got to do something about this," she says, squeezing my hand with those dead-frog fingers.

"We've got to," Rupert nods.

"It could be real bad if we don't get that nasty Mr. Bunson here to us by the time we have our little get-together tonight," Kitty says. "Real bad for a whole bunch of people."

She levels her gaze at me, making sure I understand.

And I do. Loud and clear.

I want to ask about the "get-together," but I also *don't* want to ask about it. I can't imagine these people with friends. I can't imagine them socializing or doing things humans do around other humans.

"10 p.m. I think you're catching our drift, Clark. Ain't you?" Rupert asks.

Kitty waves him off like it's no big deal. "Oh, Brother, don't scare the boy. He knows the consequences of failure, don't you, son?"

"He sure does, Sister. He sure does," Rupert says, and winks at me.

Someone emerges from inside the house, standing there in the curtained doorway. I smell them first—body odor and feces. It's a woman who might be

31

in her mid-thirties, but she looks prematurely withered, like someone who has spent the last few months in a prison camp. Her cheeks are sunken. Her hair is filthy, twisting and winding in some places or coming out in patches in others. It's all matted down by the headphones that are perched on her head. The loose cord dangles near her waist.

"I finished," she says, and thrusts a black notebook at Rupert.

Rupert and Kitty smile politely, like they've been approached by a mentally disabled person while in line at McDonald's. Rupert takes the notebook, looks at the wild, incomprehensible nonsense scribbled on the page, and shakes his head as he hands it back to her.

"No, sweetheart," he says. "This ain't right. I'm sorry to say."

The woman's face drops. She holds the notebook in her hands and just stares down at it. She doesn't understand. As it flops in her hands, I can see the pages of fine, tight script. With each page, however, the writing starts to unravel. Her text gets bigger and sloppier. She has doodled in the margins, drawing bizarre occult symbols. The open page reveals pieces of words, childlike drawings, and unintelligible scribbles, all in a red pen.

"Maybe take yourself a little nap before you get back to it," Kitty says.

"Can I go home?" the woman asks.

Kitty and Rupert exchange astonished looks. "Well," Rupert says, "Darling, you can go home any time you like. Any time at all. Heck, we'll have Helper drive you home."

Helper. His name is Helper?

"But I tell you what," Kitty says, "If you just get a little bit of a nap, you're gonna feel a whole lot better. Good as new, I bet!"

"Yeah," the woman nods. "Okay. I don't want to leave. Not really. Not 'til I'm finished."

"That a girl!" Rupert says. "Have some tea."

She moves like she's sleepwalking and just obeying orders. She grabs the pitcher of tea and guzzles it. Tributaries of it spill out of her lips and down her stained shirt. When she's done, the pitcher is empty. She doesn't wipe her lips.

"Whoa! Thirsty gal!" Rupert says.

She mumbles to herself, but before she can disappear back through the curtains, someone else emerges.

And I'm paralyzed.

It's a woman in a floor-length coat. Rubber gloves. And a gas mask.

My tongue does nervous jitter inside my mouth. "Umm ..."

The opaque lenses of the mask regards me. It's an old one, stitched together and threaded through with extra hoses and wires all intersecting at some sort of apparatus belted to her abdomen. It clicks and hisses, barely audible at the back of the room, some wheezy ghost. Her movements are precise and slow, the quiet grace of a praying mantis.

Dr. Void.

Dr. Void is real.

Dr. Void is real and standing here in front of me.

It's like walking into a room to find Scooby Doo or Magneto standing there, and impossible cartoon, plucked from my youth. I'm taken by vertigo as my brain tries to catch up.

Rupert smiles and gestures to the woman in the mask. "Now sweetheart," he says to the mumbling, disheveled girl, "Why don't you go on ahead with the good doctor. She'll get you some medicine and get you all nice and rested. How about that?"

Dr. Void takes the mumbling woman by the elbow and leads her into the darkened hallway. The doctor says nothing.

Thank Christ.

"Okay," I manage to say as I stand. My knees shake, and the shock of icy sweat down my spine gives me goosebumps. I push away Kitty's hand and it sloughs out of mine like a swath of dead skin. "Yeah, well … I'll leave you to it."

"You want that tea to go, Clark?" Rupert says, all of his gravitas gone back behind the yellow smile.

"Oh no. I think I'm just going to shoot some tequila and chase it with a fistful of Xanax, but you guys get down on that, okay? We'll see ya! Bye now!" I say to them as I back out of the sun room.

Bobble-headed, they grin and nod at me as I leave. Nearby, Helper tips his hat and smiles.

"Hey, we'll catch up later, Helper, buddy. Maybe get some sunblock on, okay?" I say.

He just smiles at me like he has no idea what I'm saying. A mover carrying a high-backed chair regards me with suspicion as he passes.

"Yeah, maybe don't drink the tea." I tell him.

My hands are shaking by the time I get to the car. Zeke sits in the shotgun seat, his eyes growing wider with every moment I don't say anything.

"Oh shit," Zeke says. "What did they do? They pull some weird shit? You didn't drink anything, did you?"

"We just need to leave."

Zeke looks over my shoulder, as if he's expecting someone to be following me.

"That bad?"

"Oh, hell yes," I tell him.

"I told you!" he says, and punches at the air. "Creepy old white people! Did they touch you?"

"She touched me. They're very touchy. It was gross. It was like holding hands with an octopus."

"Why were you holding hands? Is it weird Jesus stuff?" Zeke says, recoiling from me like whatever happened might be contagious.

"You're going in next time," I tell him.

"Fuck that. If I go in there, it will be to whip some ass."

"Let's hope it doesn't come to that, but we've got to find this Bunson guy."

"That's all they said? Just 'find him'? Or did they drop some threats?"

"We've got until 10. The threats were implied."

"I knew it! I'll go in there right now," he says, and reaches for his red bag.

"I don't know, man. There was a girl and I thought she was a prisoner at first and there was iced tea and … did you know that the albino dude's name is Helper? They just call him 'Helper,' like he doesn't have a real name!"

Dissatisfied, Zeke stares down the house. His lip curls. If there weren't things like police and lawsuits and all of that dumb bullshit, I'd give the greenlight for some patented Ezekiel Silver explosive violence right now.

"Did you see Harvey's arms?" I ask Zeke.

"Harvey? Yeah. I guess. Had some evil tattoos. Looked like he'd done some time."

"It was necromancy. Those were ancient necromantic seals meant for summoning and manipulating the dead."

"Like with the bird! That shit ain't Christian. Or sanitary," Zeke says with a snarl.

"So, if I were a geriatric necromancer on the lam, where would I go?"

\*\*\*

# CHAPTER FOUR

We hit up two Chilis and an Applebee's before we find Marianne Reznicek. It's lunchtime in the suburbs, so all the khaki-wearing, badge-carrying business casual drones are out for their sixty-minute reprieves from purgatory. There are at least three different tech companies within spitting distance of each other, situated among the Home Depots and Bed, Bath, and Beyond, creating a hive of workers with pressed Polo shirts and BMWs they can barely afford. Right now, they're slamming margaritas and talking about sales forecasts or college football. But it's not sales or football Zeke and I want to talk about. It's necromancy.

Rez is at the Applebee's. We spot her car in the lot, a spotless, leased sedan sporting an official Occultex bumper sticker. Zeke and I burst into the Applebee's and stride right past the perky hostess. We're still in our stained surgical scrubs. Zeke has torn the sleeves off his. He looks like an ER nurse who just wrapped up a particularly nasty shift in the apocalypse.

Rez is at a table with a bunch of other assholes, all of them choking down appetizers and bitching about work at Balefire, Inc. They freeze when Zeke and I approach. Rez made the poor choice to invite Zeke and I to one of her soirees at her house a few months back. We got to mingle with the Eloi. It was delightful until I started loudly ridiculing one of her coworkers for drinking Bud Light, and Zeke put her manager in a headlock. That was the last time Rez invited us to anything. Chris, the rat-faced guy sitting to Rez's right, remembers me. He probably remembers the headlock, too. The Southwestern SuperBang Steak Roll nearly falls out of his mouth when our eyes meet. He shrinks in his chair when he realizes it's Zeke next to me.

"Hey, sweetheart," I say to Rez with a smile.

Rez's eyes widen. Immediately, she stands. "Oh! Hi! What … what … what are you two doing here?"

Before we can answer, she's working her way around the table, over to us.

"We're looking for an old dude who smells like farts. Farts and weed. His name is Beaker," Zeke says.

"Wrong Muppet," I say. "It's Bunson."

The grin affixed to Rez's face doesn't say *I'm happy to see you.* By the time she gets over to us, it says *I'm going to kill and eat both of you.* She digs her nails into my arm, turns to the table, and says, "Sorry. Be right back. They work at the hospital I volunteer at. This'll just take a second. Chris, could you get the check?"

Chris nods as the rest of them exchange suspicious glances. Rez doesn't wait for an answer. She drags us back into the parking lot.

"What in the ever-loving fuck are you two dipshits doing here?" she asks.

"We lost a necromancer," I tell her.

"What? Jesus Christ, what are you talking about? You can't just storm into my lunch hour when I'm doing lunch-business things and talk to me about necromancers!"

"Are we not welcome in Applebee's?" Zeke asks.

Her manicured hands curl into fists. "Why do you look like you work at a hospital in a horror movie?"

"Because we just left a hospital from a horror movie," I say.

"Are those cats dressed as doctors? What the hell is happening right now? You know what?" she says. "I don't care. I really don't care. I love you two stupid jackasses, but I just really don't even care what all of this bullshit is."

"A lunch meeting. Are you guys hiring?" Zeke asks.

"No, asshole. You look like a crazy person and you have no skills aside from ghost murder and kung fu," she says.

"I'm pretty good at Mario Kart," Zeke says, sounding wounded.

"Yeah," I say. "Are you guys hiring any video game experts?"

"I'm going back inside. Please leave," she says, but I grab her by the arm before she can go.

"Harvey Bunson," I say. "Do you know him?"

Rez throws her hands up and is about to yell at us when more khaki-people pass by.

"Marianne," they say and smile, each of them stealing furtive glances at Zeke and I.

Rez turns on a glowing smile and is suddenly the picture of middle-management in her stylish skirt and expensive shoes. "Hey, Greg. Theresa," she says to them.

I wonder if they know she can talk to dead people, if they have any idea of what she's seen or what she's really capable of. It's probably not something she puts on her Linked In profile. Once they pass, Rez drops the facade.

"Who is Harvey Bunson?" she asks.

"Well ..." I say. "We fucked up."

"Because of course you did."

"He's this old dude," Zeke says. "Like maybe seventy. Got lots of tattoos."

"Necromantic stuff. Legit. He talks to ghosts," I tell her.

"I have no idea who this person is," she says.

"You guys don't all know each other?" I ask. "You don't like ... go bowling with your necromancer club or something?"

"I'm not a necromancer, dumbass. Necromancers like … control the dead. They summon spirits. It's real dark, weird shit. I'm not into that. I just see ghosts," she says.

"I know this," I say and turn to Zeke. "I knew that. That's my bad."

Touching up his mohawk in the reflection in the front glass, Zeke says, "Dude said he was trying to score something called cairn root. You know anything about that?"

"Ooh!" I say. "Detective work. Yes! Do that. Very cool."

Rez is taken aback. "Cairn root? Ooh. That's intense. Not a lot of places you can get that."

"What is it?" I ask.

"It's a plant. Or something. Necromancers and other magic people use it to get high and expand their mind. Almost like astral projection or something. I don't know. I stay away from that shit," she says.

"Dude!" I say. "It's a wizard drug? I want to do wizard drugs!"

"That's on brand," she says and rolls her eyes.

"Where do we find wizard drugs?" Zeke asks her and turns to me. "You're not doing wizard drugs."

"Fine," I say and frown.

Rez leans in close, like she's sharing a secret. "You want to go to the witch market."

"Third Moon Coffee?" Zeke asks. "Down by the lake?"

"That's the one," she says. "They don't sell cairn root out in the open, but you can get it there. And all sorts of other nastiness."

"You're awesome," I tell her.

"I know," she says and turns to go back inside, "But if you just show up when I'm with my coworkers again, I'm going to murder both of you with a hammer. Just call me next time."

"We go straight to voicemail," I say.

"I know!" she smiles. "Okay. Love you! Bye!"

***

Third Moon Coffee is a bougie joint situated on the shore of Lake Austin in an area I will never ever be able to afford. With its wooden decks, soft, Andean folk music, and fair trade, organic, seven-dollar coffee, it's not really on my radar. Zeke and I cross the parking lot in the shade of massive and ancient oaks. There's a peacefulness here that washes up from the lake and cascades over the coffee shop, a stillness I'm not really used to.

"You can buy wizard drugs at a coffee shop?" I ask Zeke.

"I guess. It's not just a coffee shop, though," he says. "It's a witch market."

"This place? Like white women in their late thirties who are discovering crystals and dream catchers?"

Zeke shrugs, but as we approach their courtyard, I see the tables and booths spread out among the indigenous foliage and the hand-carved patio chairs. Banners advertise tarot reading services or witch-themed jewelry with silver-crescent moons or dainty pentagrams. Palm reading. Ceremonial daggers. Powders, herbs, and oils to bring you luck, health, or money. I don't recognize any of the vendors, but I know the type. They're nice and a little awkward, hawking witchy wares here or on their Etsy store. They've got some questionable tattoos of goddesses or some quote they found in an old book and they're all really into Harry Potter.

Over the last year, I've seen some weird things, things that I can't quite explain. The world doesn't work the way I thought it did. In that time, I've met people who made bold claims. Some of them claimed to be sorcerers. Others, warlocks, witches, or necromancers. Apparently, there's a distinction between all of those and an arsenal of strange magics for each of them. Most of the people who make those claims are dilettantes, though. That's probably all most people ever meet, someone who, in the search of some sort of spirituality that can't be found at the First Baptist Big Box Store of Salvation, bought a book at Barnes & Noble that taught them how to focus their energies or mix together stuff in a pot on their stove that might bring them "good fortune." Maybe they joined a message board about how to harness the energy of angels. Maybe they're an Instagram witch who really identifies with Winona Ryder in *Beetlejuice*. They read horoscopes and have a few Tarot decks. When they're trying to cast a spell or read your fortune, they hedge their bets. *You never know,* they'll say, like they secretly, really know that it's stupid. It's Pascal's wager, but for witches. They're all here tonight, selling the equivalent of knock-off handbags. Sure, it *looks* like a grimoire and it *says* it's a grimoire, but most of the stuff in there was pulled from a Wikipedia page or another binge watch of *Buffy the Vampire Slayer*.

In the past, I laughed at them. It was all a fun game of *Let's Wear Black and Pretend Magic Is Real!* They weren't any different than I was, really, when I was trying to be a paranormal investigator, running around empty buildings in the middle of the night. We'd chase noises with our cameras and try to coax some sort of magic out of a world of insurance claims and fast food. After things soured for me and I really started to appreciate just how much of a clown I was, everything changed. My friends vanished. I met Zeke. Fought some demon kids and an evil ghost lady. The scales fell from my eyes. Before,

I thought the world was terrifying, merciless, and ready to chew you up. Now I *know* it's all those things, but also with *ghosts*.

I walk past the tables as the vendors all make eye contact and smile and I want to sweep all their crap onto the ground and tell them to go home.

Stop trying to cast spells. You're not a witch. Be a Buddhist. A Mormon. A Shriner. Anything else. Please. You don't want this.

But that's what crazy people do.

Then I see her. A warm current of sparks rushes just beneath my skin and I start to stare. She's got her leopard print heels off and her feet are propped up, toes painted lime green. Neon purple hair. Ripped jeans. A corset with Alfred Hitchcock hand-painted across it.

Andromeda Thorn.

Of all the dilettantes and Instagram witches, Andi is the real deal. Either she's a witch or she dosed me with some sort of PCP/peyote cocktail in the moments before we thought we were going to get eaten by the living dead back at the Oswald Academy. Regardless, she makes me feel like I've got little sex-elves throwing a party in the lizard part of my brain. Or I'm having a stroke. She's kicked back, reading a *Hellboy* comic and sipping tea. And she's staring back at me with a sly smile.

Zeke nudges me. "You got a little slobber on your chin, bro."

I wipe my chin. It's slobber-free. I glare at him.

"Metaphorical slobber," he says. "Now go talk to her and quit staring. You look like Michael Myers. Go."

I hesitate and pretend to look at a table full of herbs in silk pouches.

"Deep breaths. You can do this. Just don't be weird. I'll be shopping," he says, rolls his eyes, and wanders off.

I nod and smile as I walk over to Andromeda. Halfway there, I realize I'm still in those damned nursing scrubs. Too late to back out now.

"Andi! Hot damn. What's a girl like you doing in a place like this? Aside from bringing down the property value. Don't you usually hang out in dive bars and opium dens?"

I pull up a chair and slide into it like I'm not scared of her witchcraft or vagina.

"Clark, doll, it's so delightful to see you. Surprised to find you two loitering about. Are you adopting the lifestyle? Or was it just a hard day at the ER?" she says, arching a pierced eyebrow at my scrubs.

"Oh this? I'm a surgeon. Didn't I tell you?"

"No," she says with a giggle.

"Yeah. Didn't go to med school or anything. Just thought we'd try it out one day and what do you know? I've got a real knack for it."

"Oh, really?"

"Yeah. Just performed an appendectomy this morning. Easy-peasy."

"And the patient, they're …?"

"Dead. But we got the appendix out. That's the important takeaway here."

"Mmm. Noted," she says with a purr that turns my bones into Stretch Armstrong. "I'll be sure to make an appointment next time I'm feeling under the weather."

"Are you offering to play doctor with me, Andi?"

"Oh, don't be crass, dear. I think you're charming, but my current paramour might disagree."

This day keeps getting shittier.

"Ah. Boyfriend," I say, and all of my charm gets tangled in my mouth. "Yeah. Cool. How's he?"

She narrows her eyes and grins, amused. "He's off somewhere working. Morocco, I think."

"Morocco. Nice. I think I might be able to find that on a map," I say, and start looking around for Zeke. Zeke can probably kill me quickly with a blow to my neck. "What about you? You look like you're working hard."

She tucks the comic book back into her bag. "One of the perks of being fabulously wealthy. Comic books in the middle of the afternoon are often on the menu."

The Thorn family is indeed crazy rich. Old money. When Andi and I get married one day, it won't be for the money, but that will be a nice perk. Maybe I can get Zeke to kill her boyfriend.

"So…" she says and leans forward to sip her tea. Her full lips wrap around the brim of the cup and my brain starts to shut down. "You two are dressed like there's a story to be told. So, tell it."

"Right. That," I say, wishing that *this* was my afternoon, just sitting here with her, sipping tea beneath the sprawling limbs of the oak tree. "We're looking for somebody."

"Ooh. Are you a private investigator now? I didn't know Occultex was in that business. That's sexy. Maybe some bounty hunting?"

"It's for the Lazlos."

"Is that so?" Andi says, sits upright, and crosses her arms. That's the reaction I get when I mention that name. People clam up. They go cold. Sometimes they disengage entirely. "I thought you were getting out of the life, so to speak."

"Me? No. I'm fine. This is fun. Better than working a desk job, you know?" I punctuate it with a shaky laugh.

"Clark," she says, leaning over the table, "in spite of your … history, you were thrown into the proverbial deep end, dear. I'd heard you weren't coping so well."

"Who'd you hear that from?"

"Oh, you know. I'm not one to gossip."

"Uh-huh."

"My point is, darling, that if this is too much for you, then just walk away."

"It's fine, Andi. I'm fine. This is all kind of ... *cool.*"

"Honey, I'd give you a good slap if I thought you actually believed that."

"What?"

"There's no shame in extricating yourself from this world, Clark. If you want out, then get out while you still can."

I smile and look out over the lake. The words won't come. I can feel the hysteria, reminding me it's still there. If I open my mouth to speak, I'm not sure if I'll laugh or start screaming.

She puts her hand on mine and something inside me cracks. I bite the inside of my cheek and take a deep breath.

"So anyway," I say, and decide to skip over the details. "A guy named Harvey Bunson. Old man. I think he's a necromancer. Do you know him?"

"Those who traffic in the dead aren't really the type I choose to associate with. Doesn't ring a bell. What's the skinny?"

"He's bad news, apparently. We've got to track him down before tonight or I think there will be ... consequences. For us."

"How dire. And you think he might be here?"

"Rez sent us this way. Bunson was looking for something called cairn root. She thought he might be able to score it here."

"Ah," she says, her voice sharp with suspicion. "One of those types. Tell me these aren't the circles you're running in now."

"I don't even know what cairn root is. Is it like kale? Or some probiotic thing? 'Cause I'm morally opposed to all of that."

"No, silly," Andi says with a laugh. "Cairn root is mind-altering."

"Okay. I'm back on board."

"It's like DMT, but for practitioners of the art. It's a bit of a cheat, if you're looking to expand your mind and thus amplify your abilities. There are, quite naturally, myriad side effects."

"Such as?"

"Addiction. Madness. Possession," Andi says, lowering her voice to a conspiratorial tone.

"Ooh! All the fun stuff. But possession? Seriously?"

Her eyebrows dance when she tells me this, mirroring the playful melody in her voice. "Oh yes. Cairn root is a shortcut that enables you to peel off your skin and bones like a cheap suit. You let your soul out for a walk. And well, if *you're* not wearing the suit ... something else might slide into it."

41

"Ugh. Damn it. I just want to finish this job and go home. I thought he might be trying to score some here," I say, looking around at the tables, all draped in their black sheets. "But this all looks pretty benign. I think Rez was just trying to get rid of us."

Andi's lip curls into a half smile. Any time she speaks, it's like she's letting you in on a delicious secret. "Oh, Clark Vandermeer, you're adorable," she says.

"What?"

"This isn't the *real* market," she whispers. "You think we of the Disciplines conduct our business out in the open, for any uninitiated Dim to see? What you're looking at here is just a swap-meet for dabblers. The real Third Moon market is closer than you think."

I twist in my seat and look around. I don't know what I expect to see. A flickering glamour of magic, concealing the true nature of the coffee shop? A bunch of witches, hiding beneath the tables, selling necromancy drugs?

"Is it like … in the bathroom? Do I have to flush the second urinal three times and say the password?" I ask.

"Clark, my dear, you know what I mean."

"Do I?"

She looks into my eyes like she's searching for a lie.

"You're sure you can't see it? After our little astral escapade, you exhibited a certain aptitude, one that surprised me," she says. "Not to bring up things we'd rather not talk about, but if you're still denying the truth after what we went through at that dreadful school, then I might not be able to help you."

"Proficiency? You mean the thing with the …"

"You cast a spell, Clark."

"Well. You helped."

"I was just the guide. You used my charm bag, sure, but the casting? That shouldn't have worked."

"Come on, Andi. It was the bag."

"I made the bag, dear. It wasn't the bag."

It slaps me in the face like it was yesterday. It's been months since I heard that sound— the shriek of the tapes we found—but I still see Iris Angel floating over me when I wake up in the middle of the night. I still check the closet for children with sharp teeth. The taste of cinnamon in the back of my throat lingers. A glass of whiskey. A gallon. Tacos. Video games. Sleep. No sleep. Work. More sleep. Vomiting. Tears in the middle of the night that I hope Zeke doesn't hear me shed. None of that helps me forget.

I change the subject with a nod to the cane propped against her chair. "How's the leg doing?"

"It only hurts when I move. Or when I sit still. Fortunately, the scars I'm sporting across my abdomen are just the right shade of sexy." She brushes off her trauma. "The candy was your first brush with the Discipline, Clark. It doesn't go away, not really."

"Okay," I say, "So if I wanted to go in there and poke around, maybe ask some people if they've seen him ..."

"If you cast that astral projection spell back at Oswald Academy—and you did—you'd be able to see it. You'd feel it. Once you do, for the first time, you'll never be able to shake it. The more magic you use, the more you can see such things. The world blossoms open for you."

She leans back again like that settles the discussion and punctuates it with another smile. I turn in my chair and look at the booths again.

A rail-thin guy with white hair and a tie-dyed shirt is selling scarves and handmade jewelry. A Hispanic woman in a kimono and cat's-eye glasses sells framed charcoal drawings of pop culture witches. *The Craft. Charmed. Sabrina.* Each of them has a pithy quote to accompany it. Another lady, the one I stare at the longest, has an assortment of small, burlap pouches on her table. This seems the closest to legit, but she's not glowing or sparkling or anything. For all I know, she's just hawking potpourri.

A barista arrives with two more cups of tea, one for Andi and one for me. Andi motions to it.

"Sip. Relax. Breathe."

"What's in this? Is this dosed? I don't think I'm ready for another magical mystery tour." I say, smelling the cup.

"Kava, you fool," she says, and her voice brushes across the back of my neck like warm velvet. "Drink it slowly and be present, be *here*."

I look at her, at the tea, then back at her. She nods to the tea again. I frown and hold the cup to my lips. "Just kava, huh?"

"Kava," she says, and slips a tiny, black vial out of her purse, "with a little boost."

One drop. Two drops. She smiles at me over the steaming tea and puts the vial away.

"Make no mistake, this is no sort of indoctrination into the Disciplines. You're still just a tourist."

"What was that?"

"Nothing harmful. It will help open your mind and reactivate those senses a bit, the ones that allowed you to go on that horrible trip at the Oswald Academy." She slides the tea over to me. "But this will be peaceful, so long as *you're* peaceful. So, breathe."

This isn't what I wanted. If that bizarro astral trip back at the school was magic, then magic and I don't get along. For a few moments—or maybe a few hours—the world turned into a nightmare. I nearly got my friends killed and then I woke up and vomited. But like looking at a gruesome car wreck as I pass, I can't resist. I sip the tea.

"There," she says. "Take a few more. Focus on your breathing."

I try to relax. Focusing isn't something I do very well. Neither is being aware of my surroundings. Honestly, I'm kind of a dumb sack of meat stumbling around in search of a burrito, but I do as she says.

"Taste the tea," Andi says. "Feel the breeze. Listen to the birds. Take it all in. Open yourself up to the world around you. And then open yourself some more. Close your eyes."

I close them and roll my tongue through the kava. It's bitter and earthy, with a hint of spice mixed in. I can smell similar earthiness in the oak and cedar around the coffee joint's courtyard, the hints of the lake water beyond. Grackles bark, shuffling around the branches of the oak. Murmured conversations. Sales pitches. The hiss of the coffee machine. Beyond that, cars passing on the street. Water, lapping against the shore. The heavy, soothing burn of roasting coffee wafting across the market. Harmless acoustic tunes drift along, mingling with that scent. All of it weaves together in a fluid tapestry.

And I taste the cinnamon. Cinnamon candy.

I open my eyes.

"You felt it. I could see it on your face," she says, still smiling.

My skin buzzes, and I wonder if this is what real relaxation is.

"Is this going to make me think I'm a lizard? That happened in a Cheech and Chong movie."

"Shh," she says. "Look around."

Again, I turn in my chair and look back at the market. Everything is limned in the faintest aura, a soft buzz. Every leaf on the tree. Every sound dancing out over the lake. Even the back of my hand. I'm aware of it and its place among everything else, slipping through the air, connecting with the edge of the table.

"Yeah," I say, rubbing my eyes. "I'm definitely high."

Ordinarily, I would appreciate the opportunity, but right now, after getting attacked by a goddamned ghost bird, getting high in the middle of the day seems inappropriate, at best.

"Look again," she says, and I can almost see the words escape her lips and tickle my ears.

When I look, there's a path I hadn't noticed. It's slight, but I can't believe I didn't see it before. Right between the guy selling meditation CDs and the old lady with the jars of carnivorous plants is a small, dirt path.

"Is it … is that it?" I ask Andi.

She nods slowly.

I stand, afraid to take my eyes off the path and afraid to get too close. It's not like the tables moved apart or now there's some magical portal. A new angle was revealed, a different way of looking at it. I see the folds in reality, the parts of the world I would just walk past before. The tea or the meditation or the residual hoodoo in my system shifted my perspective, and there it was, waiting for me as if it had been there all along.

Zeke emerges from the warren of dreamcatchers and handmade jewelry. I point at the path. He stares at the tables, takes a few steps sideways, and then looks back at me. "What?" he asks.

"You don't see that?"

The woman at the booth, dressed up like a cartoon gypsy, smiles and shows her wares, ceramic fairies holding quartz crystals. "Come take a look," she says.

We ignore her. I grab Zeke by the arm and point to the path. "There. Right there. You don't see that?"

The fairy vendor looks to her left and her smile fades. "What? What is it?"

"Not now, lady," I tell her.

Andi rises, gives the woman an apologetic smile, and says, "Now boys, please don't make a scene. He can't see it, Clark. Just lead Zeke through."

The vendor shakes her head and goes back to reading her paperback mystery.

I shake my head and lean so I can peer down the path, behind the black curtains that act as a backdrop for the vendors. The path winds back behind the tables and beneath a mimosa tree I hadn't noticed. The air back there is different, a shift in the light. It's shaded, yes, but the sunlight flickers around the path rather than shine directly on it, a perpetual shadow, keeping this secret world-behind-the-world just out of phase with what most people see. There are people milling about back there, browsing, selling, and chatting. More tables under the tree with people selling wares I can't make out from here. The hidden market, the real Third Moon.

"Let me put it in terms you'll understand," Andi says. "You've just taken your first step into a larger world."

"Oh! You showed him how to do the thing!" Zeke says. "Right on."

"And there's stuff like this just … everywhere?" I ask.

"The more you see, the more you can continue to see," she says.

I stare down the path, half-expecting to see fairies beckoning or some sweeping vista of Narnia.

"We probably ought to get to it, know what I'm saying?" Zeke says. He throws a glance over his shoulder. Behind us, standing in the parking lot, is Helper. He's wearing white pants and a white polo that somehow still isn't as bone pale as his skin. Usually, he's smiling, but now he's just shamelessly staring at us, some thirty yards away, standing behind a Prius.

"What the hell is Powder doing here?"

"I don't know," Zeke says. "Dude's been watching us pretty much since we rolled up. Followed me around for a minute but kept his distance. I asked him what's up, but you know Whitey ain't real chatty."

The Lazlos are keeping tabs on us. I think of their wrinkled, ventriloquist-dummy faces and Rupert warning me about the consequences of failure. I don't know what that means but seeing Helper's ghostly stare curdles my gut.

"Yeah. Let's do this," I tell Zeke.

"Clark," Andi says. I turn back to her and there's a hint of concern on her face. Andi never worries.

"Yeah?"

"You're guests at the market, yes? Not a boy, but not yet a man, as the saying goes. They very well may see you as a Dim encroaching on their little witch party. Please do try not to embarrass me, dear," she says and again arches that pierced eyebrow. The silver hoop glints in the sunlight and it, too, gives off its own faint vibration.

I nod, but she's really asking a lot of me. I don't even know what to expect here. Will I vomit when I pass through this mystical veil? Will I feel untold forces course through my blood? Will Alan and the rest of my missing friends be waiting in the shadows, staring at me with hungry, inhuman smiles?

"The cairn root ..." I say.

Andi's usual melody hardens around the edges. "It's there. Practice some discretion if you don't mind. If you can't get any leads, try the RV down by the shore."

"An RV?"

"Bela Koth is her name. She lives in the RV and carries on with all sorts of unsavory types. Give her my name if you must, Clark, but do be on your best behavior."

"Discretion. Best behavior. Yeah, got it. Come on, Andi," I say with a nervous grin. "Trust me!"

***

# CHAPTER FIVE

I stand at the threshold and look down at my feet, wondering if I've already got my toes inside this invisible fairy land. There's no obvious delineation of where the real world starts, and this other hidden world begins. I stick my hand out, expecting to feel a pull or crackling energy, but there's nothing.

"Will I be able to get back?" I ask. "And Zeke can come, too?"

I take a step forward and feel the air shift, like the pressure drops.

Behind me, Zeke and Andi are watching, bemused parents. Zeke chuckles and puts his hand on my shoulder, as if I'm guiding the blind. In a way, I guess I am. "Bro," he says. "It's fine. I can follow you."

The timbre of his voice has changed, ever so slightly. There's an electric undercurrent to it, a soft buzz that lets me know he's not really next to me anymore, not exactly. He's coming through the invisible barrier, his voice carried across a connection that isn't quite real or true. He beckons for me to come.

I take a few more steps. There's no zapping sound or whoosh of air. No magic sounds at all. I still hear the birds squawking in the tree, still hear the waves lapping on the shore. Behind us, Andi gives a coy wave and returns to her comic book. Her slight wave, the slender fingers bedecked with rings across pearl-white skin, stirs up memories of her smell. She's clean and crisp with the hint of gin on her breath and across her neck.

Zeke laughs. "Man, she doesn't need to slip anything into your tea to hypnotize you."

"Shut up," I say, drawing an even bigger grin from Zeke.

Back behind the tables with the dreamcatchers and meditation CDs, the Tarot cards and the Pagan self-help manuals, is the real market. It's busier, livelier. The clientele is weird, but not a Mos Eisley assortment of werewolves and freakshows. Some tiny spark of imagination in the back rooms of my brain was hard at work crafting a picture of warlocks in black cloaks cavorting with vampires and floating, spectral phantoms. It's none of that, and I feel a slight tug of disappointment that this rabbit hole is so near to my own experience. They're like Andi. They've got colorful hair and intricate tattoos. Combat boots, gauged ears, and looks in their eyes like they know something you don't. They're the "interesting" people you meet at parties or the ones you see playing pool when you start to suspect you've come to the wrong bar. Not dangerous. Not evil, but pointedly and intentionally different.

The wares are different, too. You can't find any of this at a mall kiosk or from your favorite Mary Kay dealer. The scents take hold of me first. Tendrils of incense writhe in the air, wrapping around me, filling my lungs with the promise of magic. It burns in braziers with sage shrubs at every turn, making sure that none of this gets out of hand. Tiny bottles of it are displayed on black velvet, scents with names like *Lughnasadh, Prophetic Dream, or Eightfold Hearth.* The next table is all additives and components for spells—sandalwood, Libra oil, and hematite. Inside the shadowed space of a makeshift tent are flickering candles displaying reliquaries and tiny bottles full of bone or insect carcasses. None of this is daring jewelry you'd wear to your next book club meeting or even something exciting to spice up your love life. It's all in the service of witchcraft.

From where we're standing, we can still see the false front, the dilettantes at their own tables, going about their normal business. *Dim* business. It seems like if they wanted, they could easily poke their heads around the black curtains that act as backdrops to their booths. They could just part the sheets and get a glimpse of this other world. But none of them do. They sit in languid silence, sipping their coffee and smiling at people browsing on their way to get their Americanos or their lattes.

I try to look casual, but the light is disorienting. It's the unreal half-light of that moment when the sun passes behind a cloud on a summer day. Perpetual twilight. Zeke seems unmoved by it. He slides along with his usual, lazy gait, but I'm watching him for cues. The way his feet move like he's trying not to be heard, even when he doesn't realize it. The way his eyes shift whenever someone laughs too loudly or moves too quickly.

"Should I be ready for something?" I ask.

He smiles, knowing he's been caught. "We're hunting a necromancer on drugs. Yeah, bro. Be ready."

"You think Harvey's dangerous?"

"I'm not worried, but the dude does have some skills. That bird kinda kicked your ass."

"I wasn't ready to be attacked by a ghost bird!"

"Well then ... be ready."

We take our time, prowling through the aisles. There are maybe twenty tables, laid out in four vague, winding rows. Larger tents sit off to the side, thin wisps of smoke slithering out from the parted curtains. As we pass, we can hear chanting from some of them or the fevered patter of a séance reaching its climax. Seances usually end with screaming, don't they? Then someone faints. I've always thought they were a rowdy bit of theater that asked the participants to give themselves over to its trembling, breathless fantasy. Now I'm afraid to step inside. I've seen nothing here that you can't find at an herbalist or *curandero*, but all of it assembled in one place is a bulwark against whatever shattered skepticism I have left. Without that as my shield, I feel like a whipped dog, vulnerable, with my belly upturned.

And we're being watched. The witches steal glances at us over their coffee cups. Their eyes spark with recognition, but I've never met any of these people. Every time they whisper, I imagine it's about me. Zeke and I probably look like escaped mental patients. I try not to make eye contact and if I accidently do meet their gaze, I smile politely and pretend to browse. Still, I feel them watching, waiting for me to do something.

"This is weird. We're not supposed to be here," I whisper to Zeke.

"We're good. Just be cool."

"I'm being cool. They're still staring."

"It's because I'm Black," Zeke says.

"What?" I say way too loudly. "Seriously?"

"No," Zeke says and grins.

"Dude, don't mess with me. This is heavy shit. I can't deal with witches *and* racism right now."

"They're staring at us because you're acting strange. Stop it. Be cool," Zeke says without looking at me.

"I'm trying to be cool, but I've got questions, Zeke. I've got lots of questions right now."

"I'm listening."

"Do I have to stick close to you? Like when we did the spirit journey astral projection peyote trip with Rez and Andi?"

Zeke laughs to himself. "Nah, bro. This ain't that. That was some grade A magic. The good shit. This? This is just … Do you know what a glamour is?"

"Yeah. Like an illusion?"

"Pretty much. That's all this is. This part of the witch market is still here on earth as we know it, I guess, but the Dim can't see it. That's it. That's all."

"Okay, but it's safe? Like reality isn't going to collapse or the doorway shuts and we're stuck here in this market with these people for all eternity and we have to eat them to survive?"

"This discussion turned to cannibalism really quickly," Zeke says.

"I just want to find this asshole and get out of here before someone puts a curse on me. Do you see him yet?"

"Nobody is gonna curse you. Not here. There are rules. Decorum."

"How do you know? There are curse-y things everywhere. All of this stuff they're selling, it's for curses and evil witch shit. That's what they do with it!"

"When was the last time you were in a restaurant and a food fight broke out?"

I roll my eyes. He's not taking me seriously. "Umm. Never. I guess?"

"Exactly. Because of the social contract. You don't start food fights in restaurants, you don't go to the grocery store buck-ass nekkid, and you don't put curses on people when you're just browsing at the witch market. Now calm down."

"Where's your red bag?" I ask.

"Bro, if anyone tries to curse you or pulls any magic foolishness ..."

"It's karate time?"

"I will karate time all up in their face. I promise. But nobody is going to pull that here. Trust me."

I swallow and nod. Now eyes are all on us. When they see Zeke and I emerge from our discussion, they all look away, pretending to be busy with their grimoires and social media. One of them looks familiar, sitting on the fringe of the market, removed from the other tables. She's selling hand-illustrated Tarot cards with suits I've never heard of, like *the Three of Eyes* or *the Knight of Goats.* Her hoodie is ratty and gray, washed so many times the logo on the back— some punk band? —has faded into a blur of white and purple. The sleeves are torn off, and the hood is up. The rings on her finger aren't rings at all. They're repurposed garbage—hex nuts, neon yellow pipe cleaners, and braided twist-ties. Behind her circular sunglasses, she can't be more than twenty years old.

"Is that ...?" I ask Zeke.

"Wanderers Guild. Gotta be," he says.

The Wanderers Guild is an anomaly in the paranormal investigation scene, equal parts urban explorer, mystic, and gutter rat. With the other teams, even the ones who pretend to be vampires, I can trace them back to their mundane lives. Nights and weekends, they prowl around empty buildings, searching for signs of the unknown. By day, however, they work at sandwich shops or marketing firms. They're mostly normal people with normal hobbies. *Dim,* I guess. The Wanderers Guild is something else, though. They're *other,* living in crawlspaces or abandoned cars. They trade in handmade art or mystical garbage they scavenge from dumpsters or abandoned buildings. If there's a living embodiment of the secrets of this city, the Wanderers Guild is it. I don't recognize this one, but I know a few of the others, as much as one can claim to know a Wanderer, anyway.

"Alright. Let's split up," Zeke says.

"What? Split up? But ..."

"I'm gonna go shop for magic swords. Maybe a *karambit.* I could go to work on a fool if I had a magic *karambit.*"

"Karam? What? Is that a witch thing? Don't leave. We can't split up. I'm—"

"You're fine. If you see Beaker—"

"Bunson."

"If you see *Bunson,* just yell. He's old. He can't run fast. I'll catch him, punch him in his old face, and we can go get some barbecue."

Zeke strolls away without a care in the world, leaving me standing in the middle of the row while some guy selling candles looks at me like he just saw my girlfriend dump me in public. Everyone else, however, is watching Zeke. They whisper when he passes by and the broken tension left in his wake is a collective exhalation. I look at my scrubs to make sure we're not covered in blood. I don't remember encountering any blood, but life comes at you fast. There are stains, but just coffee and hot sauce, the usual culprits, nothing to make us look like we just murdered someone. Maybe it *is* because he's Black. Or the cat scrubs. Could be those.

The Wanderer sits at her table, her decks of cards displayed in front of her. Customers are browsing, but she's watching me, waiting. Wanderers are always like that. They like to make you think they know something you don't. I brace myself for some fortune-cookie vagaries.

"Hey," I say as I walk up to her, "You're a friend of Violet's, right?"

Over her glasses, the gold flecks in her brown eyes glint with that preternatural, elven spark that so many of them seem to have. I almost ask her if they hand out novelty contacts whenever you join the guild.

"Hello, Clark," she says, and her voice has the weight of a thousand years, of wisdom and magic only she and her friends can truly comprehend.

"Have we met?" I ask, knowing that we haven't.

"Would you like a reading?" she asks, and fans a deck out across the table.

The cards are beautiful and primitive. Crayons mix with chalk over found pencils and whatever pens they stole from banks or restaurants. All of it blends into something both bizarre and soothing, beautiful and wholly alien.

"Nah," I say. "I got out of the card game when my mom threw out my Magic: The Gathering collection."

"Free of charge," she says and smiles, revealing a tiny sapphire in a silver grill over one of her teeth.

"Free? Since when? Everyone else here is charging. Gotta pay for those grills, right?"

"Free for you. Violet said so. She said you would need it."

Something in my stomach flips over. It's not the tacos. The Oswald Academy. Since it all went down, I haven't seen many of the others. Some of them got together to bond and hash out what happened. It was group therapy that from what I hear devolved into drunken sobbing and people storming out. They were trying to make sense of it, asking the same questions over and over and not coming up with any answers.

Was it really supernatural? Will anyone believe us? Are we safe?

Yes. No. And no.

I dropped off the email list right away. I don't want to see those people. If I see them, I see Jojo and his ravaged corpse. I see John Elder and his mangled face or Belinda getting murdered right in front of me. I see Iris Angel. Poking at that weekend with a stick while we sit in a Starbucks with shell-shocked looks on our faces is not going to help me. They can wring their hands and cry all they want.

"I'm good," I tell the Wanderer.

She's not dissuaded. She shuffles the deck and starts to lay them out in a manner I've never seen. There's a process to reading Tarot cards. The order and placement of them is important. I'm not convinced that it works at all, of course. I'll hang on to that until I absolutely have to let it go. Over the last year, too many things I've dismissed as bullshit have been revealed to be inexplicable and horrifying. I'd rather live in a world where Tarot cards are just cards. The Wanderer's smile tells me she knows this, but she keeps working the deck anyway. I can't help but watch. I'm not going anywhere. She knows *this,* too.

She places them all in a spiral, edging closer and closer to the center. As each one is displayed, she regards it, thinks on it for a second, and moves on to the next. I have to keep myself from asking, "Okay, what does that one mean?"

I swallow down the lump in my throat. *The Seven of Goats. The Priest of the Sea.* She made these things up and I'm still transfixed, terrified of what she'll say when she completes the spiral, but unable to walk away.

The last card falls. *The Storm Beyond.* A lurid red-and-black thunderhead roils beneath a blanket of stars. The girl stares at it and her face falls. When she looks back up at me, her eyes are heavy with pity.

"Is that bad?" I ask. "That looks bad."

Never with a direct answer, she says, "This is your future, Clark."

"What does it mean?"

"*The Storm Beyond* is chaos. It is madness. It is the purest state of the uber-verse before it was birthed with song. It is the unformed, raw and hungry, sitting at the edge of everything."

"Okay. So, you're saying it's bad. Is this about the tacos we ate this morning? 'Cause I feel fine."

"You take care of your friends, Clark. You always do. Stay true to that," she says, and sweeps up the cards with a sad smile. "I'm sorry."

"About what?"

She doesn't answer. My stomach flips again. My friends. Alan. DJ. Melissa. Travis. Sure, I take care of them. Right.

I shake off the memory of screams through a radio, the howling noise from the tapes, and the bottomless pit in the Lighthouse.

"Hey, do you have any drugs?" I ask her.

She cocks her head. The gold flecks glint again in the half-light. "What do you need, Clark? You're a friend of the Wanderers. We can find anything for you."

"Cairn root. I heard I can get that around here."

"Ah," she says. "Don't go rushing into the Storm just yet, Clark. Those doors will be opened for you all too soon."

"Okay. I don't know what that means. But if I were going to buy some cairn root around here and get super high, where would I do that?"

Before she can answer, a large guy with a shaved head and a dwarven beard lumbers up next to me. He's too close, thrusting out his broad chest wrapped in a denim jacket. "Hey. Seriously, man? That's inappropriate. Not okay," he says, and I can tell he's deepening his voice to intimidate me.

"Listen, Gimli. I'm just here trying to score some wizard drugs, okay?"

"Maybe you didn't hear me. That's inappropriate. You can't just come up in here and start talking like that, sir," he says, and gets close enough I can smell the vetiver in his beard oil.

When I look back over to the Wanderer, she's gone. The cards have been swept off the table, leaving only the black velvet and an empty chair. Typical Wanderer.

I turn back to the beard guy. "Hey, you look like you're friends with Gandalf. Can you ask him for me? Tell him I'm good for it. I'll pay cash."

"Alright, buddy. Let's go," he says and grabs me by the arm.

Great. An ass-beating in the parking lot. Like I haven't had enough of those.

We don't get far. When he turns to drag me away, Zeke is standing there, arms crossed. Beardo stiffens and takes a half step back.

"Umm..." he says, but even that syllable chokes and dies in his throat.

"Oh, hey," I tell Zeke. "Nancy Reagan here got mad 'cause I'm talking about wizard drugs."

Zeke looks Beardo in the eye then shifts his gaze to the man's hand gripping my bicep. Beardo lets go.

"Mr. Silver. I'm sorry," he says with a stammer. "I didn't—"

"Walk," Zeke says.

The big man holds up his hands in surrender, nods, and walks back into the market. Everyone stares as he passes, then turns to watch Zeke. The air is sharp and quiet. Even the birds have stopped singing.

I turn to Zeke. "Well, that was awesome. Why did he call you Mr. Silver?"

Zeke looks past me and gives a polite wave to the small crowd that's keeping its distance. "Sorry," he says to them and flashes his biggest smile. "Everything's cool."

They all look away, at their books and their wares and the other shoppers. They do anything but look at Zeke.

"What is going on? Did you kick somebody's ass when I wasn't looking?" I ask him.

"Dude," he says, "What did Andi tell you?"

"Umm. Which part?"

"Back there when you were all goo-goo eyed, sipping tea. Were you paying attention? What did she tell you?"

"She said she was probably going to break up with her boyfriend and maybe we'd get married?"

He purses his lips and stares at me.

"She said be discreet," Zeke says. "And I don't know why I trusted you by yourself to *be discreet.*"

"I was just asking where to buy wizard drugs. Is this not the place for that?"

"You were starting a food fight!" he says and throws his hands in the air.

"I'm sorry! I don't know all of your dumb magic rules."

"They're not magic rules, Clark. They're *don't be an asshole* rules. You can't just walk up to people at a goddamn table and say 'Hey, do you have drugs?'"

"You weren't here. You don't know what I said."

"Holy shit. That's what you said, isn't it? That's *exactly* what you said. You just started asking people if they have drugs, didn't you?"

As our voices raise, the people in the market start to stare again. It's with the wariness of someone who knows a fight is about to break out. They don't want to look directly at us, but don't want to miss anything, either.

"Now who's being indiscreet?" I ask him.

Zeke crosses his arms and leans in to whisper to me. "The RV is down by the water, jackass."

"Oh yeah!" I say. "The RV!"

"Were you paying attention to Andi at all?"

"I'm sorry!" I say as we start to walk the trail down to the lakeshore. "She's really pretty, and it makes me all confused, and I forget things."

"This is on me," Zeke says and frowns. "I knew better than to take my eyes off you in a place like this. You got no finesse."

The throng of shoppers parts to let us pass on our way to the lakeshore. I mutter apologies to anyone who makes eye contact with me. We break away from the rows of tables, and I can feel eyes on our backs. When I cast a glance over my shoulder, everyone looks away, afraid they've been caught spying.

"Hey, if I get cursed, how will I know?"

"You'll know," Zeke says.

"Will it be like … I don't know, something simple like going blind? Or diarrhea until I die?"

"Again with the poop."

"Or something really heinous like demonic hallucinations? Or … Jesus, what if they curse me and all food just tastes like cold Burger King? I guess curses are only limited by the imagination of the witch, right?"

"You are my curse. I think I understand that now," Zeke says.

"I'm sorry," I say. "I've never bought drugs before, wizard or otherwise."

"Neither have I, but you don't do it like that. Besides, we're not buying the drugs, we're just trying to find Harvey. Haven't you seen any tv shows with detectives?"

"Let's just find the RV."

"Please. Try not to piss off any witches," Zeke says. "I left my bag in the car."

\*\*\*

# CHAPTER SIX

A footpath winds down a gentle slope through green grass not yet baked by the heat of the oncoming Texas summer. I wonder if others can see this path, if people out at Third Moon, just enjoying a cup of coffee, would ever notice it, or if it's always hidden by the glamour. Some real estate agent on her lunch break decides to take her shoes off and walk out under the shadow of the mimosa tree and suddenly finds herself surrounded by bat corpses preserved in jars and people who call themselves *Elzevir* or *Slayne*.

"But seriously, if we buy some cairn root, do you want to take it with me? It sounds kinda rad," I tell Zeke.

"Oh, hell no," he says. "I'm not putting anything like that into my body. And neither are you. Besides, you don't have the money for cairn root."

I'm about to unleash a volley of questions at him—

How do you know cairn root is expensive?

Why was that guy scared of you?

Why are people staring at you like you're a cop?

But the RV reveals itself as we round the corner. It's a hulking, boxy thing with broad green stripes down its side, reminding me of my grandmother's greenhouse, but on wheels and with drugs inside. It's less *Breaking Bad* and more *The Hills Have Eyes*. Dirt cakes the sides in filthy halos around the wheel wells. The windows are blacked out with layers of tinfoil and faded newspaper. A talisman of feather and bone hangs from the rearview, dangling along with a troll doll at the end of a tiny noose. The back is festooned with peeling and cracked bumper stickers.

My other ride is a BROOM.

Cat on board.

My money and my daughter go to Miskatonic University.

Of course this is where you buy the drugs. Framed by the gentle waves of Lake Austin, it's grotesque, a giant wart on the shore. There's no way the city would allow this thing to sit here or anywhere else within the sight of decent people. Even as it rests idle under the sun, I can imagine its grinding engine and the rattling, smoking cacophony when the wheels turn and it rolls down the city streets. Magic is the only explanation for why this thing is allowed to exist.

A threadbare canvas awning extends out over the front door. Sitting in a lawn chair, smoking a cigarette, is an old woman in a house gown. Her head is shaved to a short buzz. A lifetime of cigarettes and sunlight have stolen her youth and masked her true age. Under the leathery skin, she could be anywhere from fifty to ninety.

When her gaze lands on me, I stop in my tracks. Her milky white eyes don't quite fix on me. She stares just past my shoulder.

"Howdy, y'all," she says with a deep drawl.

Detective, I think. Be a TV detective.

"Hi. Name's Clark. Clark Vandermeer. I'm with Occultex. We're looking for someone. Hoping maybe you've seen them," I say.

Zeke turns to me, eyes wide. "Seen them?" he mouths.

"Don't know if you noticed, hun," the old woman says, "but I ain't seen shit."

"Okay," I say, trying to keep explanations and apologies from spilling out. "Harvey Bunson. Necromancer. Heard he might be around here."

She shrugs. "Ain't heard of him. Sorry."

"You're Bela, right?" I say, daring to step a bit closer.

"That's my name."

"Andi Thorn told me you might be able to help us track this guy down."

Zeke crosses his arms and plants himself right there next to me. She cocks her head, as if she can feel his presence.

"Little rich girl playing at being a witch? She don't know me," Bela says, and grins with a set of teeth she must have borrowed from a carny.

"Bela," Zeke says, and the bass in his voice makes her flinch.

"Zeke Silver?" she asks, and her voice is suddenly a weak wheeze.

"Goddamn right," Zeke says.

I turn to him and whisper, "Is this a good cop/bad cop thing? I didn't know we were doing that."

Zeke leans in—just a little—and Bela can feel it. She squirms in her lawn chair and even though she can't see, she averts her eyes. "Listen," she says, "we don't want no trouble."

"Well, if you've got the old necromancer in there, you've got trouble, 'cause here I am," Zeke says.

Clearly, whatever I have to say next isn't going to be worth a damn, so I just turn to look at Zeke and try to figure out exactly what's happening right now. Bela's hands tremble as she lights another cigarette. There's a pile of them in a green glass ashtray on a folding table. She's out here morning, noon, and night, a nicotine-soaked sentinel.

Finally, after a few drags, she nods. "Yeah. Yeah. Okay," she says and turns to yell at the door of the RV. "Harvey? Come on out here for a second!"

Inside there's a rustling noise. Harvey and whoever he's with are either in mid-coitus or trying to hide the drugs. I take a few steps back so I can see the full breadth of the RV. If this is anything like a TV cop show, Harvey's going to crawl out of a window and run along the shoreline. He won't get far. Even I could catch him, and I get winded drying off from a shower.

Bela turns in her chair and bangs on the door with a gnarled fist. "Harv! Get your ass out here!"

Nothing.

Zeke turns to me. "I guess we're going in."

Bela waves her hands, flinging ash everywhere. "He's tripping balls in there, smokin' the root. I ain't got nothing to do with that. He didn't get that shit from me. I can't be held responsible."

"You keep telling yourself that, sweetheart," Zeke says, and opens the door.

Body odor. Grease. Rotten eggs. Smoke. Vanilla. The odors hit us, thick and heavy. Both of us squint and recoil from the doorway.

"Jesus," I say, and cover my mouth and nose. "Smells like poached asshole in here."

The inside of the RV is filthier than the outside. Fast food cartoons are strewn about, mingling with empty packs of cigarettes, a stray lighter on the floor, and a lone, hole-riddled sock. A heavy curtain blotted with mysterious stains separates the driver's cabin from the rest of the RV.

"So not into this *Trainspotting* shit," Zeke says under his breath.

"If I get poked with a needle, I'm going to punch that old lady in the face. I don't care if she's blind," I say.

Behind the curtain, there's music and mumbling. I lean closer and listen.

"I think it's Insane Clown Posse, " I tell Zeke.

"Don't do drugs, kids," Zeke says, and parts the curtain so we can take a better look.

Harvey sits on a bench, the barkcloth cushion pocked with cigarette burns. Along with two others, he's huddled over some sort of bong they've MacGyvered together from duct tape, a car battery, and an old CRT television. Hoses cannibalized from vacuum cleaners snake out from the TV. Harvey and his friends have their lips wrapped around them. A motor runs for a second, and a light flickers in the otherwise dark TV tube. The junkies breathe and shudder. The motor cycles down, and the spark in the TV screen fades. Harvey laughs and leans back as his head rolls on his shoulders. To his right, a girl who looks like a gender-swapped Gollum exhales faintly green tendrils of smoke from between cracked lips. Wisps of hair from her mostly bald head hang down, brushing across the neck of her ragged Strawberry Shortcake T-shirt. To Harvey's right is a short guy with only one hand and a sigil tattooed on his neck, the mark of *Valac*, a demon from the *Goetia*.

Harvey's eyes drift up to us and narrow with recognition. He nods to the bong. "Come hit it."

"Get your ass up, Harvey. Now," Zeke says.

"And no ghost bird business this time," I say. "That was a dick move."

"Come on, guys," Harvey says with a slur. "I've been locked up for a while. Just chill out for a bit."

Lady Gollum and One-Hand aren't paying much attention. She stares straight ahead, through One-Hand. Through the wall. Through the folds of reality itself. A flurry of realizations spark in her rheumy eyes, revelations just for her. One-Hand is mumbling to no one in particular.

"I didn't know you were here," he whispers.

"Harvey," Zeke says and motions to the bong, "if I have to come over there, I'm going to shove this little art project right up your ass."

"You don't know what you're missing," Harvey says with a smile.

Zeke looks at the squalor all around. "I've got a decent idea."

"Wasn't talking to you," Harvey says, and his bloodshot eyes land on me.

Zeke says something else, his words sharpening, but I can't focus on it. Just behind Harvey, there's someone else, a fourth person I didn't notice until now. He's not sitting in shadow, but he *is* shadowed. I can't look directly at him, but he's there. Sitting. Floating? I can't see his eyes, but I know that he's staring at us. If you asked me to describe him, I couldn't. He's a man and he's wearing clothes. Plain clothes. Unremarkable. It's not like he just appeared. He's been there all along, like when you're looking for your phone, only to realize it's been in your hand the whole time.

I start to say something to Zeke, but Zeke is moving. He kicks the makeshift bong aside and swats One-Hand out of the way to reach for Harvey.

Then the Man is there, standing between Zeke and Harvey. The Man didn't move. He was sitting just past Harvey, like the old necromancer's shadow. And then he wasn't. Caught off-guard, Zeke flinches and takes a half step back. The Man's face shifts, a blur, like looking at someone through your tears. From five feet away, he reaches out, and his arm doesn't elongate, but it touches me anyway. He plants a frigid hand on my chest and shoves. The push isn't hard, but I'm knocked off balance from the shock. I pinwheel my arms, trying to stay upright, trying to get away from him. In the narrow path, my feet get tangled. I grab for something and snatch the curtain down on top of me. The body odor and the funk of stale beer crawls down my throat. I fall backwards into the driver's seat and kick out blindly.

Something shifts. The RV rocks. We're moving. Through the driver side window, the lake bumps and jerks.

"Oh damn!" I yell.

My elbow hit the gear shift as we fell. In the back of the RV, I see Zeke catch himself and look over his shoulder at me. "You good?" Zeke says.

"Get him!" I yell and throw the grungy drapes off me.

Twisting around, I fumble for the gear shift. Outside, the water races past, picking up speed. The RV bucks and jumps. It bangs and rattles. I'm tossed around, trying to stay upright.

Too late.

We slam into something hard, and I'm hurled into the floorboard. The windshield cracks. Zeke staggers back and tries to brace himself. Someone in the back yelps in surprise.

The RV is canted at an angle, nose-first. My hands are wet. Water is leaking in through the driver's side and filling up the floorboard. We're sinking.

"Shit!" I yell. "Shit, shit, shit!"

Zeke looks back at me. "What happened!?"

"I think we're in the lake!"

Lady Gollum scrambles. She hops over Zeke, crawling like a lizard, and bolts out the door just as a torrent of lake water rushes inside.

"Oh boy …" Zeke says and looks around as water sweeps up the debris.

We both look to the back of the RV, where Harvey is bracing himself against the fold-out bed. He's not worried. He's laughing at us, like he just won. One-Hand is tearing open a crude hatch in the side of the TV bong and clawing for the payload inside.

"No, man," he says. "Oh, come on …"

Zeke leaps to his feet, but the RV lurches, and the angle of the floor shifts. He slips in the water. It's pouring in through the side windows now. I grab the wheel and pull myself up as brackish cold steals my breath and tries to consume me.

In the back, as Harvey cackles, the Man takes hold of his arm. The back glass blows outward, sending shards and shredded newspaper flying. Blinding sunlight explodes into the sinking RV. Harvey and the Man rocket out of the window and into the afternoon sun, taking flight. In seconds, they're a spiraling speck in the distance. A whirlwind of ash and rolling papers is left in their wake. Over the growing roar of the water, I can hear Harvey's fading laughter.

"What the hell?! Did they just fly away?" I ask.

The RV lurches again, now in a full-on dive into the deep. The door is submerged. Lake water roils and pulls at me, threatening to drag me down.

"We gotta climb!" Zeke says, and begins to grab at door handles and edges, pulling himself upward.

I follow as the water rises. The cold numbs my hands, making it hard to hold onto anything. Zeke quickly makes it to the window with his ghost-fighting ninja parkour.

"Come on, dude," he yells and hoists up One-Hand by the arm.

The water catches up to me. Rather than pull me down, it raises me up and spits us out the back window just as the lake devours the rest of the RV. I kick for the shore, but the surface churns, trying to drag us back down after the sinking vehicle. I'm sucked under. The cold blue of the sky battles with the colder darkness of the lake as I fight. I open my mouth to scream, and muddy water fills my mouth.

Hands grip me under the arms. I hear Zeke growl and pull as my feet find a purchase. We stumble back, tangled up in each other, and collapse on the shore. Eddies of RV-junkie trash swirl, the only thing left of the battered caravan. One-Hand, soaked and scared, scrambles to get away from the scene.

"My baby!" Bela screams. She's dancing a mad jig on the bank, like a spider missing most of its limbs. "That was my house! My home, you sons-of-bitches!"

The crowd is spilling out of the market. They stumble down the slope, slack-jawed and helpless. They look at Bela, at the quieting spot in the water where the RV vanished, then over at us. Their gazes twist from horrified amazement into disgust.

"Oh, they're pissed," I say.

"We out," Zeke says, and jumps to his feet.

We cut through the crowd and try not to look anyone in the face. People are beginning to murmur. They try to comfort Bela as she spits frothy invectives at us. She wails something about a curse, but I try not to listen. If I don't hear what spell she's going to cast on us, maybe it won't work.

LALALALA! You're not going to turn my insides to liquid shit! LALALA!

We move up the path with the quickstep shuffle of soggy clothes. The vapors of lake water cling to us. When we break back into the regular market, the light shifts again, back to normal sunlight, and I shield my eyes from the intensity. We're out of the glamour.

The regular market, the one where the *Dims* shop, is moving along, quiet and polite. From here, we can't hear Bela's yelling. The commotion is only thirty yards behind this façade, but it might as well be on the other side of the world. No one suspects a thing.

Until they see us tottering away like wet rats. The small crowd, still full of curious soccer moms and old Austin hippies, freezes in place to look at us with wide eyes and gaping mouths. I start to make some awkward apology, but Zeke grabs me by the arm and pulls me along behind him. We beeline for the parking lot when we see Andi hurriedly tossing her bag into the passenger seat of a baby blue Volvo P1800. It's completely intact and in pristine condition. The only thing marring the restoration is a black bumper sticker that reads *Siouxsie Is My Copilot.* She jumps behind the wheel.

And suddenly, I don't feel the biting cold of the lake water soaking me or the rough asphalt beneath my bare foot. I'm not worried about the angry mob of witches or the Lazlos' thinly veiled threats. I'm riding shotgun in the Volvo, blissfully buzzed on margaritas as Andi blasts Dean Martin and races down an empty highway past Elysian Fields. The windows are down. She's grinning. I'm warm and filled with soft sparks and maybe finally happy.

But she spots us and the look we get cuts through all of that. It's colder than the lake water. The picture in my mind blows away like Harvey vanishing into the daytime sky.

"You two are unbelievable. Un-fucking-believable," she says through the open door of the car.

"Andi ..." I say.

I try to catch up to her, but she slams the door and races out of the parking lot. We stand there, dripping.

"Ooh, girl, she mad at you," Zeke says.

"Me?" I ask, turning on him. "She's mad at me? She said *you two*. Two. That's us. She's mad at *us*."

Zeke looks back toward the lake and sneers. "I'm gonna whip Harvey's ass."

"What in the hell was that thing? That guy with him. Was that a person? What was that?"

Zeke shrugs and heads for the car. "Some dark spirit. Kinda pissed at myself for not noticing."

"Great. So, necromancy is real. I didn't need this today," I say.

Behind us, people from the market are gathering at the edge of the parking lot. They're pointing us out to management. A few of them are on their phones, probably talking to the police. We slide into the car and when the doors close, we're trapped in there with the funk of stale lake.

"The car is going to smell like this forever," Zeke says.

"I need a shower. Maybe two showers," I say, and pick bits of debris out of my hair and off the soaked surgical scrubs. "And maybe some antibiotics after going into that RV."

Stuck to my shoulder is a piece of paper. It peels away like a layer of dead skin.

"What now?" Zeke says, his hand poised on the gear shift.

Behind us, a manager with his stern *I'm-a-manager* face is walking over to us. He's wearing his black apron with authority, but I can't be bothered. The piece of paper in my hand is trash. I should have just brushed it off and tossed it into the floorboard with the rest of the garbage, but I can't. I'm holding it, staring at it, like it's something I should remember. The purple print on white paper feels like a string around my finger. It's the fragment of a dream that comes to me hours past waking, a reminder I wrote to myself while in a drunken stupor.

The manager taps on the glass and knits his brow. I think we're about to get grounded without witch privileges. We ignore him.

"Excuse me," he says and raps on the window.

"Let's get out of here before you have to karate this guy," I say, and stare at the receipt as if just looking at it long enough will cause it to reveal its secrets.

Zeke backs out of the parking lot. "Where we going? We ain't giving up, are we?" he asks, as the manager throws his hands up in indignance.

*The King's Crown Motor Inn* is printed across the top of the receipt, along with today's date. In the rearview, I lock eyes with Helper. He's standing apart from the crowd, still there, unmoving, a porcelain-white scarecrow in a field of cars. The look on his face is placid, but focused, like he's reading my thoughts writ large across my brain.

"Let's be TV detectives and follow a lead. Maybe we should get sunglasses and a bad ass car," I say.

"I'd settle for dry clothes," Zeke says as we haul ass out of there.

"We've got a half tank of gas, a bag full of swords, and we're chasing a necromancer," I say.

"Let's do it."

\*\*\*

# CHAPTER SEVEN

7 p.m.

Shit.

"So let me get this straight," Zeke says through a mouth full of potato chips. "We are following up on a lead based on a piece of trash that was stuck to you?"

"Right."

"It's literally a trash lead."

"Yeah, but … I don't know. It felt significant."

We're standing in the parking lot of an abandoned motel in North Austin, just off the interstate. The faded wooden sign, listing dangerously forward over a patch of weeds littered with empty beer cans, advertises a laundry room and free HBO with your stay. The windows of the Pioneer Motel are smashed or covered with graffiti-tagged panels of wood. As the streetlights begin to glow and all the summer's nocturnal insects noisily stir, defeat descends over us with the dusk. Standing here with our sodas, splitting a bag of potato chips, we look like we just wrapped up some unlicensed surgery. The scrubs got all crunchy and stiff as they dried, and they don't smell any better. Over the last few hours, we've gone to every seedy motel in the Austin area. All the decaying eyesores that charge by the week or month, every place that looks like the last refuge of degenerates and bedbugs. None of them were the King's Crown Motor Inn. No one we asked has heard of it. It's not showing up on any map or in any of our web searches.

Zeke is examining me, nodding as though he finally understands. "That's magic, bro," he says.

"Huh?" I ask, taking the chips away from him.

"The receipt. It's significant. I'm sure of it. It's Synchronicity."

"Did your Magic 8-Ball tell you that?"

"I'm serious, dude. The more you use magic, the more magic shows itself to you. That receipt? That was magic—or the universe or whatever—helping you out. It's called synchronicity. Be careful."

"Am I a wizard? Is this the part where you take me to Hogwart's? 'Cause I don't know if I have the patience for those little bastards right now."

"I'm just saying: the more you use it, the more it uses you."

"And I'm just saying that if I can cast *Magic Missile,* I'm gonna do that shit all the time."

"If you start casting spells, you're gonna have to find another roommate."

"What? Why wouldn't you want to live with a wizard? I'd be a badass wizard!" I make little spell-casting motions with my greasy fingers, accidentally flinging chips onto the cracked asphalt.

"I have to explain to you how the dishwasher works literally every time you use it."

Twenty yards away, cars fly past on the interstate. We sit on the hood and watch them, lost in thought. I'm totally going to cast spells *and* I'm going to do it to cheat at video games. He can kiss my ass. It's going to be awesome.

And I'm going to bring back Alan, wherever he and the others might be. With wizard powers, I could do that. If that damned door at the Lighthouse sent them to the Phantom Zone, then I can reopen it. But seeing Alan at the Oswald Academy, staring back at me from a gulf of shadows, makes me question if I even want to.

"She text you back yet?" Zeke asks.

I check my phone, which is miraculously still working after our little swim. No new messages. My heart sinks a little deeper, a shrinking little cube of ice sliding into the pit of my stomach.

"No," I say, and remember the snarl on Andi's face.

"She's mad. She'll get over it. That shit wasn't our fault."

"It was kind of our fault."

"A little bit, but what were we supposed to do? That old son of a bitch won't listen to reason, so we had to flex on him a little."

"Yeah, about that …" I say and turn to him for an explanation.

"What?"

"You know what. The people back at the market, they were scared of you. What's that about?"

Zeke shrugs. "I wasn't always your partner."

I cross my arms. "Yeah, I'm gonna need a little more than that."

"In the past, I've had to smack down some witches," he says and shrugs. He watches the cars pass on the highway with a thousand-yard stare reserved for war veterans and people who work retail.

"You've got stories you're not sharing with me, and it's kind of hurting my feelings."

"You'll be fine," he says, still not looking at me.

"When I'm a wizard, I'm going to cast something cool and make you tell me."

Finally, he turns to me and grins. "You cast one spell on me, I'm going to kick your head right off your shoulders. *Right. Off.*"

"Wizard vs. karate! Round one! Fight!"

My phone buzzes, and I snatch it out of my pocket. It's Andi. *Ask Violet*, it says. I show the text to Zeke. He winces.

"Just two words?" he says. "She's so pissed at you."

I rush around to the passenger side of the car. "Shut up. We're going to get married and have magic babies."

\*\*\*

Downtown Austin has its secrets. Among all the gleaming towers and bars with $20 cocktails, there are still things hidden in the spaces in between. The Wanderers Guild lives in these spaces. The empty apartments. The vacant storefronts. The alleys you never noticed. The Wanderers call these places home. Technically, most of them are vagrants, but even that isn't entirely accurate. They are the forgotten and overlooked, invisible people that slip through the cracks. They're the keepers of the city's mysteries. Violet is their leader, and if anyone knows where to find this motel, it's her.

It's Friday night, and the revelers are starting to come out in droves, looking to fuck or fight or just drink themselves into oblivion. It used to be my scene, bouncing from joint to joint until I ran out of money or reached my limit of liquor and shame. The bros in their muscle shirts and hair products chase the girls in their glittery skirts and heels. All of them titter at us or offer vague looks of disgust. Our scrubs are painted with brown shades of lake water and mud. That's my life.

I wish I really were a wizard. I'd turn into a werewolf or a dragon and make some dudebro cry. *Who's laughing now, you little shitbags?!*

I guess you could say I'd be an *evil* wizard. I'm okay with that.

Down an alley that smells like hot garbage and stale pizza, a smaller path breaks off and leads us into a winding, urban labyrinth. We hop over construction barricades and through tunnels under Sixth Street. The air is acidic with the stench of urine. I'm reminded of rotting drywall and children with sharp teeth, and I have to swallow down the anxiety. The notes of a baritone sax drift through the air, a lonely dirge. It gets louder with every turn.

A rickety fire escape takes us four stories up the side of a dark office building nestled in between two larger buildings. As we climb, I realize we're following the sound of the saxophone. The melody is loose and languid, with long, mournful notes casting out over the city.

"We *are* detectives!" I say to Zeke in an excited whisper.

"Just move your ass, Harry Dresden," Zeke says.

When we top the roof, I see a grinning and fanged Lon Chaney, his face towering over us, displayed on the side of an adjacent building. The image flickers in black and white as a projector softly hums. We join a small crowd, maybe twenty people, sitting cross-legged on blankets or in camping chairs, all sprawled out, watching the film. A rooftop theater. They sip cheap beer from coolers at their feet and snack on street food. Just left of the screen, where Lon Chaney prances about in his top hat and trench coat, is the saxophone player. A tarnished and long baritone sax rests between his legs, providing the score to the silent film. Like most of the others here, he's wearing shredded denim and combat boots, his with a tattered Operation Ivy t-shirt. The audience is transfixed as a bug-eyed Chaney chews up the scenery, menacing his victims.

The sensation of being untethered from reality washes over me, chilling me to my marrow again as I recognize the film they're watching. I turn and look over my shoulder. Austin sprawls out before me, looking like it always does. The pink of the capitol dome. Skyscrapers. Endless construction cranes. It's still my city. It's still earth, as far as I can tell, yet once again, I'm unmoored. This time, it's because of a movie.

"You alright, bro?" Zeke asks.

I point at the screen and I'm not sure how to explain it. I must be confused. "It can't be." I say.

"It is," a soft voice whispers.

A few feet away, so close we should have seen her approach, is Violet. She's smiling, and her eyes—one lavender and one pale green—spark with an almost preternatural light in the glow of the projector. If she coasted inches from the ground, held aloft by fairy wings, I wouldn't have been surprised. She always seems to have one foot in some other world, like she's not really from around here.

"Damn, Vi," Zeke says. "You're gonna scare me right off this dang roof."

"Hello, Zeke," she says, and her voice vibrates with the softest timbre, coming to us over a radio from Middle Earth. "I'm so glad to see the two of you here."

"Violet," I say, unable to take my eyes off the screen. "Is … is that *London After Midnight*?"

She smiles, pulls her hoody up over her head, and slings a backpack over her shoulder. "We should hurry. You don't have much time."

"For what?" I ask.

She heads for the fire escape and starts to descend. "You have a long night ahead of you, Clark. If we're going to get you to the motel, we should leave now."

She disappears below the lip of the roof. Zeke shakes his head and gives me a flat stare. "You tell her where we were going?"

"Nope."

"You know I hate it when she does that shit," Zeke says and starts to follow her down.

I take a second to stand there and watch the movie. I'm not paying attention to the story or even really listening to the moody undercurrent of the saxophone's score. It's a reckoning. I have to stare this in the face and accept it. I spent years poking around abandoned buildings and reading about demons and grimoires and all the things that existed outside of our world of 401k contributions and changing your oil every five thousand miles.

Then I found it. That night in the Lighthouse, the night my friends vanished, *the other* revealed itself to me. And it won't stop. Like a fractal, it keeps expanding into elaborate and new designs. All those things in this *other* happen and exist outside of what I know. Ghosts are real. Death isn't final. People can manipulate the natural order of the universe with methods I'm only beginning to comprehend. But it's not in my home. It's outside my door, but I can always retreat to the safety of video games, reruns of my favorite sitcom, or McDonald's French fries.

But then there's this movie.

Even casual film fans know that *London After Midnight* was destroyed in a fire back in the 1960s. It doesn't exist, not anymore. Yet here it is. Lon Chaney grins at me like he knows what I'm thinking. He knows he's got me. He opened the door to my house and ransacked it, letting me know that even the things I thought I understood are null and void. There is no veil. There is no difference between life as I knew it and the *other*. I have to deal with this. And what am I supposed to do? Sometimes one of your friends tells you they saw an alien spaceship, an actual UFO. They describe the night in detail and finish the conversation with, "Yeah. Crazy, right?" And that's it. That's the end of it. They go back to their life. And I always wonder how. How do you see something like that and then just go home and watch Netflix or worry about your taxes?

Now a mysterious woman is going to lead me to a necromancer who's hiding in a motel that doesn't seem to exist. This is my life now. Lon Chaney's leering, toothy face watches me as I descend the fire escape after Zeke and Violet.

Violet grins up at Zeke. "I like your cat doctor shirt."

***

The parking garage is cavernous. The echoes of our footsteps dance ahead of us into the empty gloom. We walk down a spiraling road, heading deeper, and the concrete traps the summer heat, making the air thick with humidity and the lingering scent of motor oil and exhaust. Violet skips along ahead of us like she's on a hike through the greenbelt. Zeke and I follow. I keep shooting wary looks over to him, tacitly asking him if this is cool. If he sees me, he doesn't acknowledge it. I can't tell if he's completely at ease or ready for something to go down. With him, those two things are often the same. As we descend, I get the feeling that this stopped being a parking garage two floors back. It still *looks* like a garage, but now it's endless, a tunnel winding down in a brutal spiral of cement and fluorescent lights.

I don't know how long we walk. Just as I'm expecting the concrete to give way to bare rock and limestone, some portal to the underworld, the ramps of the garage level out, and we reach the bottom floor. Still no cars. Not another soul in sight. Even our echoes have abandoned us. The endless ramps have stopped. The only way to go, other than back up, is a battered metal door set in a nondescript wall. It looks like a maintenance closet. The door handle is greasy, and the face of the door is scuffed where delinquents have tried and failed to kick it in.

Violet, of course, has a key. She barely slows as she unlocks it and passes through. Zeke and I both hesitate at the verge, unsure if we should follow. She walks ahead into a long and dank stone corridor dimly lit with flickering, industrial lights.

Zeke cocks an eyebrow at me. "You trust Violet, right?"

"You read my mind."

He sighs and follows her. "She couldn't just tell us to take a right at the Chili's, just past the highway, and the motel will be on your left?"

"I'm starting to think it's not that kind of motel," I say under my breath as we head into the dingy hallway.

"I left my bag in the car," Zeke says, frowning. "Should I go back and get it?"

"Hell no. And leave me here? Plus, I don't know that we'd ever be able to find this place again."

The hallway breaks to the right and ends in a small, basement-like room with a low ceiling. My heart crawls up into my throat. Violet is standing there in the middle of the room, her back turned to us, facing four colored doors.

I freeze up at the threshold and grip the door frame to keep from falling over as all the blood rushes to my head. They aren't the same doors that I saw in the Lighthouse, but the memory of Melissa standing there in front of the one I think my friends passed through—*screaming the entire time*—triggers a flood of pants-wetting paralysis. Four metal doors, painted red, blue, yellow, and green. My eyes race over every inch of the cramped room, searching for symbols, the weird and ancient markings that I should have seen as warning signs.

There's nothing else but the naked bulb in the ceiling. It's a bare room made of concrete slabs. Bits of dirt and other debris collect in the corners, but there are no warning signs and nothing telling us where the doors might lead. No magic seals. I fight the urge to grab Zeke by the arm and drag him back out. We can't go in here. This isn't worth it. We'll find Harvey some other way.

Violet sets down her backpack and smiles over her shoulder at us. She roots through the pack for a moment, past the tarot cards, flashlight, and dice carved from animal bone, and pulls out some sort of gadget. It's a black, circular thing with four brightly colored buttons.

"Is that a Simon?" Zeke asks incredulously.

"Mmhmm," Violet says, and sets the electronic game on the floor in front of her. She sits cross-legged in front of it, still facing the doors, and places her hands on it with the delicacy of someone touching the planchette of a Ouija board. Zeke scrunches up his face in confusion and looks at me.

I shrug. "I don't even know anymore, man."

The game beeps at her, the buttons lighting up in random patterns. Violet ignores us and plays for a moment, repeating the patterns as the memory game gets progressively more difficult. She doesn't miss a beat as it buzzes increasingly complex sequences. Zeke and I don't speak. We hold still and let her focus, as if the slightest sound could derail her streak.

Finally, the blue button on the Simon lights up and begins to pulse. The game has stopped. Violet turns and looks over her shoulder at us again, still smiling.

"Congratulations?" I say. "Do you have a Gameboy in there, too?"

"The blue door will take you to the motel," she says, as if it's the most obvious thing in the world.

Zeke and I exchange glances as Violet packs the Simon away and slings the bag over her shoulder.

"Is this an underground motel?" I ask.

She walks past us, heading back into the tunnel. Before she leaves, she says, "Be careful. Things will be different after tonight. If you live."

And then she's gone.

"Okay!" I shout after her. "Good seeing you. Text me, I guess."

Zeke takes a deep breath. "You ready?"

He grips the door and braces himself.

"When you open that, if there's screaming or Pinhead is standing there or something, I'm just going to go home. Fuck Harvey."

"Stand behind me," Zeke says.

\*\*\*

# CHAPTER EIGHT

A warm night breeze flows into the room, carrying with it the faint scent of algae and chlorine. Zeke stands there, looking through the doorway but not moving. There's another dark room just past this one, littered with empty buckets and hoses cast into the corner. A derelict water pump is decorated with a thick and sprawling spider's web. Beyond that, an empty swimming pool.

Zeke gives me a *WTF?* look and walks through. We step out onto the deck of the drained pool. A murky, sludge collects in the bottom, around the legs of a mangled pool chair. A neon sign blinks yellow and blue. The King's Crown Motor Inn. The crown at the top flashes yellow at cars passing by on a lonely stretch of highway. It's the kind of place we were looking for—a single-story mausoleum for the living and the desperate, the kind of place where secrets are kept, and the sheets are never changed. Weeds worm through the cracks in the sidewalk and crowd around the edge of the building. The rough flora continues into the trees, spreading out all around for as far as I can see in every direction. Shingles are missing from the roof, giving it the broken grin of a madman leering at the moon.

Lon Chaney's sharp teeth.

Behind us is the brick maintenance shack, long abandoned. Now it's a place for drifters and stray dogs to get out of the rain. The door is closed. We didn't close it or even hear the click of the bolt. It's not blue on this side but a rusted gray, and we both know that if we open it, it won't lead back to the parking garage. A message is sprayed in pink across the bricks of the shed. *The Storm Is Coming.* Above it is a smiley face with a deranged grin.

The Storm. Not *a* storm, but *The Storm.*

"Does that mean something?" Zeke asks.

"Let's just go."

Zeke leads the way, and I really wish he hadn't left his red bag back at the car. I know he's got multiple knives hidden in places I don't even want to think about, but I'd feel a lot better if I had one.

We exit through a waist-high wooden gate at the edge of the pool, out into a half-full parking lot. The motel itself stretches in a straight line, parallel to the road. On one end is the pool. At the other, the office. The noise of multiple televisions blares from behind many of the doors, blending into an uninterrupted slurry of gunshots, canned laughter, and commercial jingles. Occasionally, it's interrupted by someone shouting unintelligible fragments of rage or laughing inappropriately loud.

"Office?" I ask.

Zeke answers with a nod, and we walk along the sidewalk that passes by each of the rooms, slowing any time we can peek through the gap in the olive curtains.

"Just so you know," Zeke says, "I'm probably gonna choke him out. Like right away. I don't want to give that dude a chance to pull any bullshit."

"Can you kick him in the face, first? Or choke him out and then *I'll* kick him in the face?"

"I'm good with both of those options," Zeke says as we walk through the glass doors into the office lobby.

It's red shag carpet and wood paneling, the kind of place you didn't know still existed. A neon Coors Light sign glows over a mini-fridge, and a small TV mounted on an arm hangs from the wall. On the screen, a man in a gas mask and a lab coat dances around a cardboard graveyard, jabbering about another old horror movie. If it's Lon Chaney, I'm running down the highway and not looking back. The guy behind the counter is staring up at it, his chin resting in his hands, looking at the show but not really watching. With his buzz-cut and Buddy Holly glasses, his black tie and crisp, short-sleeve white shirt, he completes the tableau of decayed Americana. This is Route 66 gone wrong. He doesn't so much as twitch as we walk through the door.

Zeke and I stand there for a moment, waiting for him to acknowledge us. I clear my throat. He blinks a few times and looks over at us before standing up straight and smoothing out his tie. He takes his time with all of this, like he wants us to know he's got power over us.

"We've got an opening down at the end," he says, and checks the book behind the counter. "Forty-five per night."

"We're not here for a room," I tell him, putting a little gravel in my voice, like I've been smoking cigars and yelling at perps all day. "We're looking for someone."

"Okay," he says, and the TV tugs at his attention as his eyes begin to wander.

"The name's Harvey Bunson. Got a lot of bad tattoos, like prison tats, all up and down his arms," I say, unsure if I should tell him that Harvey's a practitioner of the dark arts.

"He's a real dickhead, too," Zeke adds.

"Sounds like a lot of people around here," the guy says in a dead, flat voice.

I feel Zeke bristle next to me, sparks jumping across his skin. He steps forward. "You got a lot of people named Harvey Bunson around here?"

The clerk doesn't flinch, but finally gives us his full attention. He narrows his eyes. "I'm not saying one way or the other. We respect the privacy of our guests. That's kind of the whole point of this place."

Zeke snorts, a bull ready to charge. "For real, bro? We're in a fix here, you know what I'm saying? We need to find this guy, okay? Real quick. If we don't, there's gonna be problems. And if I've got problems, I'm going to make them *your* problems."

The clerk sneers. Zeke's chest-thumping swagger bounces right off him. "Yeah. Okay," he says, unimpressed. "You think I don't have crackhead warlocks in here every night, threatening me? Talking to me about whatever crazy shit they're going to summon or all the curses they're going to put on my bloodline? Now I'm supposed to be scared because you have a mohawk?"

Zeke takes a half-step back, just as surprised as I am. He's not used to getting shut down.

"Now, do you want the room or not?" the guy says, redirecting his attention to the black-and-white horror show on the TV.

"I'm with Occultex Incorporated, and I want to speak to your manager," I say and cross my arms.

The clerk raises his eyebrows and gives me a long, level look. "You sure about that?"

He eyes a door behind the counter that leads to the back office but doesn't seem to want to look directly at it, like he doesn't want to acknowledge it.

"Yeah," I say. "Go get your manager, pal. I want to have some words with him."

The clerk stands up straight again. His Adam's apple bobs in his throat. He steals another glance at the office door. "Maybe you guys can call your friend. Or wait outside?"

The dull bluntness of his tone is gone. He looks at the door again like he's expecting it to fly open and for something unfortunate to come wailing out into the office.

"Manager," I say. "Now."

"Okay …" he says, and again smooths out his tie and tucks in his shirt before walking over to the office.

From his belt he pulls a mass of old iron keys, the kind you find in a dungeon, not some roadside motel. As he fiddles with the tangle of jangling metal, I see that his hands are shaking, and a stripe of sweat sticks his shirt to his spine. When the right key slides home into the lock, he glances over his shoulder at us once more before turning it. Zeke and I cross our arms and look down our noses at him. He disappears into the room, opening the door as little as possible so we can't see inside.

Zeke and I relax. "Asking for the manager. That is the whitest thing I've ever done," Zeke says.

I rush over to the counter and find the ledger. No automated systems here, just a registry bound in cracked and peeling faux leather. Inside, it's page after page and line after line of the same, precise serial-killer script. This guy must never get a day off. I find Harvey's name near the end.

"116," I say, and toss the ledger back behind the counter.

Zeke nods and we slip out into the night, the bell over the door announcing our escape. I move a little faster than normal and have to keep myself from breaking into a full-on sprint.

"We're in a hurry now?" Zeke asks.

"Yeah, I think we are," I say, and look over my shoulder into the glass-encased office. The clerk still hasn't emerged from the back room, but I have a feeling I really don't want to stick around to meet management. The guy wasn't warning us for his sake. He was warning us for ours.

***

"I hear grunting," I say with my ear pressed to the door of 116.

"Like … *that* kind of grunting?" Zeke asks.

"I'm afraid so. And other noises. More grunting. Maybe some moaning."

"So, grunting in the company of others? Group grunting?" Zeke asks, his face curled up.

I step away from the door. "Yeah. Sounds like Harvey and his friends are having the kind of good time you find in the darker corners of the internet."

Zeke's face further twists with disgust. "Should we wait?"

"I don't think we have time."

Zeke sighs and waves me aside. "Alright."

"Is it game time?" I ask.

"It is," Zeke says, and stares down the door like he can break it with the force of his will.

He takes a half step back and kicks it so hard the blast of the impact rattles car windows in the parking lot. The door slams open. In the dimly lit room, people scramble away. It's worse than the RV. A dirty sheet is thrown over the lamp, casting a murky glow over the grungy carpet, and the bed is riddled with cigarette burns. A thin, greenish haze lingers in the air. On the bed closest to us, Lady Gollum sits across from a young guy with greasy, long hair and a Rugrats T-shirt. Between them is a Ouija board covered in lines of powder the color of dead grass, all partitioned out and ready to snort. Another guy is passed out on the floor, a thick tendril of saliva working its way down his cheek and onto the carpet. Judging by his clothes, he clocked out of his shift at the call center and came straight here. Standing in front of the mirror is an older woman who's been turned to beef jerky from a few decades in the sun.

Her skin is pocked with sores, and she has the glossy eyed gaze of someone who has fully and completely achieved liftoff. She grips the edge of the mirror for dear life, staring deep into it, and doesn't bother to so much as glance at us.

On the other bed, Harvey is on his back, tangled in the sheets and literally caught with his pants down. On top of him is … something. I can't quite make it out. It's a mass of shadows in the vague shape of a woman. Round breasts, flowing hair, and spikes jutting from her back, all of it undulating in a phantom breeze. She—it? —turns her head to look at me, and the stare alone makes the room spin. Two opalescent eyes glisten in the center of the black, writhing shape. I grip the door frame as the gravity of the look pulls me in. Tearing away from those flickering points is a physical sensation, a gentle tug on the front of my brain.

"Oh, what the fuck?!" Harvey says.

And he's there in the bed alone, his bony fingers clutching at nothing but the vacant space above him. "Harvey, I think you might be bad at Tinder," I say.

As the two dumbstruck goblins on the other bed look at us, bloodshot and uncomprehending, Harvey glowers. Something moves in the periphery of my vision. It's a flicker in the air that my mind registers as a person, flashing across the room at us, a shark unseen under the surface of reality. Zeke steps into its charge and thrusts out his arm. The shimmer slams into the blade in Zeke's fist and stops dead.

I'm looking at it, but I can't see it. Not really. It's a man. It has a face. It looks like any other face. It has hair and clothes, but even as I look at it, I can't describe them. It's there in the room, but it's nothing, a cipher.

No one moves. No one breathes.

It shudders, impaled on the end of the knife. Zeke wrenches the blade downward, widening a wound that does not bleed. I'm aware of the thing's hands flying up in agony. With his left hand, Zeke drives his balled-up fist into the wound.

The moan comes from every corner of the room. From under the bed. From the television. It's heavy with dawning despair. The lights flicker. Zeke grits his teeth. His hand works around inside the thing, the quasi-void that floats there at the end of his arm. With a quick jerk, he yanks his hand back out. The moan is cut short.

The spirit is gone. It doesn't vanish so much as it's just not there anymore, an empty spot in the room. In Zeke's hand is a bundle of sticks, dripping with hazy, gray slime. Feathers and tiny, yellow charms are tied to the sticks with thin, red string. They're teeth, some of them animal, some not.

The crack of the wood makes everyone flinch as Zeke breaks the sticks over his knee and casts them into the corner. The guy on the floor is stirring. He looks like he'd be more comfortable at a sports bar, throwing back happy hour beers and shouting at the screen until his wife texts that he needs to come home and take care of the kids. He's sitting up on one elbow and raises a hand at us. His fingers twitch and dance.

Zeke points the knife at him. A runner of gray ichor slides off the tip of the long blade and collects on the carpet.

"Try something," Zeke says to him. "See what happens."

The man lowers his hand and looks away, withering under Zeke's stare.

"Listen," I say to the room, "We've had a long day and my friend here could stab people all night, so Harvey ... put some pants on and let's go, buddy."

As Harvey grumbles and worms out of the sheets, a voice from the parking lot calls out, "Enjoy your stay!"

Everyone in the room freezes and looks at the door. You'd think it was a police siren.

"Enjoy your stay!" the voice bellows again. "Enjoy your stay!"

Harvey, wide-eyed, hitches up his thrift store jeans. "You dumb fuckers got the Manager's attention?" he says, scrambling for his shoes.

The room explodes into a frenzy. They clamber over each other and around us, grabbing their things. The guy on the floor bursts past us and out into the night like he's fleeing a burning building.

"Enjoy your stay!" the voice comes and carries across the motel, drawing closer. It's less an exhortation than an announcement, a warning from the town crier.

"Don't just stand there, assholes!" Harvey says, and rushes to the door. "Let's get the hell out of here."

The junkie is still transfixed by the mirror. Her head lists to one side, rolling lazily on her shoulders. Her mouth is open and her lips are moving, but only a quiet wheeze escapes. And I see what she's looking at. Instead of her reflection, the mirror shows a vast sea of stars, black and endless. I take a half step toward it, drawn into that sparkling infinity until the voice from outside snaps me out of it.

"Enjoy your stay!"

Harvey pokes his head out the door, checking to see if it's safe. Shoes in one hand and a baggie in the other, he runs. Zeke shrugs at me and gives chase, trotting after the old man as Harvey hurries barefoot across the asphalt.

Outside, doors all up and down the motel are flying open. The rooms vomit out their occupants. Each face is etched with vivid panic. They dart blindly into the night. Engines roar. Tires screech. Some just run for the fields.

Making his way slowly down the sidewalk is a tall man with mismatched clothes and aviator sunglasses. Reedy-thin, he walks, his hairless head nearly bumping the yellow sodium lamps. He must be over seven feet tall, and at first, I think he's taking careful steps atop parade stilts. His clothes look plucked from the lost-and-found, articles left behind in rooms or dropped in the parking lot. Mismatched socks. Two watches on one wrist, one of them hot pink with Hannah Montana's smiling face. The faded Hawaiian shirt rides up his torso, exposing a pale belly, and his praying-mantis arms stroke a sock monkey cradled next to his chest.

"Enjoy your stay!" he says, and his lips purse with an officious smile.

A step behind him, the desk clerk has accepted something horrible and inevitable. It's the look of someone the instant they see a car crash. He's here to bear witness, an attendant to whatever nightmare the Manager brings.

"Dude!" Zeke shouts to me. He's halfway across the parking lot with a knife in each hand.

"Enjoy your stay!"

The Manager inches closer. I run.

\*\*\*

# CHAPTER NINE

"Real talk, Harvey—what kind of STDs can you get when you put the sex on a shadow demon thing?" I ask.

"I guess I'll never know," Harvey says, growling at me as he steps gingerly through the gravel on the side of the road.

We're on a dark stretch of highway I don't recognize, but we can see the Austin city lights gleaming in the distance. I figure if we just keep heading in that general direction, we'll stumble across something familiar. A mile behind us, the King's Crown Motor Inn has finally faded from view. There hasn't been anything else as we fled, not a passing car or a single streetlight. We're alone under the stars.

It's almost 9 p.m. We might be fucked.

"Anything?" I ask Zeke.

He holds his cell phone up to the night sky, trying to find a signal.

"Nothing," he says, and tucks it back into his pocket.

Harvey slumps down into the dirt and starts pulling on his shoes. I take the opportunity to snatch up the Ziploc full of yellow powder he brought with him.

"Hey, come on!" he says.

I shove it into my pocket. "No, Harvey, you lost your necromancer orgy drug privileges when you sicced a ghost bird on me."

"I ought to whip your ass for what you pulled with that Spoorn," Zeke says.

Harvey's melted-candle face sags into scowl, "That bundle of sticks is the least of what I can do. Give me some time and I'll craft some shit that will make you want to cry for your daddy."

"You so much as think of perpetrating some necromancy on us again, and I'll kick you so hard you'll poop your mom jeans," Zeke says.

Harvey grumbles and clambers to his feet. "How much farther? I'm too old for—"

A distant scream cuts through the darkness. We turn to face it, but the night is silent.

"Sounds like the Manager caught up to somebody," Harvey says. "Can we keep moving?"

"Agreed," I say, and we turn to hike down the road at a brisk pace.

I want to know what the Manager is and what he does to those he catches, but not right now. Right now, I just want to focus on getting away from him, and I've already experienced enough of the inexplicable today. I don't know if I can process it. My sanity is still running with the needle in the red, trying to keep up with ghost birds and whatever the hell a Spoorn is.

As we walk, the rhythm of our shoes crunching, we take turns casting wary looks over our shoulders. Zeke periodically pulls out his phone to check for a signal, grunts, and puts it away.

"This is a liminal space," Harvey says, like we should understand what that means. "No signal."

Down the road, coming from town, a pair of headlights grows closer. I want to rush off into the weeds, but Zeke sees it on my face. He extends a calming hand, as if to say *hold on*, and in his other hand, one of his knives.

A brown station wagon stops in the middle of the road, taking up both lanes. Helper is driving, his face glowing white, a crescent moon behind the wheel. Two more men climb out of the passenger side. Their faces pale in the darkness. When they come around to the driver's side, I take a step back. Zeke tenses and tightens his grip on the knife.

"Oh God damn it," Harvey says, and his voice cracks with defeat as he steps behind Zeke.

When I see the men, I blink. My mind spins, reaching for an explanation for what I'm looking at. The two of them, both clad in tan coveralls, are identical. Albino white. Hairless. Toothy grins. They look like Helper, *exactly* like Helper. There's no single detail to distinguish them from the man behind the wheel—not a mole or a scar, no difference in weight or height.

We're trying to take it all in when one of them opens the driver's side back door closest to us. With a cordial tip of the hat he's not wearing, he motions for us to climb inside. His grin gleams like the frost blue of his eyes.

Zeke looks at me. "Did you call an Uber?"

Another scream in the distance. Everyone turns to look down the highway. Helper and his friends cock their heads, dogs staring at a television.

"Nope," I say, "But I'll take it."

As I step toward the open door, the second Helper extends a hand to block me. He wags a bony finger at me before pointing it at Harvey. Behind us, Harvey deflates.

"Oh no," he says, and his voice is a choked plea. "No, no, no."

All of Harvey's bravado, his profane posturing, and threats of using the dark arts against us wither. He holds up his hands in feeble defense but doesn't run or fight. One of the Helpers moves for him. Zeke intercepts, putting a hand on the Helper's chest. The Helper looks down at the hand as if he doesn't understand, even through the unbreakable smile.

"Hold up," Zeke says. "I don't know you people."

The one standing by the car door again gestures for Harvey to step inside. Harvey stands stock still. A single bead of sweat glistens in the glow of the headlights as it tracks down his temple like a stray tear.

"We got a job to do," Zeke says. "We're supposed to deliver Harvey here to your creepy bosses, not you. So, unless you want to give us all a ride back into town, you can just drive your white asses on down the road."

The smiles fade. All at once, the artificial cheer is gone. Their faces are slack, jaws agape with stupid emptiness.

"Unh," the one behind the wheel grunts.

"Unh," the other two grunt in response.

The one coming for Harvey knocks Zeke's hand aside and keeps moving for the old necromancer. Zeke shifts his weight, clutches the guy's wrist, and in one fluid motion, has the Helper in a hold with the man's arm wrenched up behind his back. I wait to hear the snap of bone. The Helper keeps struggling.

"I'm gonna break it, man," Zeke says to him.

The Helper wrenches his own arm. There's a *pop!* like a wet chicken bone. With his arm snapped in half just below the shoulder, the Helper slides around and grabs Zeke by the throat.

Zeke says, "What the—" and lets go of the floppy arm.

The Helper's smile returns. He shoves hard and pins Zeke to the car.

Moving like a ghost, the second Helper strides in. I lunge at him, leading with my shoulder. I throw my weight into his stomach. He bounces off the car, spins, his limbs jiggling and twitching, before sprawling onto his back in the middle of the road.

The one holding Zeke leans in and tries to snap at Zeke's face with perfect, pearly teeth.

"Seriously?" Zeke says, staying just out of reach of the bite.

Zeke gives him a right cross to the jaw. The Helper's eyes spark with excitement. Zeke hits him again. And again. Harder each time. It barely seems to register on the Helper's face, even when his jaw goes soggy and slumps to one side. Teeth and milky white fluid pour from his ruined mouth. But his eyes still gleam. He still won't release Zeke's throat.

The one in the road jumps to his feet, and without making a sound, rushes at Zeke. His arms flail in the air above him, but his face is still dumb and still. Zeke takes the Helper on top of him, shifts his weight, and hurls the man into the charging one. They crash into each other and tumble in the dirt. Helper #2 grunts once.

He reaches out for Zeke's leg, wrapping his spindly fingers around his calf. Zeke lands a solid, hard blow to the side of the Helper's head. Helper #2 collapses, his strings cut. He begins to seize. His limbs thrash. His head jerks and his eyes roll back.

They melt right out of his skull.

Milky white fluid gushes from the sockets. He vomits up more of it as his tongue liquefies. The rest of him follows. As his arms and legs tremble and kick, the watery sap comes running out of his coveralls. It spills from the cuffs of his pants and his ears. He flings it everywhere, spattering the asphalt and the side of the car with sticky excretion. Waxen bones appear beneath the eruption, and those too dissolve into the white slime. In seconds, there's just a puddle leaking out of a pile of gooey clothes.

The other one grunts at us, looks at what's left of his friend, and stands. His shattered jaw hangs. Zeke nods and shows the Helper his fist. The one behind the wheel of the station wagon just says, "Unh."

The Helper in the road gives us one last look and climbs into the back seat. He lays face down across it, like he doesn't know how cars work. The driver calmly puts the car back into gear and drives away without another word. We watch them leave until their taillights fade into the night.

Zeke turns to me and shakes his head. "The fuck?"

"Ugh," I say, and step back from the mess with my arms held out away from my clothes. "Oh God. It's on me. I got Helper juice on me."

***

Harvey shovels pancakes into his mouth with mad abandon. He takes quick, gulping breaths in between bites, syrup dripping down his chin and onto his secondhand T-shirt. I'm not eating. I *can't* eat. I'm dipping my napkin into a glass of water, scrubbing white goo out of my scrubs and hair. Zeke slowly chews his bacon and eggs, gazing out the window of the diner and into the parking lot, waiting for someone to come.

After about an hour, we made our way to Cody's Cafe. It's no-frills white linoleum with pictures of local high school sports teams on the walls and locals with unironic trucker hats. Judging by the curious and guarded glances, we're the only ones who aren't regulars. Probably because we look absolutely squirrel-shit insane. Usually, Zeke's mohawk is enough to get everyone's attention. You take a muscled black man with a mohawk into the hinterlands of Texas, people start to get twitchy. Tonight, however, we've brought them the entire travelling sideshow. The stains on my scrubs are accumulating into some sort of smelly Jackson Pollock experiment. I kind of recognize the road we're on, one of the many winding trails through the Texas hill country. We're just outside of Austin's orbit, where the gentrification of craft brew pubs and upscale coffee bars gives way to the real Texas of wide-open spaces and people who don't chase magicians. It's 10:30. We've missed the deadline, but none of us want to say anything. There are decisions to be made, choices that Zeke and I are clearly ignoring.

I scrub the skin on my forearm raw after finding another white speck that's coagulating into something thick and crusty. "So … I think we can all agree that I've been really good about not asking questions. We've got things to do, you know? I don't want to interrupt it by questioning every weird thing I experience. But today, man … today has been hard. I'm just trying to go with it, you know, but I've got to be honest … the *what-the-fucks* are really starting to pile up."

"Heh," Harvey says, and continues slurping. His face is inches from the plate, and I'm afraid he'll get a little too zealous and stab his eye out with the fork. The waitress returns and tries to hide her sneer as she brings him yet another beer and a plate of pork chops.

"Don't sweat it, brother. We're good," Zeke says to me, not taking his eyes off the parking lot.

"Oh, are we?" I ask. "Are we good? Today I've crashed an RV full of stoned witches into a lake while some sort of dark spirit flew away with a necromancer."

"Spoorn," Harvey says with a mouthful of food. "It was a *Spoorn.*"

"Whatever. Spoorns. Necromancers. Movies that shouldn't exist. Motels that can't be found on any map. The Manager! What the hell was the Manager?! What *was* that?! And you, Harvey, you were engaged in sexual congress with something that I … I …"

"Elaine," he says, and with one arm, swipes the empty plate aside to replace it with the pork chops. He digs in, tearing with his teeth. "Her name was Elaine."

"Oh!" I say, and nudge Zeke with my elbow. "Her name was Elaine! That's great. The incubus was named *Elaine.*"

People are starting to stare. Two college students sitting at the counter turn to snicker at us before returning to their conversation. I don't care.

"Succubus," Zeke says without really joining the conversation.

"Succubus. Incubus. Whatever!" I say.

"Succubus is a lady sex demon. Incubus is a dude," Zeke says.

"Nope," Harvey says, before continuing to stuff his face with French fries.

Zeke now turns to look at him. "Yeah. Succubi are women. Incubi are men."

Now Harvey doesn't look up. "That's dismissive of the gender spectrum of infernal creatures. C'mon man. It's way more complex than that. You'd think a guy wearing a shirt with cat doctors on it would understand."

Zeke frowns at his own shirt. "My bad," he says.

"I'm not finished," I say, and scrub harder. "Zeke punched a guy so hard he melted. *He fucking melted!*"

"Those aren't guys, sweetheart," Harvey says, and shoves away another empty plate. He reaches for the menu.

"What?" I ask.

Seemingly at random, Harvey picks something off the menu and starts to wave it at the waitress across the diner. She gives him a forced and polite smile before going back to helping other customers. "Those white assholes?" Harvey says. "They're not people."

I look at Zeke, who only shrugs. He pulls out the headphones for his Walkman and starts to listen to something thrashing and angry.

"Yeah, Harvey," I say, "I'm gonna need a little more than that."

"They're created. Drones. They don't even have souls. The Lazlos make them somehow. Sorcery," he says and keeps waving the menu at the waitress like he's trying to guide a plane onto the runway. "Darlin'! I need some cheesecake over here."

"Yeah. Sure. Drones. Why not?" I say, mostly to myself.

The waitress comes again but doesn't say anything. She just looks at Harvey with her pen hovering over her pad.

"Slice of cheesecake," Harvey says, "And some of that peach cobbler. And keep the beer coming!"

Zeke pauses his music and arches an eyebrow. "Seriously, dude?"

Harvey turns back to the plates that are stacking up to his left and right to scoop up stray bits of scrambled eggs. "What?" he says.

"Order away, Harvey," I say to him. "Might as well. We're picking up the tab anyway and we're flush with cash, right? Oh … wait. We're probably not getting paid."

"This fool's eating like it's his last dang meal," Zeke says, grumbling.

Harvey's face drops. He swallows and just stares at the greasy tabletop. "Yeah. I am."

"What does that mean?" I ask him. "You've probably got a string of people you've pissed off. One of them finally caught up with you. Deal with it."

Harvey's lip curls into a rueful smile. All the hedonistic, jagged edges fade away. "I never crossed the Lazlos. Not once."

"Not our problem," I tell him.

"Then why didn't you hand me over to those drone bastards?"

"The Helpers? Because … I don't know. I've seen movies like this," I tell him. "We hand you over to them and then the Lazlos claim they don't have to pay us because *technically* we didn't deliver you ourselves. No, we're going to do this right. I'm going to drop your nasty ass off on their doorstep, collect our money, and be on our way."

And the Lazlos owe me so much more than money, Harvey. They owe me explanations. Answers.

The waitress comes and sets the cobbler and cheesecake down in front of him. He just stares at it, doesn't even raise his fork.

"So, you don't know why they want me, do you?" he asks. "You never bothered to wonder why?"

"I don't give a shit, Harvey," I say.

"Yeah, you do. I think you're probably good guys. A couple of dumbasses, sure, but you're not like them. Rupert and Kitty Lazlo are bad actors, and you know it."

No one says anything. We just watch him as he stares at the desserts, with a look that acknowledges devouring it all won't help him.

"I'm eating like this is my last meal, fellas, because this *is* my last meal. Those fuckers are gonna kill me," he says, and finally pushes away the plates.

"What? Like a ritual sacrifice? I've always wanted to see one of those," I say, and take a sip of my soda.

"It's for their damned book," he says. He tosses his fork down on the table and I see tears welling in his eyes. "I'm gonna die so they can finish their fucking grimoire."

Zeke sees the spark of interest in my eyes and shakes his head. "Here we go."

"Grimoire, huh?" I ask. "What grimoire?"

"Nothing you've ever heard of," Harvey mutters.

"I've read a lot of grimoires, Harvey. Try me."

"*Vocea Fortunii*. The Voice of the Storm," he says, and the words hang over the table like a curse.

My stomach sours. I see the churning red cloud from the tarot card. Chaos. Madness. My future.

"You *have* heard of it," Harvey says with surprise.

"No," I say, thinking that if I deny it, it won't get too close. "I mean, not really."

"*Vocea* what?" Zeke asks. "That's no grimoire I've ever heard of. I think you're making that up."

"I said they haven't finished writing it, jackass," Harvey says.

"Harvey," Zeke leans in to make sure he's understood, "I've been through some shit today, understand? And that's because of you, so I'd go easy on who you're calling a jackass."

"Have I not made it clear to you two dipshits that I've got nothing left to lose?" he says, his voice cracking with defeated laughter as a tear spills down his cheek.

"We're listening," Zeke says, relenting.

Harvey wipes the tear away and takes a deep breath. "There's lots of grimoires, right? More than I can count."

"Yeah," I say. "And they're all bullshit."

"Most of them," he says. "Most of them are just paranoid screeds from seventeenth century monks or some dickhead with a useless master's degree and a lifetime supply of mascara."

Zeke turns to me. "He's not wrong."

"But some of them," Harvey continues, "Some of them are the real deal. And the *Vocea Fortunii*? It's … vile. Profane."

"What makes this one different?" I ask.

"The Lazlos and some of their cronies in the Specter Society found something," Harvey says.

Now Zeke is invested. "The Specter Society? Those old weirdos are still around?" he asks.

"Yeah, but most of them stay out of the spotlight now. You've got your covens and your dabblers, but those are basically just book clubs, right? Knitting circles," Harvey says. "But not the Specter Society. After the seventies, everyone thought they went out with disco, just faded into the background, but they didn't. Not at all. They found something, a signal, a noise off in space."

As Harvey speaks, I realize I'm squeezing my toes into fists. My teeth grind, and the lump in my throat won't go away.

"That noise," he says, "they tune into it, and it's the real shit. You know what I'm saying? If they know where it's coming from, they're not saying, but it's speaking to them. And they're documenting it in that damned book of theirs. It's the first creation of a legitimate grimoire in years. They say it's the voice of the Storm Beyond, telling them the secrets of the universe."

It's cool inside the diner, but a thin sheen of sweat has beaded up around my hairline. I take a sip of my soda, and the ice rattles with my shaking hand.

Harvey rubs his face and sighs again. "They've been finding these signals all over the world and recording them. Now they've got translators coming in by the dozens, trying to pull the message out of these horrible sounds. The noise—Jesus Christ, you wouldn't believe the noise—it's like Hell itself is getting torn in two, and the entire universe is screaming along with it."

I bite my lip hard enough to cause my eyes to water. He has to stop talking. He *has* to. I don't want to hear any more.

"Elder," Zeke says flatly and looks over at me.

These are the sounds that John Elder was playing at the Oswald Academy. I know the Voice of the Storm. We both do. The Specter Society made these cassettes, recording noises from all over the world—sounds from bottomless pits and abandoned factories. They went to the forsaken places of the world and captured howled spells on magnetic tape.

Harvey keeps going. I want to jump from the booth and excuse myself. Let him explain this to Zeke while I try to vomit out what I just heard into the diner's toilet. But I don't move. I sit there and let the train roll right over me.

"All of these sounds," Harvey says, "They've got these people translating, but guess what? Guess fucking what? The people they've hired are going out of their minds. Full on psychotic breaks. They're done. You get that sound inside you and it messes you up, man. It'll turn your brains right into scrambled shit, but the Lazlos don't care. They're full speed ahead."

The woman at Candle House. She was broken beyond all measure. Her mind had snapped, and her health was following. I remember her pungent smell as she stood in the doorway, trying to hand Rupert the black notebook containing her work. The Lazlos sent her back to the millstone with a cold drink and a swat on the ass. They chuckled the entire time, as though she was one of their grandkids getting into trouble and not someone whose mind had been shredded by those damned tapes.

"So how do you figure into all this? They want you to translate?" Zeke asks.

"No, not me," Harvey says, and his voice chills again. "I've got other skills."

Harvey twirls the tines of his fork through a smear of peach cobbler and cheesecake.

"I wouldn't call being a nasty old man a skill of any value," Zeke says.

Harvey ignores him. "I can hear the Voice of the Storm," he says. "Mediums can. Not all of us. Just some. You get somebody with the right sensitivity in there, and they can pick up on this signal. You don't even have to find one of those goddamn pits with the microphones and all that bullshit. They put me in a trance and use me as a receiver. I start spouting off that heinous shit and they record it for their book. It just flows out of me. I'm the conduit."

"You've done it before?" Zeke asks.

"Nah. Hell no. A friend of mine did when they tried it a few years ago," Harvey says, his voice going quieter as he falls back into some black memory. "Burned her right up. Just hollowed her out, soul and all."

Harvey is full of shit. I know this. He *knows* I know this. Harvey is the kind of guy who will tell you whatever lie he pleases, sometimes for no reason at all. There's probably very little that comes out of his mouth that has any hint of truth to it. Right now, I know what he's trying to do. He's trying to save his own ass. I can't say that I blame him. I don't know what it means exactly to "hollow someone out," but I can imagine. If I were him, I'd be fighting tooth and nail to get away from us. I'd lie. I'd cheat. I'd send ghost birds to attack people while they're just trying to drink their goddamn morning coffee. Finally, Harvey tosses the fork down and throws his hands up.

"But fuck it, right?" he says. "I mean … I'm dying anyway. Channeling that shit … that's a hell of a way to go, I guess. Maybe the Voice of the Storm will possess me with the knowledge of the cosmos. On my deathbed I will receive complete and total consciousness. *Gunga lunga* and all that shit."

"That's it, Harvey. Just lay that self-pity out on the table," I say. "You're dying anyway. Yeah yeah. We get it."

Zeke shoots me a look but asks anyway. "You're dying?"

"Yeah," Harvey says and nods. "Cancer. I'm seventy-fucking-three, though, you know? I mean, that's part of the deal when you get this old. Cancer. On a long enough timeline, everybody gets it. I guess it's my turn. Whatever. I've been pretty shitty, a real dickhead to just about everybody …"

"You don't say," I tell him.

"I guess whatever those sick fucks have in store for me is better than laying there in some bed hooked up to a bunch of machines. Bring it on. Bring on your horrors from beyond space and time. I'm ready for that shit," he says and snarls.

I sigh. Both Zeke and I lean back. We're simpatico. He looks at me and neither of us have to say a word.

"Damn," Zeke says, and waves for the waitress as he chews on a toothpick. "And I was looking forward to getting paid, too."

I rub my eyes, understanding that the shitshow is just warming up. "I wish I'd never met you, Harvey."

***

"On a scale of one to ten, how pissed do you think Rez is going to be when we knock on her door?" Zeke asks.

We're crammed into the back seat of a rideshare that reeks of vanilla. The driver hasn't said a word to us. She's a Mexican woman with a Prince T-shirt and bad Pop 40 playing on the radio. Her smile melted the moment she saw us crossing the parking lot. Then Harvey asked her to round up some friends so we could all party later. After an uncomfortable laugh, she turned up the radio and just stared daggers at us through the rearview. I don't blame her.

"Well," I say to Zeke. "She does love it when we show up unannounced."

"She threatened to shoot us last time," Zeke says.

"Yeah, but that was different. We were running from the cops. We have a better excuse this time."

"Well, now we have a necromancer," Zeke says.

"What's this chick's name?" Harvey asks. "Marianne? Is she cute? Does she like older guys?"

"Please. Seriously. Don't fuck with her," I tell him. "She will tear your face off."

"*After* she tears Clark's face off," Zeke adds.

"My face? Why mine?"

"Because she's gonna know this was your idea," Zeke says. "I'm gonna tell her, the second she opens the door, 'This was Clark's idea.' And she'll believe me, because she knows I would never ask this kind of thing of her."

"We've got to hide him somewhere," I say.

"And you know what her next question is going to be? How long is this old bastard supposed to stay here? And we don't have an answer for that," Zeke says.

"We just … wait for this to blow over," I say, and it sounds like a guess.

"You just heard that on a TV show. Shit like this doesn't just blow over," Zeke says.

"I don't need a babysitter, fellas. Let's just go get a handle of Jack and some smokes. I know a guy down in Laredo who can put us up for a few days. You don't have to worry about me," Harvey says.

"There's an ancient Chinese proverb, Harvey. I have saved your life," Zeke says. "Now I'm responsible for it."

"That's not a proverb. That's some Zen nonsense you heard on a TV show or in a Shaw Brothers movie," I say. "You don't even—"

The headlights of the oncoming car pin us in place. We're flash-frozen in that moment. It's too close, too fast. No one has time to shout a warning. No one flinches. We just lock eyes with the inevitable, in that paralyzing instant before impact.

\*\*\*

# CHAPTER TEN

The burly men in purple hockey masks and coveralls hover over me. I can't move my arms or legs. Lights flash overhead in one of those *Get this man into surgery!* perspectives as I'm pushed down an austere hallway. One of the dayglo Jason Voorhees assholes has a baton that crackles at its tip with the ferocity of a summer squall. He jabs it into my side. Lightning zips into my body and locks up my muscles. I grit my teeth and scream as the lights go out again.

\*\*\*

I surface. My vision swims, and everything sounds like it's coming to me from the bottom of a well. I blink away the tears and am aware of strong hands under my arms. The tips of my shoes rake across the linoleum. The purple-headed thugs to my left and right toss me into a small, empty cell. I hit knees first and buckle. As I roll over and try to catch my breath, I see one of the masked men taking one last hate-filled look at me before he slams the door. His mask is split down the middle, revealing a swelling eye and a misshapen nose that gushes blood onto his coveralls.

I laugh with what little breath I can draw. "Heh. You pissed Zeke off," I say to him.

He slams the door. I black out.

\*\*\*

When I come to again, the first thing that hits me is a wave of shame. Everything is sterile and white. The cold of the floor bites through the thin cotton of the scrubs. Overhead, the fluorescent is unrelenting. It gleams off of the stainless-steel bench jutting out of the wall. There's a toilet with the same lifeless sheen. It triggers a flood of memories, and I have to lay there for a moment and piece everything together.

I crawl to my knees on the spotless white floor, and the realization constricts around me. I know this room. If not this one, then dozens of others like it. This is Cavendish. We're back at the nursing home.

Scrambling to my feet, I push my face to the small window in the door. I recognize the hallway outside, bland and institutional white. The door is locked. I don't bother banging on it or trying to kick it open.

No windows. No ceiling tiles to crawl through. No air vents. Just me, a toilet, and a metal bench that I guess is supposed to be a bed. The other rooms we saw, like the one we freed Harvey from, at least had televisions or modest furniture. This is a holding cell.

The shock of waking up in here starts to bleed away and a slow, pulsating pain replaces it, a bone-deep ache all the way up and down my right side. The pulses get deeper and faster, an insistent and aggressive percussion.

There was a car crash.

I remember the headlights and the split-second before unconsciousness, when the world was turned into a kaleidoscope of rent metal and shattered glass. I want to scream out for Zeke. The car slammed into the right side—my side—so I took the brunt, but Zeke could have been thrown free. The car rolled. I'm almost sure it did. I remember flashes of the world spinning out of control, end over end. He could need an ambulance, but they tossed him in a room like this. After seeing the shattered mask and the mess he made of the guard's face, they probably have him bound. He could be laying there in a straight-jacket, bleeding internally.

"Step aside," a voice says through the door.

The purple mask lingers in the door window like a scene from a bad slasher film. Strange runes etched into its surface crackle with unnatural energy, like the embers of a cigarette. I recognize some of them. *Strength. Ferocity.* Something about werewolves, I think.

"Where's my friend?" I ask him.

He holds up the stun baton and makes the sparks at the end dance. "Obey my commands, or I will be forced to take punitive measures."

"Oh, don't you try to sweet talk me," I tell him. "Go find Harvey. He's into some weird shit. And he's a lonely guy. I've got a good feeling about you two."

The door opens, and the big guy looms there. He's massive. His jumpsuit strains to contain the girth of his arms. He's not the one with the shattered mask. That guy is probably applying frozen peas to his busted face. Using his baton, he points to the steel bench in the corner.

"Go sit over there. Hands in your lap. I won't tell you again."

I go sit. "So do you guys have room service, or is it just a continental breakfast?"

Leaving the door open, the guy steps out into the hall and carts in an old CRT television with wood paneling on the sides and an antenna with one limb snapped off at the end. Its cable snakes out through the door and down the hall.

"You're not going to make me watch *The Hills* are you? Or like *the Real Housewives of Little Rock?* If it's any sort of *Real Housewives* thing, I'd like for you to just zap me again instead."

He snarls at me over his shoulder, hunching to turn on the TV. It crackles to life, but there's nothing on the screen, just darkness that occasionally buzzes with errant, soft static.

"You keep talking. Ain't no one ever gonna see you again, smart guy," he says.

"So, tell me about this ensemble you're wearing," I say to him. "Is this like a sports thing? Or did you guys all get together in the break room and decide that purple was really intimidating?"

He storms off and shuts the door behind him, leaving just enough room for the power cord. I pretend not to stare at the door. It's cracked. I could run. If I'm where I think I am in the building, the back exit we took last time isn't that far. But last time, the purple goons weren't on high alert. They must be the nursing home's special team for the high-risk ward, the muscle they keep around to slap down witches who won't take their meds. There's at least one of them in the hallway outside, maybe more, and I can't leave without Zeke.

The TV flickers, but nothing starts. There's no other device hooked up to it, no VCR or streaming box, just the broken antenna. The black screen reminds me of the moment before the FBI warning on old video tapes. I reach forward to change the channel. The knob is a bulky, plastic dial with only fifteen notches. I switch through the other channels, but only get snow. When I come back to the dark screen, it flickers again. A tinny, warbling tune plays through the speaker. The jaunty notes come out warped as the old tape stutters and shows a picture of the Cavendish Assisted Living Facility on a sunny day, a photo right out of the brochure.

"Welcome to Cavendish," the warm voice says. "A great place to spend eternity."

"Eternity?" I ask no one in particular.

The nursing home dissolves in a dated star wipe, revealing the lobby. Orderlies in crisp, white outfits with crisp, white smiles buzz about. Each of them takes a moment to nod at the camera. They're all soft around the edges with dulled colors, growing incrementally blurrier every time the phantom video tape plays.

"At Cavendish," the voice says, "You'll find everything you'll need to prepare you for your journey. Our qualified and caring staff are available to you twenty-four hours a day. As you approach your golden years, Cavendish will be there with you to escort you to our fine, post-living facilities."

All the patients grin big for the camera. They look at me and nod knowingly.

"We have the most up-to-date accommodations. Modern amenities, but with all the safety measures of old."

A priest, the one we saw earlier this morning, smiles placidly, and bows his head as the camera pauses on him before more slow pans across the cafeteria and the recreation room. It cuts to a shot of an office. If I didn't know any better, I'd think it was stock footage. It's the platonic ideal of an office, with a large desk, papers stacked neatly, books along the walls, and a picture of a family angled just so the camera can see their kind and vacant faces. Outside, the manicured lawn of the nursing home, softly illuminated by solar-powered lights that line the sidewalks. I'm chuckling at the artificial pleasantness of all of it, trying to ignore the fact that my heart is racing, and my breath keeps catching in my throat. The winding hallways of the Lighthouse, in one form or another, catch up to me. A quiet, insistent part of my brain whispers that they have a room for me, a room next to Alan and the rest of my friends.

A man in a white lab coat comes into frame and sits behind the desk. He could be one of the picture-frame people. He's generically handsome and nondescript, a nothing-person who could be anywhere from twenty-five to fifty-five. His hair is kept short and is the same shade of basic brown as his eyes, the kind of person you have to introduce yourself to five or six times before you just start referring to him as *that guy*.

"Hello," he says with the charm of an automated phone system. "Welcome to Cavendish. Or should I say welcome *back* to Cavendish. I'm the Administrator."

He folds his hands atop the desk and stares into the camera. The soothing elevator music has stopped, and I can hear the air conditioner rattling in the video. The camera rests on him. He swallows and blinks, his lips pursed in a soft line. I turn to look around the cell, wondering if I'm missing something.

"You are Clark Vandermeer, correct?" he says, looking at a paper from the stack on his desk.

"Umm," I manage to say as I search for cameras around the television. "Hello?"

"Yes," the Administrator says. "Can you hear me all right? Please feel free to turn up the volume."

"Oh. You're ... you're really talking to me," I say. "Yeah. Yes. Hi. I'm Clark."

"Hello, Clark. I appreciate your patience. This really is a regretful turn of events, but I think it will all turn out for the best. I'm sure you have questions, and—"

"You hit us with a fucking car," I say, and all the anxiety bleeds away. *Fuck this guy.*

He winces. "That was regrettable. Insurance will cover the damage to our van, as well as the poor Uber driver's minor medical expenses. I hear she's already been released from the ER and is doing quite well, if you were worried."

"Where's Zeke?"

"Mr. Silver is in a separate holding room, not unlike the one you're in now. He, too, is waiting to be processed," the Administrator says like it's the most natural thing in the world.

"Processed? Processed for what?"

"We here at Cavendish are equipped to handle a great deal of guests such as yourself, but after all of the unfortunate hullabaloo with Mr. Bunson this morning, our board decided it was best to relocate you to a more ... *secure* facility."

"Guests like me? What the hell are you talking about? We're paranormal investigators," I tell him. "Well. Kind of. We're *kind of* paranormal investigators."

In the murky suburban gray in the yard behind him, something moves. A face emerges from the hedges. It's blurred into a howling Rorschach blot, and the body is gaunt and pale, floating out of the bushes with twitching feet scraping across the earth toward the window. My stomach drops, and I swallow the impulse to warn him.

"Oh, that's awfully modest of you, Mr. Vandermeer," he says. "You're not as dumb as you look, but I assure you that our Gehenna facility has every amenity to suit your needs."

Another wraith surfaces behind the first, slithering through the air, and then another. They move by inches, creeping up over the Administrator's shoulder, getting closer to the window. As they move in, their haggard and wailing faces do not come into focus, just black blotches for eyes and a yawning smear where the mouth should be. I try not to look, to let on that something's behind him.

"Gehenna facility?" I ask and shake my head. "Listen, pal, my needs are pretty simple. Tacos. A good internet connection. A moderately comfortable couch. I'm not complicated. But if you're offering me the deluxe package with strip searches and Thorazine enemas, how could I say no?"

The wraiths are right up on him, almost pressed to the glass. He smiles at me and I see for the first time that there *is* something behind his dead eyes. It's not vapidity or even the crushing wheels of healthcare bureaucracy. It's ravenous, a feral dog lying in wait. The faces over his shoulder are no different. They're blurred approximations of human faces, expressions just a portrait of their misery. If I squint my eyes just right, he looks no different from one of them. I can see one of those things, squirming just beneath his skin. When he reinforces his smile, they smile behind him, dark slashes across their faces turning up at the corners in hungry leers.

I sit back on the bench, recoiling from the conversation. The Administrator leans in. In the next frame, the wraiths are gone, just snipped out of the narrative like they'd never been. But I share a look with the Administrator, one where I can't deny that what I saw scared me and he knows it. We understand each other.

"Mr. Vandermeer, I see now that I was right. Keeping you here as our guest for a while may well resolve the difficulties you'll cause for us in the future," he says, sharpening at the edges, the syllables weighted with a threat.

"Hey, there weren't going to be any future problems. Believe me, I regret ever setting foot in this joint, then you went and hit me *with a fucking car*."

"This has all been a regrettable mix-up, but I'm sure we can make this all up to you during your stay in Gehenna. Guests with your skills can be put to good use," he says, and as he looks to the door—my door—it opens, and the purple-clad guard returns for the television. As the guard carts him out, the Administrator's eyes follow me. "It was wonderful to meet you, Mr. Vandermeer," he says. "I look forward to providing you with top-quality care until chaos claims the known universe."

"After a while, crocodile," I say and try not to let on that my brain is blinking red, trying to shut down for a little panic nap.

The slamming door snaps me out of my paralysis. I don't know what any of this means. Digesting that along with everything else that's happened today is asking a bit too much of me. I could chalk it up to some graphics design nerd with a laptop, conjuring up rudimentary special effects. The old TV didn't hurt, either. A spooky message from some asshole in a lab coat only gets more potent when shown on something like that.

I give myself another sixty seconds of rationalizing, of crafting a tale about how that *wasn't really* some cadre of infernal apparitions and their meat-puppet relishing the fate they have planned for me.

Toss that in the vault. Throw some dirt over it. Move on. It's fine.

They took my phone. I search my pockets. No wallet either. Nothing but the small baggie of what I assume is cairn root. They overlooked it. The powder is a dull ochre under the sharp lights. I don't know how long until I'm "processed," but I'm pretty sure I don't want any part of this "Gehenna" the Administrator guy mentioned. Anything that's named after some aspect of hell, I try to avoid. Cavendish is bad enough with its scheduled medications and white walls, like *One Flew Over the Cuckoo's Nest* for practitioners of the dark arts. Zeke and I don't fit into that category, but I don't think they care. This room is temporary. Gehenna must be a more permanent solution for people they want to hide away forever. My mind begins to spin hot and frantic, conjuring up ideas of a dingy federal prison, but instead of murderers and thieves, it's all necromancers and demons. Zeke might be able to hold his own in there. Hell, he'd probably get his own crew. Me? I'd have to become some warlock's girlfriend to survive. Whatever happens, has to happen *now*, before they come for us.

You peel off your skin and bones like one of your cheap suits.

I open the baggie. The scent is earthy and tart, sawdust mixed with tangerines. The first whiff makes my head spin, sending a faint electric cloud crackling through my brain. It's like the first sniff of a good Scotch after a long day, one with just enough bite to get your attention and make the hairs on the back of your neck stand on end. I don't have some bizarre, MacGyver'd bong to smoke it out of. I don't even have a lighter or even know how much I'm supposed to use. I dip my finger into the powder and draw up a small mound on the tip of my pinkie. I've never snorted anything before. Except one time in fifth grade. On the playground, I snorted Pixi Stix on a dare. That didn't kill me. I had purple snot for about a day, but otherwise I was fine. This should be easy.

I sit on the bench, staring at the yellowish pile of powder on my finger. They might find me choking on my own tongue or frothing at the mouth. Maybe it will kill me instantly. Or maybe they'll come in and find that I'm the new home to some ancient demon who happened to be passing by and thought my twitching body looked nice and warm. That would be super disappointing for both of us.

Buy the ticket. Take the ride.

Here we go.

\*\*\*

# CHAPTER ELEVEN

The taste isn't the best. The earthy tang slithers down the back of my throat. I choke it down and wait. Will it be a shock of energy? A quick wave of euphoria? A cool numbness that starts in my fingertips? It's one of those moments when you're not sure if it's working or not, sitting there asking yourself *Am I high? Do I feel any different?* And I do. There's a low buzz sparking across my skin. It's nothing dramatic, like being enveloped in warm flannel. The pain in my side is gone. Beyond the walls of this room, sounds begin to detach and float around. I don't so much hear them as I am just *aware* of them.

Water rushing through pipes.

A car passing by on the street outside.

Down the hall, a conversation about sandwiches.

I only catch bits and pieces, and when I try to latch onto something, it drifts just out of reach and dissipates, dandelions on the breeze. Just when I think I might need to take a bit more, I look down and realize the baggie is not in my hand. It's in someone else's hand, someone sitting right next to me.

*Me*. It's *me* on the bench, shoulders slumped and a vacant, bloodshot stare gazing off into nothing. A thin tendril of drool creeps over my bottom lip and onto my pants. The side of my face is swollen and mottled with a blossoming bruise, the aftermath of the crash.

"Oh. Oh shit…"

Staring at myself, I can't feel the cold of the steel bench beneath me. I can't feel much of anything. The weight is gone—my own weight, the weight of my dead friends, the weight of being trapped in here. It all fades, and I can feel the universe expanding all around me. I can feel its endless emptiness, beyond the roaming souls anchored to the ground by meat and beyond the radio waves and the substrate of dreams and nightmares. I can feel the stars.

Damn it. I hate astral projecting.

Zeke.

The thought comes like a jolt of electricity, shocking away the miasma. Zeke. I have to find Zeke.

The room doesn't change. I don't drift away like some ghost, passing through walls. I'm just *somewhere else*. This isn't the same kind of trip I had before. The cairn root is different. This is astral projecting on rocket fuel.

The walls in this new room are white, too. Blinding fluorescent and brutal sterility. For an instant, I'm worried that this is the end, that we did die in that car accident and "processing" is what waits for us on the other side. We're stuck in here, waiting to be judged.

Zeke is sitting on the floor, smoldering. His right eye is swelling shut, and his lip is split open. There are new tears in his scrubs, and fresh blood spatters the front. I don't think all of it is his.

"Zeke!" I yell.

Zeke raises his head and looks around as if he's not sure he heard anything at all.

"Hey man! Can you see me? You can see me, right?"

Zeke narrows his eyes and stands, keeping his back to the wall. I get right in front of him and wave my arms.

"I don't know how this works, dude! Can you hear me? I took some of Harvey's drugs, and now I'm all floaty."

Zeke steps around me with slow, predatory paces. He's not looking right at me, but he knows I'm here. He knows *something* is here.

"Don't worry! I'm going to try to find Rez. Can you hear me? I'm going to —"

His hand lashes out faster than I can see. It cuts through the gauzy, languid haze, something fast and sharp and solid. The blow catches me in the chest. Starbursts of white pain erupt throughout my body. The world flickers. The room vanishes and reappears, rapid fire. Frames are missing from the film and in those gaps, there is a vast and howling darkness.

And suddenly I'm in the parking lot.

"Damn it! Come on!" I yell, but Zeke is gone.

I'm aware of the night breeze, but I don't feel it. I don't smell the rosemary lining the sidewalk up to the front door of Cavendish. It's all there—the asphalt, the stars above, the cicadas in the trees and their rhythmic chirp, and me. At the heart of it all is a tug, a string around my finger, something I'm not supposed to forget. My body, sitting slumped over in that cell, connected to my astral form with an ephemeral umbilical.

Nearby, a trio of Helpers stands next to the brown station wagon. They're not doing anything, just standing there watching the nursing home, waiting for a command. After we put up a fight, they must have reconvened and grabbed more friends. How many of these weird fuckers are there? Can the Lazlos just make infinite minions? Because I could get way more done in my day with a couple of these creepy bastards running errands for me.

As one, they turn to look at me.

"Umm. Hi," I say. "Can you see me?"

No response. They're not smiling. Mouths hang open just enough to show perfect white teeth and pink tongues.

"Hello?" I say and wave my hands.

When I take a few steps to the side, they follow me with their icy, vacant eyes. Just past them, something catches my eye. I can't tell how far away it is. Distance feels like intuition more than measurement. From here to there is gauged in feeling rather than feet. I step around the trio of idiots and walk toward an empty field. There was no field when we were here this morning. It was suburbia. There were roads and convenience stores and a CrossFit gym.

Everything is quieter in the field, and when I look back over my shoulder, the nursing home is just a streetlight in a sea of darkness. I try not to look too deeply into the starless black all around. If I do, I know that something will look back at me.

Something like Alan. If I find him out here, could I lead him back to the world? Just find a door to usher him through and then *presto*, everything would be fine?

But it wasn't Alan, was it? It was something *like* Alan.

He and DJ and the others, waiting for me on the threshold back at Oswald Academy, beckoning me. Are they still out here? Roaming around? This might be my only chance to find them.

I shake it off. If I think of that school, I might project myself there.

Focus, asshole.

Andi and Zeke warned me that the possibility of getting lost forever was very real.

This field is lifeless. No cicadas. No cars passing by or even the wind in the trees. It's dead grass and weeds, standing motionless under a blank canvas. A familiar dread creeps into me. There's another parking lot, this one empty and shattered with age. The tall grass had hidden it from me until I was close. This parking lot has no building, just the slab of a foundation. But there *was* a building here. Bits of debris litter the grass—chunks of concrete and cast-aside drywall.

The dead grass reaches up to hide the sign out front, too. The sign is sun-faded and scrawled with lazy, black graffiti. If there's a message in that tag, I can't read it, but the sign beneath reads *No Trespassing. For Inquiries call 888-555-7475.*

The numbers and letters drift as I stare at them, like trying to read in a dream.

I'm standing on the slab before I realize it, and I'm aware of the ghost of the building that was. The walls wind around me, invisible, but still there. Closed doors. Ruin. Cats. The scent of ammonia. The building was destroyed, but its soul remains.

This is the Lighthouse.

Then there is a keening, low and quiet, coming to me from across a vast gulf. It picks at my brain, the seductive whisper of a needed cigarette. The sound is far away. I feel this, but it's getting closer, gathering steam. With my attention drawn to it, it gets louder, and I can't help but listen. I crouch, putting my ear to the slab. Beneath the concrete is a vast void, every bit as empty as the nothing behind the night sky. The sound is still muffled by tons of cement, but I know that won't stop it. The sound's power grows, picking up speed, a semi-truck barreling toward me from the bowels of the earth.

The weeds in the field shift, the dry rattle of old bones. The stars above flicker and wane. I step away from the slab, but the sound from within wails now. It claws its way out of the earth, splitting the concrete with raw, concussive force.

I close my eyes.

Rez. Find Rez.

The sound stops. The grass under my feet is still dead. Texas summer hasn't quite sucked the life out of everything, but the grass here is yellowed and brittle. When I look up, the slab is gone. The empty field has given way, becoming an unkempt lawn. In front of me, a house the color of a traffic cone.

I'm in the courtyard at Candle House. Great. *Fucking great.* It's mostly dark. The moving team is gone, and the Green House is quiet but for a few lights inside. Oddly, it's less menacing at night. The fluorescent paint of its various houses doesn't glow like a garish challenge. I haven't been inside this building. The door is propped open with a box fan lazily spinning. Rez isn't here, but I step through anyway. I drift, the anchor of my body pulling less now. It's a name on the tip of my tongue, the sensation of walking into a room and forgetting why you're there.

"That's probably bad," I mutter to myself as I go deeper into the house.

Stainless steel tables line an institutional room of linoleum and hospital tile. Stacked boxes. Dead computers the color of cream with deep black-green screens. It reminds me of my high school chemistry classroom. Four people—two men and two women—sit hunched over tape decks. The decks are old and blocky, with the faux-metal and sharp edges of the 1970s. Big orange buttons and Maxell cassettes with labels on them:

*Sikonge, Tanzania, October 17, 2016*
*Ft. Davis, Texas, March 02, 2019*
*Flint, Michigan, August 08, 1936*

In the center of the table is the box, the box of tapes from the Lighthouse.

The tapes play, and I don't need to hear it to know what sounds slither up the coiled wire and through the headphones over the ears of the listeners. One woman closes her eyes and rolls her head on her shoulders, gripped in ecstasy. She makes raspy non-words and stretches her fingers out to the ceiling. Her hands are pocked with sores. The nail on her right index finger is missing. Next to her, an older man whose jaundice seems to sweat out through his sagging skin writes feverishly. His hands spasm across the page of the notebook he's using to transcribe, and he's starting to chew a hole into his bottom lip. The third guy just stares straight ahead. His lips move along with the profane howls coming through his headphones, but he makes no sound or effort to write them down. The fourth, a woman with a thick shock of curly blond hair, may be dead. Her chin rests on her chest, and the blood that poured from her nose has turned the color of rust. The stain paints over her lips and down onto her shirt. An old couch is shoved to the side of the room, where a young man— unshaven, with clothes that shine with filth—stares up at the ceiling, his mouth agape.

"I am in the house of the Weeping King," he says with a cracked whisper. "He suffers the Storm, and within it sleeps his court, the Court of Eight."

And he begins to cackle. After the first round sends him into a wheezing fit, he laughs harder, bucking and thrashing on the couch. The laughter peals into the hot room, and he sits up, his teeth bared. With a wild look in his eyes, the laughter hardens. He forces it out, casting it at the others like firing a gun. The older man turns to look at him and pulls off the cans, letting them dangle by the cord. The third guy, the one whispering the forbidden words as he hears them, turns to face them. They start laughing with him, too. Their voices are ragged, tearing out of their throats as they lean into it, red-faced and straining.

I back away, and the house changes around me. The floor moves beneath my feet. Doorways pass overhead. The laughter fades, and I can't hear it or see it, but I know that it, too, is now just another island in the darkness, somewhere on the periphery.

I don't see the shift when it comes. I'm in Candle House, and it moves around me and then it's *not* Candle House. I'm looking at a field of stars. They're arranged in unnatural stripes on the horizon, stretching up to the sky. Streaks of green and red. They pulsate and flicker, trying to communicate with me in some ancient tongue of the stars.

No, not stars. They're headlights and taillights, stretching down the interstate.

I'm at a window overlooking the city, twenty stories up. It's the Austin skyline. A riptide of vertigo threatens to pull me under. The sensation of geography being obliterated and rebuilt around me while I blink threatens to unmoor me. My mind struggles to keep up, to right itself. I close my eyes and take a breath and realize I don't have lungs. I don't have eyes. I don't have anything. I'm an essence, stretched out at the end of a leash to my meat sack. Will it rot while I'm away? Can I find my way back?

At the base of my skull is a feather-soft tickle. That tickle trails back into darkness, a tail extending off into nothing and eventually landing at my cold and still body. It's hard to grab onto now, a memory of a cloud.

Shapeless panic bubbles up within me but is immediately quelled by a smell that I don't smell. I'm aware of gin. The cold sensation of juniper wafts across the dimly lit apartment, dancing with the sound of ice cubes clinking in a glass.

Andromeda Thorn is behind me, sitting in a high-backed, black leather chair that looks like Vincent Price could have owned it. It's big enough to devour her as she draws her knees up to her chest and wraps herself in a midnight blue chenille. On the TV is a documentary about ancient Egypt. In her hand, a tumbler with the last sip of gin and tonic. The apartment is a delicately cultivated balance of gothic and mid-century modern, equal parts Eames and Addams Family. Elvira on velvet over a blonde, hi-fi stereo cabinet. It flirts with the borders of bad taste, and I want to walk around and explore everything. I've never been in an apartment this expensive. I've never been in *Andi's* apartment.

"Andi ..." escapes my mouth without thinking.

Andi sits up. She listens, muting the large flatscreen mounted on the wall. Camels cross in silence through a sea of brown.

"Andi?" I ask, louder now. I wave my hand in front of her face.

She swats it away like you would a mosquito and stares past me, through me.

"Andi!" I say, yelling.

My voice feels like it dies when it leaves my lips, this place sucking the life from my words before they can reach her. I jump up and wave my arms, yelling her name.

Andi slides out of the giant chair and limps across the room with the soft steps of someone who hears an intruder. She goes to an old chest, sitting next to a stack of magazines. It's banded with tarnished brass etched with Enochian sigils.

"Andi! It's Clark! I know you're pissed at me right now and I get it, but I need to help Zeke! And the old guy, I guess. That necromancer? Yeah, real pain in the ass. He's super gross, but the Lazlos, they're ..."

Andi pulls out a box of matches, a burnished metal brazier, and a fistful of sage. Her eyes scan the apartment, and I can't help but laugh as she prowls to the center of the room, moving like someone who knows there's an errant bug in here. I'm a fly she intends to swat.

"Andi! Please! It's me!"

I swat the glass tumbler from the table. It flies off and rolls onto the rug, scattering its ice cubes across the apartment. Andi doesn't seem to notice. She's whispering a quiet incantation, and the words hang heavy in the air, taking shape and lingering there. Latin phrases take on incomprehensible forms and float, crowding me as each syllable of the prayer drifts from her ruby lips.

When I look down, the glass is still on the end table, and the riptide comes again, threatening to suck me under. There's no ice on the rug. The last sip still floats at the bottom of the glass.

"Andi!" I try to yell.

She softly blows on the sage, feeding its gentle crackle, and the scent fills the air. This too, I can feel. It snakes upward, a slow, buzzing exhalation that creeps across every surface. The edges of the apartment turn to glitter and bad reception. The shape of the hi-fi grows blurry, shifting into a kaleidoscopic funhouse of what was just there. The scent of the gin twists into a copy of itself with another copy in its wake, blue, then purple, then red. Everything shifts out of phase and sparkles with tiny flashes of light. Each ephemeral blink marks the disintegration of another boundary. The high-backed leather chair loses its shape. Andi's face elongates, just oil on the surface of a pond. It stretches and deforms until she's gone in the haze. I can't even feel her, and I reach out as I realize the miasma has consumed the room.

"Andi!" I shout.

Something ripples across the scintillating cloud—a shout? A thought? A feeling? In the undulating shimmer, Andi takes shape, if only for a second. She can't see me. Her head emerges from the fog, searching. I take another step back, swatting at what I think is a sparkle come to render me into non-existence.

"Fuck right off with your sparkles!" I yell.

"Clark?" Andi asks, her voice laced with surprise.

"Andi!" I yell again, staggering away from the cloud of sage.

The hallway behind me is dark, and I want to scurry into it and hide in the shadows, away from the crystalline softness of the smoke. Above me, moths and crane flies hurl themselves against a plastic-covered light recessed into a ceiling of rotted brown wood. Andi's apartment is gone.

I'm somewhere else. I'm in an exterior corridor lined with other, older apartments. Fast food bags spill over the lip of a metal trash can bolted to the concrete. The paint is chipped. The single welcome mat reads *Oh Shit Not You Again*. Everything sags with bone-deep sadness. I can hear cicadas just beyond the perimeter of the flickering yellow light. The cool, crisp air of Andi's apartment gives way to the thick and hot breath of a Texas summer night. I don't feel any of this. I only sense it. I'm aware of it all—the smells, the heat, and the sounds—lingering in the air. I'm just broadcast into them like an errant burst of radio static, my drug-addled brain the transmitter.

This shit is annoying.

I don't know where this apartment complex is. It looks like the rest of the low-rent quasi-slums crowded around the city. Termite-ravaged spaces with mostly functional appliances. Cars on blocks in the parking lot and duct tape over cracks in the windows. Misshapen couches cast aside next to the dumpster. Everyone here lives in a tenuous truce with their neighbors.

The door in front of me has no number. Over the peephole is a bright, smooth face. A ceramic mask hangs on a nail. It's mostly featureless, just a soft bump for a nose and lips gently parted in breath. Bold yellow stripes cross its face and matching streamers dangle down the door.

The door is open. It's just a crack. Claws of incense unfurl around the edges of the doorway. It opens when I push on it, and I stare at my hand. I clearly don't understand the rules here.

The inside of the apartment dances with the light from a dozen candles. Beneath that linger layers of cigarettes, greasy food, and stale beer. The place is littered with trash and mismatched furniture. On the couch, a man sleeps in his clothes—jeans with a hole in the seat and a black T-shirt—and has his faced tucked into the crack between the cushions.

Sitting on the peeling linoleum of a cramped kitchenette is a woman with her back to me. She sits motionless, legs in the lotus position. One hand is slack, resting in a copper bowl full of glistening oil. Her left loosely holds a fist of dry rice. The rice rattles to the floor in a steady rhythm, slipping from her hand like sand through an hourglass.

I step inside, moving before I realize it. As I cross the threshold, I can hear the woman whispering, so quiet it's almost inaudible over the rain of rice. It's a chant, a cataract of silent syllables too soft to make out. She rocks back and forth, her dress spilling across the circle of protection she's painted on the floor with cheap mauve nail polish.

I can feel something else in the room, cloaked in shadows and incense. The nape of my neck pricks with the sense of being watched and suddenly I feel like I'm standing on a stage in front of a faceless crowd. I spin around, expecting to see the Manager from the King's Crown or one of the blurry nightmare things at Cavendish. Or Iris Angel. Or the toothy, feral things that chased us around the Oswald Academy. Any of it. All my shadows are now filled with things that bite, things I didn't have to worry about before. Now they lurk in every stray thought and around every corner.

The woman in the protective circle turns her head, but I can't make out her face. "Well look at that," she says, her voice a serpentine Texas drawl.

The prickling sensation of being watched goes icy and settles into my bones. "You can see me?" I ask, and suddenly I'm afraid of the answer.

Rice skitters across the floor, piece by piece. "Now that didn't take much mojo at all. I put out some feelers and you just came right to me. Ain't that dandy?"

She looks over her shoulder, and her eyes flicker in the candlelight, milky-white stones sunken into a drawn face. *Bela Koth.*

"Bela? Umm. Hi. I don't know if you remember me," I say, as she twists into position to look right at me. "I mean, of course you remember me with the whole crashing-your-RV-into-the-lake thing. I mean ... is that insured? Do you have insurance? 'Cause that was our bad. Maybe you can just get it detailed real nice and—"

"You, boy ... you destroyed my home ..."

"Oh!" I say, taking a step back. "That was your home? You lived there? Yeah. Housing in this city has gotten pretty crazy, right?"

I glance over my shoulder. The apartment door is closed.

"Yer damn right that was my home," she says and begins to stir her fingers through the thick oil, moving them in lazy circles. "You two sonsabitches come in there like the belles of the ball, but you don't know a damn thing about what's happening, do you?"

"I'm gonna be honest with you, Bela, I really, really don't."

She drops the last few grains of rice, one by one, for emphasis. As each one hits on the floor, I'm increasingly aware of how out to sea I am.

She whispers again, guttural supplications that crawl up from her belly. "*Nashtu grut. Filkabba shashish.* Lord of the Wormwood Star, hear my pleas. Oh, mighty master, Black Goat of the Garden, help me finish this cycle by matching this foul dilettante's transgression with your retribution ..."

Though blind, she doesn't look away while she chants. I avert my eyes as the hate spills over in hers.

"Well, I clearly interrupted some *you*-time, so I'm just going to step back outside and see if I can get a ride. I'll get out of your hair. Keep doing your thing," I say and turn to the door.

In the inky well of shadows in the corner, something moves. At first, I think it's another person I hadn't noticed, someone just sitting there, watching.

"This boy, naked and dumb, has come walking along the shore of the Sea of Mon. *Filkabba shashish. Vurm. Vurm!*" Bela says.

Other shadows across the room waver, the inky pools rippling as pale masks float to the surface. Three of them rise, facing me, all staring with empty sockets and uneven features. They float in the dim candlelight, disembodied faces like the one on the door. Made of *papier-mâché*, they crudely resemble a man, a woman, and a child, all decorated with intricate crimson symbols, unholy spirals and slashes squirming across the surface. Bits of actual hair frame their faces. The woman's lips are smeared with red lipstick. In the boy's open mouth is a single, real tooth.

"Yessss," Bela says, her voice rising. "*Vurmis wol. Kathulq il rugk!*"

The mouths of the masks yawn open as Bela begins to laugh. When the moaning starts, my mind can't catch up. I reel, rocking back on my heels, trying to make sense of it. The groan bellows soft and insistent, a call from their lips that harmonizes with the others into a dirge. Bela's cackle is wet and hacking, but full of rage, full of victory.

My legs won't work. I stumble to escape, and the door seems to move, sliding across the wall. Bela wails with giddy laughter. She's smearing the oil on her face and drawing patterns across her bare chest. The floating faces collect in the center of the room and as one, they turn to watch me.

I throw the door open and rush out into the night. The masks follow.

***

# CHAPTER TWELVE

I run through the apartment complex, darting around corners, and sprinting for the cover of darkness. I move from shadow to shadow. In the night, the moaning voices carry across the courtyard. The intermittent groans bounce off each other, a call and response. As I pause, I catch glimpses of the masks drifting through the air. The mouths open and close, gawping as they search for me. All around are more brown, slumping buildings, three stories high with windows that glow like rotting jack-o'-lanterns. The only hint of people are the shadows that move inside the jack-o-lantern's eyes, wraiths in gentle glows of blue or gold. I keep moving.

Think of Rez. Focus on Rez.

I try to hear her voice, to recall every barb of disdain. I focus on that and turn random corners, expecting to find that the apartments have melted away into her North Austin townhouse.

But there are just more corridors, more suffocating buildings gone soggy in the damp night. It's a twisting warren of brown siding and mangled miniblinds.

The masks emerge from a darkened corridor, one I came from seconds before. They've got my scent. They don't move quickly, but they don't have to. They're just dumb enough to be relentless. I'm not tired—I don't know if I can even *be* tired here—but eventually, I'll stumble into a *cul-de-sac* and find them floating, waiting.

A wooden sign planted in the center of the courtyard lists to one side. Its chipped and faded letters, once a rich forest green, say *Village Oak Apartments.* I think. Those letters swim, too. The gravity of this places settles down around my shoulders and pulls at my limbs.

Rez. Please hear me.

A mask looms, inches from my face. I stop hard and pitch forward, trying to avoid it. It's the mask of the man. The eyes widen and the mouth gapes like a bell. Its lifeless groan becomes an inhalation, and past those paper lips, I see an endless and fleshy orifice. The suppurating tube stretches back as far as I can see, and the sides glisten as it waits to receive me. The mouth stretches. It distends, jaw dislocating to take me whole.

I throw myself at the nearest apartment door. The door gives, but there is no apartment on the other side. It's another hallway, this one cool and crisp with muted gray walls and cheap, industrial carpet under foot.

It's always hallways. They're empty and winding with only screaming at the end and a part of my brain, the part curled into a little ball behind all the desperation, whispers to me.

Maybe you're already dead. You're dead and this is what waits for you—endless corridors and something hungry at your heels.

The mask is gone. Its melancholy wail, beckoning me to slide into its maw, is silent. Behind me is only another door, this one plain and gray with a silver handle like the others. Bright fluorescent tubes hanging from the ceiling illuminate everything, leaving no shadows to hide within. Down the hall, I can hear the faint ringing of phones and a sea of murmuring voices.

It's an office building. I turn the corner to find row after row of cubicles, each of them separated by five-foot temporary walls. Phones chirp, and a current of soft voices flows down the aisles, words overlapping each other, uninterrupted.

I come to the first populated row. Every other chair is occupied with someone sitting over an office phone. The first guy is motionless, his back to me. Black headphones hang askew on his head as the phone in front of him beeps and blinks red. The headphones aren't even plugged in. The man doesn't move or make a sound, not taking notes or even nodding as he listens to his call. The susurration of voices isn't coming from him or anyone on this row. This row is quiet, as if it's holding its breath as I approach. The man's clothes don't fit right. They sag loose around his shoulders, and I glimpse the flesh on the nape of his neck. Flawless, it gleams under the fluorescents overhead.

A mannequin.

This entire row, just mannequins arranged to look like people in a call center. I move up the aisle, creeping by each one, peering around it to see if it's someone breathing, pretending. None of them move. There are dozens of them, men and women placed lazily in an office chair, wearing generic business casual clothes with the tags still attached. Some have cheap wigs that tangle in the headphones. Row after row, with not a real person among them. Beneath some of the desks are small speakers broadcasting the sounds of office work. The voices, the shuffling papers, and the rattle of keyboards play on a loop and as I stand there and listen to it, I can hear its pattern, cycling over and over.

Thanks for calling.

What can I do for you today?

I'll have that over to you right away.

"Hello?" I ask, but the only response is more beeps, more office platitudes.

It's just one large room, a sloppily constructed set with no one to mind it. I pass by a breakroom that doesn't smell of food. The chairs are all still in place, and there are no dishes in the sink. The trash cans are all empty.

I know what this is. The connections are being made with every step, but I don't want to face it, to give it life.

Past the rows of dead conversation, through the front windows, I can see the darkness beyond. It's perfect. There are no lights out there, no cars. There's not even an empty parking lot. Not yet. It's just null, maybe not even springing into being until I try to pass through it.

The office lobby is function over form. The front desk is unmanned. There's a telephone on the desk and a computer monitor sporting a thin coat of dust, but neither of them are plugged in. They're situated where they're supposed to be, right next to the pristine notepad and pen. It's all like a replica of what aliens imagine we look like in our native habitat.

The year 2174 has reconstructed the living conditions of the 21st century Homo sapiens and found that the primitive society weaponized monotony and unleashed it on its populace with extreme prejudice.

Over the lobby desk, emblazoned on the wall, is the powerful blue of the Lighthouse logo. Atop the lighthouse, instead of a beam of light to guide ships away from the rocks, is a radiant, golden eye. I look into it and feel it stare right back. Others may not be able to see me in this state, but the eye can. It always can. Since I first met its gaze the night Alan and the others disappeared, it's followed me. It's watched me, unblinking, showing up in dreams or peeking at me from the corner of an errant thought, while I'm in the shower or pumping gas.

I look away from it, afraid that somehow it might anchor me here. If it stares at me for too long, it can see right into me and trap me here in this place. I'll be a phantom custodian, cursed to babysit the lifeless faces of the never-ending workday.

"Nope!" I say and turn to the front door.

Two Helpers stand on the front porch, right in front of the swinging glass doors. Both are decked out in a facsimile of a butler's uniform—white gloves, black jacket, and tie. From just a few feet away, I can see the outfits are fake. It's all plain cotton sewn into a replica of a suit. Like the call center, it's a stage costume, meant to give the veneer of elegance. Empty grins affixed to their faces, they stand motionless, waiting for some interaction to trigger them.

And there are cats. So many cats. The sidewalk is crowded with them. They pace and prowl, collecting like a mob ready to rush.

At the end of the walk, just fifteen feet from them, is the edge of this island, where the darkness begins. In the waking world, these pasty Helper goons are staring out into the parking lot, cars passing on the cross streets, or maybe just the quiet night sky. For me, it's another island in the black. Every other place—Andi's and Candle House and the rest—only exist for me as points of an inexplicable geography. They reconstruct around me, vague shades of what I know, only to dissolve when I transition to the next point.

This must be death. An unmoored spirit, knocked off course to its final reward, finds itself roaming here. It's an eternity of brushing past the ones we love and the things we remember, but never touching them, never being seen by them. If I don't find Rez or worse, never find my way back to Cavendish, where my actual body lies, will I just float out here forever? Haunting Andi sounds fun in theory, but if she's going to light sage all the time and work some hoodoo on me, that's not quite the Patrick Swayze fun-times I'd hoped for.

One of the Helpers on the other side of the door tilts his head and squints to get a better look at something ahead. In the dome of darkness over this place, three white points appear. At first, I think they're more Helpers come to join the others. Three vacant faces move steadily closer.

The masks float out of the darkness. I duck back out of the lobby and crouch in the first row. They found me. There won't be any eternal drifting. These things have one directive. I can hop around to as many places as I want, but the masks will know. Eventually, they'll catch me.

One by one, they announce their presence with a long, plaintive moan. The two Helpers by the door exchange quizzical looks as the faces approach. Then the duo decides to open the front doors and escort the floating sentinels inside. Honored guests, the masks drift through the door and into the lobby, the woman flanked by the other two. They pause, hovering in the air. The faces rotate on an invisible axis, turning to scan the call center.

Near the back of the room is the hallway I came from, leading deeper into the building. I take a breath to sprint for it, but the sentinels separate. They fly off in different directions, descending into the rows to hunt for me. There is no moaning now. They are silent as they cut through the stale air, mouths opening and closing.

I bolt for the first door in the back hallway. It's heavy and metal with a push-bar across it. I hit it as quietly as I can, but I'm moving fast enough that it still makes a loud *clack!* A few feet away, the floating face of the woman starts to turn. I don't pause to see if she noticed me.

This entire place is just a box full of other smaller, gray boxes. Everything is right angles and fluorescent lights, industrial carpets with simple patterns and tasteful mauve hues. Every stretch of hallway looks like the last. It's quieter in here, but the low, busy tones of office work are being piped in from somewhere.

*Can you hold for a moment?*
*Let me know when you have the bandwidth to review that.*
Shuffling papers. Benign, digital chirps.

I jog down the hallway and look into the offices as I pass. Many are empty. Some are decorated to give only the most basic semblance of occupation. A mannequin sits at a desk, its back to the door. This one is in a cheap suit instead of business casual. The glowing screen shows an open email, never answered.

A moan drifts from the end of the hall. I freeze in place as the boy's face stares at me with its eyeless gaze. His lips work, squirming without words until the jaw finally drops and the maw stretches open. The sigils across the newspaper spark and scintillate. The moan is one of recognition, one of hunger. It moves quickly, the mouth growing larger as it zips down the corridor.

I run. Trembling panic boils up from my chest. It erupts as a giggle, and a stuttering bit of insanity escapes my lips. I keep moving, not looking over my shoulder at the inevitable, voracious thing trailing me. If I look back, it will be over. I will collapse to my knees and let the landslide of unhinged laughter just roll over me while the face starts to eat.

Rez. Find Rez.

I break left, heading into a small anteroom with overstuffed burgundy armchairs and plastic ferns placed dutifully in the corner. Two Helpers stand at attention on either side of a nondescript, windowless door. They nod to me and smile, gesturing to a sign on an easel.

Welcome. Please turn off all cell phones and recording devices.

The first tips his invisible hat and opens the door. Soft chamber music curls up stone steps, mingling with the scents of fresh pastries and expensive wine. The second Helper gestures for me to go through. I hesitate at the threshold, but the moaning of the woman's face fills the room as it appears behind me. The Helpers give it a curious look, then back to me. I rush inside, pulling the door closed as the face draws near. It hits the door with a soft thump and groans with discontent.

I back down the steps, away from the entry. The face will devour the door whole in a moment, I'm sure of it. In one swallow, it will just consume that portion of my reality and keep coming, inexorable.

Behind me, the soft strains of a cello and violin play, crackling from the horn of an old phonograph. At the bottom of the stairs is a makeshift gallery. Rugs have been cast upon the room's concrete floors and atop them are hand-carved wooden chairs and broad tables with pristine white cloths. White-gloved Helpers glide through the well-dressed crowd, carrying trays of *hors d'ouevres*. The brutal stone of the room is hidden beneath layers of expensive antiques, lending an air of quiet refinement. The twenty or so guests sit fanning themselves or exchanging whispered secrets as they wait. The furniture is arranged in a semicircle, all of it facing a small chamber at the front of the room. The chamber is a closed gray box with a wide, Plexiglas window offering a view to the darkness inside. At the back of the crowd, Rupert Lazlo is standing next to Kitty, his hand on her shoulder. They beam at the guests, at the trappings of high society they've assembled. Rupert wears his finest western-cut suit, a gray, boxy piece that settles over his shoulders like armor.

Neon-blue saguaro cacti are embroidered on the lapels. Kitty's dress matches, of course.

I swallow hard and step into the party like it's a minefield. If I'm too loud, they'll all turn at once and see me standing among them. They'll howl and tear off their fineries before pouncing on me *en masse*.

But these people look normal. They're mostly older, some of them well into their golden years, with fine evening wear and the dull look of the bored and terminally rich. Sitting off to the side, though, is something I don't believe. I stagger back when I see her. The weathered and cracked gas mask is grotesque among the nice watches and expensive handbags. It's a smear of oil on a white dress. Dr. Void. She's sitting there, a thick hose running from her mask to the clicking and hissing device strapped to her chest.

The Sinister Dr. Void! What dark scheme is she hatching beneath the gas mask that keeps her alive?!

I get a better look than I did when I glimpsed her cameo this morning. From beneath her mask, her hair hangs in long, white dreadlocks down the back of her hooded cloak. Not an inch of skin is showing. Only the thick cords of hair suggest any sort of person. Sitting in her velvet-backed chair, she looks like a space-faring nomad.

And she's staring right at me. I take a step back and look behind me to make sure she's not looking at someone else, but the dark lenses of the mask follow me. I freeze. Was I moving too much? She tilts her head and looks over to the Lazlos. They don't notice me. When she turns back to me, she stands and raises a finger to point at me.

A moan cuts through the polite whispers in the room. Dr. Void pauses and looks to the man sitting to her right, a bearded guy in a black turtleneck with about five too many necklaces. He's looking at me, too, but his eyes are hollow. They're black sockets, bottomless. His face goes rubbery and wriggles on his skull. The moan from his lips grows louder. His jaw extends, dislocates, and the face of the boy—*the mask*—grows out of the man's own face. It twists and pulls away, distending his flesh. The man stares straight ahead into the chamber, trying to see what's hiding there in the shadows. He taps his foot and checks his watch, completely unaware that he's giving birth to some spectral hound.

Dr. Void's attention is on the spectacle. She watches, rapt, but no one else in the room has the slightest idea. Even the man's date, a droll brunette in a flowing, black gown, keeps chattering at him as this second, child's face is born. The mask pulls loose from his skin with a final jerk. Behind the transformation, the man's real face is unmarred and for that I am *truly fucking thankful*. I was expecting a bloody, grimacing skull.

111

The child mask floats there next to him. It blinks, eyeless but searching. It moans and its lips twitch. Dr. Void raises her hands up and steps back, then looks to me, waiting for what happens next.

"Yeah," I say. "Super gross, right?"

The face floats over to me, mouth wide, as I dance between rows of oblivious guests. I try to keep them between me and the mask.

"If you've got any juju you can work to get these things to fuck off, I'd be grateful," I tell Dr. Void.

Inscrutable, she only watches. Everyone else shifts in their seats as I scramble around them. They look past me or right through me, waiting for whatever is about to happen in the dark chamber at the front of the room. At the back of the crowd, a second moan, followed by a third. An elderly woman's face twists and pulls away from her skull to reveal the mask of the man. Two rows over, the same thing happens to an older Asian man with a bright red scarf. He sits calmly as his face contorts into the mask of the woman. It wrenches itself free from his skin, pulling and stretching while he sits with his hands folded in his lap.

The masks rise up above the crowd to reform their floating trio. They hover overhead, gaping mouths and bottomless eyes. The woman mask twitches into something resembling a smile. When it speaks, it's not a moan or even a hungry shriek. It's a woman's voice, a thick, Southern drawl worn ragged with cigarettes.

"You can't run from me, boy! You thought you was hot shit, didn't you? Thought you could just roll up and destroy my life. Hell no. You ain't gettin' away with that. You done kicked the hornet's nest, son," Bela says, her voice booming over the heads of the guests.

The paper skin of the mask spasms with rage. I scramble, darting down rows and crawling over laps. There's nowhere to go. The masks descend.

"Oh, you ain't gonna like this none. *Heheh*. No sir," Bela says through the mask. Her voice deepens as the mouth distends to swallow me whole. "It's a special kind of hell waitin' for those that fuck with me, you hear?"

I stumble back, tripping over a purse and sprawling onto my ass. I crab walk away as the faces loom over me. There are no other doors that I see, just the stairs. As if reading my thoughts, the child mask floats over to block the way. A tendril of saliva drips from its mewling lips as I scuttle to press my back against the wall.

But there is no wall.

What looks like cinderblock draped in shadows is really a veil. The other people at the party probably see the dark end of the room, bare and concrete. I see endless black. I see a vast gulf of darkness and floating in the distance, if I stare hard enough, the orange glow of sodium vapor streetlights.

The masks close in. They take their time. I jump to my feet and plunge into the gloom. With the streetlight as my anchor, I race through the starless void. The blackness around me is all-consuming. Over my shoulder, the masks grow smaller as I put distance between us. They're still coming, direct and unstoppable. The moans grow faint, swallowed up by the endless night. There's no path to follow, and I can't see my feet. I just keep moving and hope I make it to the other side. This new island of light feels far away, just a memory, but something at the back of my skull thrums, a low bass note that draws me in. I follow this thread, like reeling myself in out of the darkness, and before long, my shoes crunch on gravel. There's asphalt beneath my feet as I draw closer to the streetlights.

The island is a small parking lot. Towering over it is Cavendish Assisted Living. My will bleeds out onto the pavement. I've come in a circle. My strings cut, I just want to sit right where I am and wait for the three masks to catch up. Right now, they're vague spots in the darkness, but moving inexorably closer. I've got maybe a minute. If I focus on the pull at the base of my skull, I can follow it back to my body. Right back where I started.

Ahead is a familiar brown station wagon. The license plate reads LAZLO-3. The three Helpers are still standing there, and I'm not sure if they've moved since I was here. I don't know when I *was* here. Hours ago? Days? Any amount of time could have passed while I went on this little astral fiasco. There are still no stars or moon in the perfectly opaque sky, no way to tell. The Helpers are blind to it all. They stare at the building, waiting, every bit as dead-eyed as the mannequins taking calls at the Lighthouse.

"Hey!" I yell at them, as I approach. "Hey!"

In unison, they turn to look at me and I can see the emptiness behind their eyes. I can feel it. It's a vacant space to crawl into. It's a closet or a box with nothing in it. They tilt their heads like dogs.

From across the parking lot comes the moaning. I can make out the faces now, mouths wide and hungry. The Helpers see them, too. They look past my shoulder and cock their heads to the opposite side.

"I need you to fight those things. Slow them down or something. Can you do that? Hello?"

The Helpers exchange looks, then turn back to their vigil, watching the Cavendish building as if I was never there.

"Ain't nowhere to run now, sugar," Bela says through one of the masks. "It's cute watching you panic, but this ain't something you can hide from. No, sir!"

I ignore her and grab the first Helper by the arm to make him look at me. He tries to pull away, but his body suddenly seizes up. His limbs go rigid, and I feel myself slide, tumbling away from everything. The world gets pulled out from under me and for the blink of an eye, there's nothing but white. My blood chills and I gulp down hot, thick air. A strangled scream. Bela's mouth must be closing over me. This is what getting your soul eaten feels like. I kick and thrash, hearing startled yelps barked out in response.

"Help! Help!" Someone yells.

I blink away tears as the night sky swims into focus. A gibbous moon hangs overhead with a field of stars as the backdrop. I stare up at it, just lying there on my back.

"Unh?" One of the Helpers asks as he looks down at me.

Something is wrong. I'm cold. Outside, the humidity of the night air clings to my skin, but my insides feel cool and grease-slick. I sit up and the first thing I see are my shoes. They're generic, scuffed penny loafers and I sit there looking at them, wondering how they got on my feet. The back of my hand is bone white, so white the nails look pink in contrast.

"Ah!" I scream.

I stand. There were three Helpers. Now there are two, wide eyed and wiggling their fingers as they try to understand what happened to their friend. "Muh?" they ask. "Een?"

In the reflection in the station wagon's window, I see a Helper. I wave at the reflection of the pale, hairless man in his midnight blue coveralls and he waves back, perfectly in sync.

"Oh, you've got to be fucking kidding me," I say, and my voice comes out as a cracked squeak.

I run my new bony fingers across the smooth face, feeling the nose, the teeth, and ears.

"Oh shit. Oh no," I say, and try to choke back the words, alien sounding as they pass my lips.

It feels *real* fucking weird, like I'm wearing a suit of clothes just pulled from the freezer and slathered with Vaseline.

"Well, you just think you're so goddamn smart, don't you?" Bela's voice growls.

The masks float over us. The woman's—Bela's—is bigger than the rest, stretched out of shape into an angry, mottled blob that barely resembles a face.

"This ain't the end of this," she says. "Not by a damn shot."

They whisk away into the night, up and off past the streetlights. I look up at the stars again and feel a surge of relief. The stars are back. The trees beneath those stars are back. If I walk down to the road, it will connect to other roads and those roads will connect to homes and businesses that have always been there. The Texas night feels different on my skin. I can actually *feel* it like I can feel the pavement under my feet.

And now I'm a Helper.

*Jason Murphy*

\*\*\*

# CHAPTER THIRTEEN

I examine my hands again and clench them into fists. I bend my legs and arch my back. Everything seems to move and work like it's supposed to, but my equilibrium is off, and I can feel myself sliding around inside this pale, skinny meat-suit. This body doesn't fit right. It's not even a body, not really. What will it take for it to dissolve into goo? If a solid blow from Zeke will do it, what about a bump on the head? A stubbed toe? If it degrades into sludge, what then for me?

The other two Helpers are watching me. "Guh?" they ask, then answer it with a muttered, "Umm. Nuh. Buh."

My head spins, and I'm not sure if it's because the colossal shit-slide of today is raining down on me or that I'm possessing someone else's body. The stars begin to drift in the sky above and I find myself slumped down on the curb, trying to grab hold of something so that my mind doesn't get cast off into the ether.

"Enh?" One of them says.

"Yeah. Help," I say to the Helpers. "Sorry, guys. Just give me a second. It's been one of those days, you know? I mean necromancers and drugs and those face things chasing me ... there was a motel ... A ghost bird attacked me in my car! And now this shit. The world is asking a lot of me right now."

"Fuh," one of them says. Blank stares.

"Yeah," I say. "You're right. It's fine. I just need to keep it together. I should ... what would Zeke do?"

"Irf."

"You're right. I don't know any ghost karate. Maybe I should just drive to Rez's place right now. We could just take your car and ... I don't know," I say, looking again at my snow-white skin. "Should I go to the ER or something?"

"Lur."

"Yeah. I doubt this is covered by my insurance."

I don't even know if I could find Rez's place, not without my phone. I can barely find my way to the grocery store without my phone. Now I know that Andi lives in a fancy apartment downtown, one facing north. That just leaves a few thousand more. She might be able to help me, but again, her number is on my phone. Finding Violet is a crapshoot. Most of the time I just locate her by sheer luck. You say her name three times in a drain tunnel, and she appears. My only other friend is locked up in a nursing home for witches, waiting to be "processed" for Gehenna. After today, I have to acknowledge that I don't have the imaginative capacity to even guess what that is. I know it's some sort of prison and that they're taking us there soon. Tonight.

"All right, listen, you two," I say and when I snap my fingers, they look alarmed and jerk back. I point at the Cavendish building. The lights in the lobby are on and from here, we can see a bored night clerk sitting at the desk, surfing the internet. "We're going in there," I tell the Helpers and try to ignore the nasal twang of my new voice.

They look to the Cavendish building, then back at me. "Ooh?"

"Yes. We're going in. You two are going to cause a distraction. There's going to be some dudes in purple. Don't be afraid. Just rush them. In fact, anyone that comes for me, you tackle them and beat their ass, okay? We're going down a level to find Zeke and my body. And an old man and some drugs. Do you know what drugs are?"

They look at me without nodding. I have their attention, but I don't know that it means anything.

"Little bag full of yellow powder," I say and mime holding a small bag.

They look intently at my hands and then back to me. "Efk."

"Yeah. Okay. You know what? Not a big deal. I'll find the drugs. You guys just don't let anyone get me, okay? Maybe run at them, screaming. That would be super scary to see one of you weird bastards running at me, howling like a banshee. Maybe take your clothes off and set yourself on fire …"

The Helpers exchange looks. One of them unzips his coveralls.

"No. No. No. Okay. Don't do that. I'm just kidding. Nobody needs to see what you've got going on down there," I say, and reach forward to zip him back up. "Wait. Do you even …?"

I look down at my own crotch for a second before shoving the thought aside. I can think about that later. Right now, we're just going to ignore the fact that it feels like I might be Ken-doll smooth.

"Let's go," I tell them, and they fall into step right behind me as I stride for the front doors.

"Aoof," one of them says.

The front of the nursing home is unguarded. The lobby looks empty except for the night clerk with the TV on the wall quietly playing cable news to keep her company. I push through the swinging front doors and walk right past her.

"Umm. Hello?" she says.

"Ehl," the Helper to my left says, but I nudge him to stay on course as I avoid even looking at the clerk.

I make a beeline for the doors that will take us to the high-risk ward. They'll be locked. I'm going to make my new idiot friends bang on them until someone answers. Then, when they do answer, I'll slip right through as my new idiot friends help them to the floor. Hopefully, none of the orderlies here punch as hard as Zeke.

It's a great plan.

Just as we get to the doors, they fly open before us. One of the purple enforcers stands there, looking at us like he can't understand what he's seeing. His stance hardens.

"Get ready," I say under my breath and look for something to hit him with.

The Helper to my left shrieks. I nearly jump out of my new skin. He throws his hands in the air, flailing and screeching as he rushes the enforcer.

"Aoooeee!" he screams.

He hits the enforcer hard. They both go sprawling. The Helper starts snapping his jaws like wind-up teeth.

Oh shit. He's trying to eat that guy's face.

The guard slams both frozen turkey-sized fists on either side of the Helper's head. The Helper doesn't flinch.

"*Agru mot!*" the enforcer says with a growl.

The runes on the man's hockey mask spark with magic. His arms bulge. His neck swells, expanding with corded muscles. I think he just called on the power of Grayskull. The other Helper and I cower against each other. I'm clutching at his coveralls, watching the brawl.

With one shove, the enforcer launches the Helper into the air so hard the Helper smashes into the ceiling. Tiles and dust rain down. The Helper comes down just as hard on the floor.

The enforcer slams his boot into the Helper's side, caving in his ribs. But the Helper rises, wearing his empty, maniacal grin.

The enforcer pokes him with his stun baton. A blue spark arcs into the Helper's chest.

Pop!

The Helper bursts like a balloon filled with milk and cottage cheese. The sludge sprays everywhere, raining down on armchairs and spattering up the wall. A wave of cold slime drenches me. The enforcer barely flinches as wet chunks speckle his mask. In a pile at our feet are the Helper's sticky clothes.

"Jesus Christ!" I yell.

"Roooisss?" the remaining Helper asks.

The enforcer looks at the mess, back up at me, then sparks his baton once again before trudging forward to grab me.

"Run! Fucking run!" I yell.

The Helper follows as I barrel through the lobby, knocking over chairs in our flight.

"Un! Unnn!" he yells.

The clerk, in shock, looks at me through a smear of white slime across her face. It drips down onto her cell phone. The purple-clad guard chases. I sprint outside and make for the trees, not bothering to see if my ally can keep up. Behind me I hear the enforcer burst through the door and the fall of his heavy boots keeping pace.

I dart between cars, trying to ignore the sparking of the baton as it pops somewhere behind me.

"Come here, freaks!" he says.

I hit the trees at the edge of the property and dive into a thick and tangled copse of hackberry and pigweed. My right foot hangs on a root buried in the brush. I lurch forward, pinwheel my arms, and go tumbling down an incline into a drainage ditch. I slide, splash down in knee-deep ditch water, and struggle to keep my penny loafers from being consumed by the sucking mud. Trying to climb out will leave me wide open. I'd slip and slide up the steep bank, getting tangled in the overgrowth just long enough for the enforcer to leap in and turn me into yogurt. I keep slogging, hooking a left and moving through the ditch that runs parallel to the building. I stay low in the culvert, keeping my head beneath the line of overgrown grass.

Somewhere behind me, the enforcer barrels into the ditch. On the other side is an undeveloped lot that backs up to another small, professional park full of CPAs and dentists. I catch a glimpse of the goon emerging from the other side some thirty yards behind me. I pause when I see him, standing stock still in the moonlight. If I move, I'll stand out like some radiant ghost trying to hide in the murk. The enforcer turns away, scanning the trees in an empty lot. I move, staying low and fast, trying not to splash around in the runoff.

As I navigate the brush, I slow down. He's losing my trail, but me slipping in the mud and getting impaled on a branch or stray rebar hidden beneath the surface will get his attention. The ditch opens into a concrete depression that extends under the dark roads and further into the city. Broad pipes, the kind murderous clowns hide in, line the edge, some trickling thin streams of stale water into the discarded cigarette packs and empty cans of Monster Energy drink.

A flashlight beam sweeps just over my head. I duck, not daring to look. The halo of silver light bounces and widens, and I hear boots stomping through the brush, getting louder. If I run, I might be able to make the thirty or so yards between here and the next bend in the ditch. Maybe. Instead, I cram myself into one of the drainage pipes. Hunched over, I can barely stand inside. It's not nearly tall enough for me to flee deeper into the sewers if spotted. I could crawl, scrabbling on my hands and knees until I found a bend in the pipe—or a precipitous drop into a vat of shit—but I really have no idea how sewers work. The pipe could lead down beneath the city, down into a latticework of forgotten service tunnels and ladders. If I can't get back to my own body, maybe life as a CHUD would suit me. This skin tone won't do so well in the sun. Might as well lean into it.

A pale face emerges from the darkness of the pipe. I jump and fall backwards out of it, stifling an *oh shit* as whatever was in there with me leers at me from the murk.

"Ugk?" the voice whispers and the Helper flashes his toothy grin.

"Seriously, man, I need you to shut the fuck up like right now," I tell him.

The beam sweeps overhead, dipping down lower into the culvert. I duck and crawl back into the pipe, shoving the Helper deeper. I press a finger to my lips and point up to warn him about the enforcer above us. A rock skitters from the lip of the ditch and lands right next to me as the beam crawls along the concrete floor. It lingers on every patch of trash and every swirl of graffiti, taking extra time to shine into the pipes on the opposite side. The Helper opens his mouth to speak. I slap my hand over his lips and try to use my eyes to tell him that I will murder him in this ditch.

A radio squawks, and my entire body tenses. "Paul, this is Truman. You got that wrapped up?"

We listen to the enforcer fumble for the walkie on his belt. "Hey. Yeah, I think we're good," he says. "Those weird little albinos ran off. Third time this week. Nailed one of 'em. Jesus, you should see the mess in the lobby."

"Nice. I think the cleanup crew is already in there mopping it up. Hurry back when you're done. Administration wants to do this Gehenna transfer before shift change."

"Ugh. Gehenna," Paul says, and the words curdle around his lips. "You guys need me for that one?"

"Don't be a bitch. We've got two combative guests and a corpse to move. That's a three-man job, Paul. We're all loaded up at the back dock. Get your ass over here."

"Copy that," Paul says, snaps off his flashlight, and trudges back toward Cavendish.

A corpse. They found me. They found my body and think I'm dead. Are they going to bury me? Cremate me?

I slink out of the pipe and give the Helper a hand.

"Oolp," he says in a tone that I assume means *thank you*.

I look down at my stained coveralls. Filthy, mud-caked, and spattered with drying ropes of Helper goo. At least no one will recognize me.

Still staying low, I run over to the edge of the ditch nearest Cavendish and pull myself up the side to take a look. Back behind the nursing home are loading docks lit with harsh, yellow lights. A van—the one that broadsided us earlier—is parked off to the side. Its front end is mangled, with the bumper hanging like a busted lip. A second van, this one all white, without the Cavendish logo across the side, idles with its back doors open to the loading dock. Two more purple enforcers wait as Paul trots up to them.

"Let's get going before this one starts to stink," one says, motioning into the back of the van.

Paul goes up to drive while the other two climb into the back. I scramble out of the ditch and start running across the lawn, right for them.

"Wait!" I shout as the van pulls away. "Stop!"

I have no idea what I would do if they did stop. My only option right now is to beg, to chase the van like a stray dog and hope for a miracle, but the van pulls away. As the taillights grow smaller in the distance, I follow its path down the service road behind the building. The trail winds around Cavendish and past the parking lot, until it connects with the street out front.

I break for the front parking lot at a full sprint. "Come on!" I yell to the Helper.

Eyes wide, he runs along behind me, mumbling, "Unnon. Unnon."

"We can intercept them if we hurry, now move your ass!"

"Oov!"

"I've got a plan," I tell him. "You're not gonna like it."

***

The van, headlights bouncing over the uneven road, skirts the edge of the parking lot as it draws closer to the intersecting street. Next to me, the Helper watches. We're crouched in the hedges, trying not to get caught in the glare of the headlights. The Helper looks at the van, at the road, and then back to me. I'm not sure if he understands. I kind of hope not, considering what I'm about to do.

The van pulls up to the road and pauses for the driver to check for cross traffic. He's got his mask off now. Paul is a flat-nosed thug who probably enjoyed the extracurricular job perks before he was fired from his job at some federal prison. He steers the van out onto the road and turns left, heading in our direction. I place a hand on the Helper's back.

"Okay. Get ready. This is gonna suck and I'm sorry, but I'm out of ideas."

"Guk?" he says.

The van picks up speed.

I count to myself, under my breath. "Four … three … two …"

I shove the Helper into the street. Tires squeal. He doesn't even raise his arms in surprise as the headlights pin him down. He looks right at Paul. Paul's

121

jaw drops in horror. Their eyes lock just as the van smashes into the Helper. Milkshake explodes all over the front of the vehicle. It sprays up across the window and showers over the pavement. The van slides and leaves a long, white smear on the asphalt.

Breathless, I lurk in the bushes as the ride rocks to a stop against the curb. For a pregnant moment, the van just sits there. No one inside moves. There's nothing but the sound of Helper juice dripping from the grill. Finally, Paul stumbles out of the driver's seat to look at the mess.

"Holy shit …" he says and steps back to take it all in. He starts to laugh and follows the white smear down the street to where the Helper's coveralls lay shredded with tire marks and soaking in ooze.

I run for the open driver's side door.

Paul the enforcer is nudging the pile of clothes with his foot when he says, "Guys, come check this out. This shit is crazy!"

The back doors open just as I dive behind the wheel.

"Hey!" I hear Paul yell. "Hey, damn it!"

I throw the van into drive and floor it. The tires screech, and for a second, we hover there in place, wheels spinning on slick pavement. Paul hurries to catch us. Before he can get close, the tires gain purchase, and we go careening down the road. The van bucks as we nail a curb, hop it, and then correct just in time to get back on the road and take a wide right into a random neighborhood. We fly through dark streets.

The cab of the van is separated from the cargo space. I can't see what's going on back there without opening a small window. As I slide through a stop sign, not wanting to slow down too much, I reach to open it. Suddenly, the van rocks hard to the right. Behind me, there's a series of muffled thuds, followed by a choked scream. I hear the spark and pop of the batons. More commotion. The van rocks left, then right, making it hard to keep the wheel straight. Another scream. I check the side mirrors, making sure we're not being pursued. The street behind is dark and silent. I slam the brakes and jerk the wheel to the right. My cargo slams against the wall. We slide into a parking lot behind a run-down hardware store.

I throw the van into park and am about to jump out when I spot Paul's stun baton rolling around in the passenger floorboard. I'm almost afraid to touch it, like if I get too close the electricity will leap out and obliterate me. It feels good in my hand, though. Heavy. I might have to get Zeke to start carrying one of these in his red bag.

When I slip out, the back of the van is quiet. The doors are closed and no one inside moves. I reach out to open it, keeping the baton charged and raised in my left fist.

"Zeke?" I ask.

The back doors explode open. A purple enforcer hurtles out of the back, headfirst. I jerk out of the way. He lands on the pavement with enough force to splinter his mask and drive the air from his lungs in a ragged gasp. When his mask breaks, he deflates a little. His muscles shrink down to normal, human size. In the middle of the street, he groans and tries to make his limbs work before finally giving up and collapsing into a pile. From inside the van comes growling and scuffling. The vehicle rocks on its wheels. Zeke comes out, tangled up with the other enforcer. They kick and thrash against each other as the enforcer tries to tame Zeke, to break him. Zeke's ankles and wrists are bound with zip ties. His face is secured with a restraint mask, but when I see his eyes, I want to run. For an instant, my mind screams that it's not him, that Zeke has been overcome by some other *thing*. His eyes flare with a blood-hunger and his bared teeth flash beneath the mask.

The enforcer is making the sounds of someone getting eaten by a shark, lots of half-spoken pleas for help that turn into spittle as he fights for his life. Zeke isn't making a sound. He shakes free and manages to get to his feet. With one quick leap, he whips his wrist restraints under his feet so that his hands are in front of him, and immediately snaps the ties.

I can't help but laugh. "You tried to hold him with zip ties? You dumb sons of bitches!"

A man with a black bag over his head and his wrists bound with the same zip ties staggers from within the van. I recognize Harvey's necromancy tattoos up and down his forearms. He throws himself to the van floor and struggles to get his hands in front of him.

"What the hell's going on?" Harvey yells from beneath the sack. "Hurry up, man! We've got to move!"

Zeke and the other enforcer smash into each other with all the force of ground zero. The enforcer dwarfs him, and for one still second, they push against each other there in the middle of the street. The purple man growls. Zeke's feet slide and he stumbles back. The beast of a guard, even now, without the mask's magical strength, howls. He bull-rushes Zeke.

Zeke waits. I hold my breath, expecting my friend to explode from the impact.

Zeke sidesteps. He spins and uses the enforcer's momentum to slam him into the ground. He rolls with it and brings his knee down onto the bigger man's chest, using all his weight. The sternum gives with a muffled snap. The enforcer gasps. The massive guard lashes out with a clumsy swing. In an instant, Zeke catches the arm and bends it the wrong direction. Another snap.

Zeke snatches loose the mask. The enforcer's face is chalk white and frozen in a building scream. His limbs wither, still massive, but not inhuman.

Zeke's face is blank. He looks the enforcer in the eye, grabs him by the throat, and begins to squeeze.

"Whoa!" I say. "Dude. Zeke! Stop!"

Zeke doesn't so much as glance at me, but the enforcer pleads as he gags beneath Zeke's grip. His bloodshot eyes beg me to help, to not let him die, as his skin turns a shade of purple to match his coveralls.

"Zeke, don't!" I yell, but don't want to get close.

The baton is heavy in my hand. Zeke still just watches the man's face deepen to the color of a bruise. We're in the middle of the street in a neighborhood full of print shops and hair salons. The lights are off, and the roads are still.

"You gonna make me chase you?" Zeke says, still not looking at me.

"What?"

"You're next. Are you going to make me chase you? If not, just wait right there," he says.

"Dude! You're killing him!"

I stab the baton at him and pull the trigger. The tongues of electricity lash out and lick at his shoulder. Zeke jerks, growls, and snatches the baton from my hand. Before I realize what's happening, he cracks it across my cheek and takes me out at the knee. The next instant, I'm on my back, trying to catch my breath. It comes in great, labored wheezes as the stars above spin overhead from the blow. The enforcer fights for air, gurgling and spitting. I get to my knees. A white drop of goo drips down from my wounded cheek, across the tip of my nose, and onto the pavement. I stare at it, frozen, not sure if it's the first of many. I brace myself and take a deep breath, wondering if I'm about to dissolve. I don't think it will hurt. The blow across the cheek was painless, just a redirection of force without any other sensation. Inches from my nose, only a few more drops of white spatter onto the street. I look up, too scared to move for fear that something will break, and I'll immediately turn to slime.

In the back of the van, Harvey is still trying to worm around and get his bound hands in front of him. He's got one leg through the loop and twists around on the floor like an idiot. Ten feet away from me, Zeke tears his knife from a strap around his ankle. He's always bragging that when he's searched, they never find *all* his knives. Still straddling the enforcer's chest, he unsheathes it, and it hangs there in the moonlight, a promise, and the enforcer starts to gibber.

"Wait. Wait, wait, wait. Please, man. This is just my job," he says and holds up his one good arm to shield himself.

"You killed my brother," Zeke says, and I don't recognize his voice. His fingers tighten around the knife.

"Zeke, it's me. I'm okay! I'm right here!" I say.

He doesn't look up, but says to me, "You've got about a five second head start before I turn you into soup. I ain't playin'."

"Oh God. Please. We didn't do anything. He was like that when we found him. I swear," the enforcer says, but if Zeke hears him, there's no indication in his face.

Zeke grabs a fistful of the man's hair and yanks the enforcer's head back to expose his neck. The man yelps, a frail animal noise. He bats at Zeke's grip as his will to live bleeds away.

"Mina!" I yell, and Zeke freezes with his blade poised over the man's neck. The word goes off like a gunshot. I keep going.

"That's your favorite knife. You named it Mina, after your first kiss," I say and start to stand.

Zeke turns his head to face me, and the look in his eyes says I might not be next to die. I might be *first*.

"Damaged. That's your favorite Black Flag song."

Zeke gives one last look at the enforcer before crawling off him. The man on the ground still doesn't dare to move. As Zeke stands, he looks me in the face and prowls over to me, his knife held loose in his hand. As he gets closer, I can see the tears in his eyes.

"You should've run," he says.

I fight the urge. I raise my hands up in defense. "It's me. It's Clark!"

He keeps coming.

"You keep an Incan coin under your pillow. Your grandma gave it to you. It's supposed to keep away nightmares. It doesn't work. Sometimes … you wake up screaming. You act like I don't hear you, but I do. So, I get up with you and we play video games 'til the sun comes up," I say and my breath shakes. "Don't do this, man."

He lowers the blade, and his face drops with it. His eyes brim with tears. He throws his arms around me and I feel his chest hitch with a sob. "I thought you were dead. I thought you were dead."

"Me too, brother."

He takes a step back and looks me up and down. "Oh no. This ain't gonna work," he says and turns to the enforcer. "Fix this shit."

The enforcer looks at the both of us and shakes his head as he wipes away tears. "I don't … I don't know what you mean."

"No. No!" I tell Zeke. "This isn't him. It's the drug, the cairn root. It's a whole thing. Tonight's been pretty fucked up. I'll tell you later."

Harvey, still tangled up in himself, raises up his bagged head. "You've got my root?"

"Shut up, Harvey," Zeke and I both say.

"Well …" Zeke says, and shrugs like he doesn't know what to say next. He motions to the back of the van. Tucked away in the back is a black, vinyl sack, about six feet long.

"Is that …?" I ask, but the words die on my lips.

"Yeah. We probably want to do something about that," Zeke says.

I don't want to get near it. Staring down into my own, lifeless eyes might break me. Hell, the shock alone might cause this Helper body to immediately erupt into goo.

"Hey, a little help here?" Harvey says, but we ignore him as we inch closer to the bag.

"Am I dead? I mean, did I look like … a dead person?" I ask.

"Yeah, dude. That's a body bag, and you're inside of it," Zeke says, but grabs me by the arm before I can climb into the back van. "Hold up," he says. "We don't know if there's going to be any sort of Time Cop business."

"Time Cop?" I ask. "What are you talking about?"

"If you get too close to yourself, maybe you'll blow up or some shit," Zeke says and tries to suppress a snicker.

"This is super weird and really serious right now, okay?" I say.

"I know," he says, "But man … I didn't think you could get any whiter."

"Yeah, you're hysterical. You're so funny."

The second enforcer pulls off the shards of his shattered hockey mask. He sits in the center of the street and stares at the pieces in his hands. "What happened? Was there an accident?"

Zeke strides over to him. The enforcer rolls over onto his back and shows his belly like a cowed dog. Clipped to the man's coveralls is an old Walkman. Zeke reaches down and snatches it away from the man.

"That's mine," Zeke says through his teeth.

And *then* he kicks the guy in the face. The enforcer's head whips to the side. As the man drops into unconsciousness, a bloody tooth skitters across the asphalt.

Zeke looks over to the conscious one. The remaining enforcer lays prone in the middle of the street. He shrinks under Zeke's gaze.

"Y'all purple motherfuckers are testing me today!" Zeke says.

***

# CHAPTER FOURTEEN

"And you're sure you can do this?" I ask Harvey as I stare at the black bag holding my mortal coil.

"Yeah," Harvey says. "Easy-peasy."

He takes a drag off a cigarette from a pack one of the goons left in the van. He blows it out the passenger window and kicks his bare feet up on the dash. Harvey has toenail fungus. Zeke's behind the wheel. He shoots Harvey a glance and shakes his head.

"You can get my soul or whatever back into the right body? No screwing around? You're not gonna fuck me?" I ask.

"Nah," Harvey says and then cranes his neck around to look at the body bag again. "Wait. How long has it been?"

"I don't know, dude. I've been on the astral plane. Time and space were irrelevant. Maybe an hour?" I say.

"Yeah. An hour is about right," Zeke says.

"Should be fine," Harvey says. "It'll be like switching the batteries in the TV remote. A small ritual and then *bam,* you'll be ready to rock."

"A ritual?" I ask. "Like with components and chanting?"

"Yeah. Something like that. I know a few spells. *El Cambio Imposible* should work." He shifts in his seat and scratches his head. "Or maybe *Lore Berria.* I don't know. One of those."

"Wait. What? One of those, Harvey?" I ask. "*One of those?* How much guesswork is involved in necromancy, anyway?"

"You'd be surprised," he says with a grunt.

"Do I need to stop at a pharmacy or a 7-Eleven or something and get some supplies?" Zeke asks.

"Nah," Harvey says. "We'll see what she's got. You said she's a medium, right? We'll get some braziers. Candles. Some chalk. If she's got a chicken—a live one—that would be groovy."

"Yeah, she's not that kind of medium," Zeke says.

"There's an herb shop on the south side," Harvey says. "An old curandero. You'll have to go in, though. I was banned after an incident."

"An incident, Harvey?" Zeke says.

"An incident," he says, and doesn't elaborate.

"It's almost midnight," Zeke says. "Ain't no *herberias* open after midnight."

"Well, none you know about," Harvey says and keeps staring out the window at the passing streetlights.

127

"Just go to Rez's," I say.

I spend the rest of the drive describing my bizarre adventure to Zeke and Harvey. Zeke shakes his head the whole time. "This is that foolishness," he says. "This is some bullshit we do not need to be involved with."

Harvey just looks stunned. "How in the hell did you hop around like that without any help? Just body swapping all night? You fucking with me? You just snorted some root and then *boom,* just like that?"

"Yeah. Just like that," I say with a shrug.

"And you just jumped right into that new body?" he asks.

"It was an accident. I reached out for the Helper guy and it just kind of happened," I say.

"You made it sound like it was easy, Harvey," Zeke says.

"Yeah, with a necromancer who knows what he's doing," Harvey says and looks me up and down, almost like he doesn't believe it.

When we pull up near Rez's house, the lights are still on. Zeke parks a few doors down and kills the engine. "I hope we're not interrupting anything," he says.

"I hope we are," I say and laugh.

Harvey grins and rubs his hands together. "Yeah, baby."

"Okay, now you're just being gross," I tell him. "Again."

Zeke says, "If we *are* interrupting her and a ... guest ... she'll shoot us. All three of us. So be cool."

"I'm cool," Harvey says with a big smile.

"I'm talking to you, Harvey. Seriously. Do not fuck with her, or she will hurt you. And I'll let her," Zeke says.

"I'm cool!" he says and lights another cigarette.

We get out of the van and walk as fast as we can to her townhouse. If anyone spots us, they're calling the police. With the way we look, no one will ask questions or see if there's something they can help us with. They'll immediately dial 911. We've got a stolen van and there's probably a silver alert out on Harvey, along with the two assholes we left tied up behind a Jack in the Box. Despite how it looks, this can get worse.

Zeke knocks politely on Rez's door, wincing as he does. She may be the only person he's afraid of. The door cracks open on its own and before I realize it, Zeke's got Mina in his hand. The frame of the door is cracked. You wouldn't notice from the sidewalk, but the boot print next to the knob tells the story. Zeke tenses next to me, and I feel a stillness come over him. He pushes the door open with the tip of his knife. We let ourselves inside and scan the living room. Rez's place is a Pottery Barn ad come to life, with furniture that matches the end table, a rug from the same catalog, and throw pillows that accent the colors on the rug. All of it is offset with the occasional quirky pop of color—a "whimsical" cactus in a bright pink bowl or a canary yellow lamp from a thrift store. Django Reinhardt strums from a Bluetooth speaker sitting on a shelf between a candle holder that matches the picture frame next to it.

"Rez?" I ask. "It's me and Zeke. And Harvey, I guess. You alright?"

No answer. Harvey stubs out his cigarette and sneaks in behind us, staying close and thankfully keeping his mouth shut. "Rez?" I say again, and my voice echoes across the stained concrete floors and up the stairs.

As he creeps around the room, checking everything out, Zeke says under his breath, "Man, I've said this before, but Rez's place is nicer than ours."

"Yeah. Maybe we should clean up a little bit."

"And get jobs."

"We've got jobs."

"Jobs that don't involve necromancers and guys in hockey masks."

"Oh! Like real jobs. Yeah. No thanks. Hard pass."

Zeke holds his hand up, and I freeze. He points to a shattered bottle of wine on the stained concrete floor.

"Shit …" I say to myself. The glass pieces aren't in once place. They're scattered, cast across the kitchen floor.

"She didn't just drop the bottle," I say, following the sparkling trail.

"You guys aren't gonna call the cops, are you?" Harvey asks, backing away from the crime scene. "'Cause I'll just hit the road if —"

"Shut up," Zeke says. Harvey closes his mouth and steps back.

The trail of broken glass stops, but *bordeaux* droplets spatter across the floor, over a chair, and onto the rug in a drunken line. Rez has the rug shampooed at least once per month. I know this because she tells me every time I come over. I'm not allowed to so much as look at it unless I take my shoes off. Even then, Rez watches my every step, waiting for me to leave some mysterious stain. Each stray drop of wine across it tells me that yes, someone has definitely been murdered. Rez killed somebody. No question. The impressions in the rug, where the chair legs left their outline, stand out. The chair, heavy, circular, and upholstered with soft brown leather, has been knocked out of alignment. Zeke and I both realize it.

"I think we're like TV detectives now," I tell Zeke.

"Like the Rockford Files?"

"But with necromancers," Harvey says.

Zeke snarls at Harvey and bends to look under the chair. He reaches beneath and pulls out the neck of the wine bottle. He holds it up in the soft light. A thin rope of white slime drips from the jagged edge and collects on the rug.

"Those mother *fuckers*," I say.

Back behind the chair is more of the goo. It pools next to the baseboards and is all smeared around like someone tried to clean it up.

"They came for her," I say. "So, she broke the bottle and got one of them."

"Atta girl," Zeke says, examining the Helper-blood that drips from the jagged glass. His voice is a soft growl.

"They just took her?" I ask, but the pieces are starting to fall into place. Once again, I feel like the floor is going to drop out from under me.

"They took her because they don't have *him*," Zeke says, nodding to Harvey.

Harvey looks at the floor.

Zeke walks over to him and stands close. Harvey won't look him in the eye. "Yeah, Harvey Bunson here won't go to them, but they still need a medium. So, they took our friend."

I sink down onto the couch.

"Hey," Zeke says to Harvey and touches his chin, making the old man look at him. "I'm reasonable, Harvey. I'm real reasonable, you know? But this is on you. This whole day? Me getting thrown into a cell, pissing off witches, and my friend getting kidnaped? That's you."

Harvey can't make his words work. Even from the couch, I can see his lips tremble. His caustic bravado wilts.

"No," I tell them. "It's not."

They both look at me.

"It's not him," I say. "Harvey, you're a piece of shit. No denying that. But this isn't your fault. You were just trying to steer clear of all of this. I get it. I'd run from us, too. This is on the Lazlos."

Harvey nods. "Yeah. That's what I've been trying to say. Those fuckers in that house—"

"Shut up, Harvey," Zeke says again, and again Harvey shuts up.

"They started this. And now they've got Rez," I say.

"Alright," Zeke says and moves for the door. "Then let's go."

"But they're not at Candle House," I say.

"What? Where are they?" Zeke asks.

"I don't know," I tell him, and my voice dies on the last word.

I don't know how to explain to them that she's in a Lighthouse, one that I've only kind of been to. It's here in town, in some non-descript call center, but that could be any one of thousands of office buildings in Austin. I don't even have any reckoning of the general area of the city. Even if we called the cops, they'd never find her in time.

Zeke turns to Harvey, "Well, you can do something, right? Work some spell so we can find her?"

Harvey shrugs as he thinks about it. "Yeah, maybe. I guess I could do that. Gotta get some components, though. Some supplies, you know?"

"Yeah. Yeah," Zeke says. "What do you need? How long?"

"I don't know. It would take a while. Two, maybe three hours?" Harvey says.

Zeke gets in his face. "Two or three hours? You can swap bodies easy-peasy, but it's gonna take you three hours to find our friend? You can't get on the necromancer internet and ask a few people?"

The clock on the wall says 12:45 a.m.

"We don't have time, do we?" I ask.

"No," Harvey says and again stares at the floor. "No, it's … it might be too late already."

Zeke hurls the jagged bottle neck across the room. His face glows with rage, and he prowls, pacing like a panther in his cage. "Fuck!" he screams.

Harvey and I both find ourselves with our backs against the wall, trying to give him space. Today comes down on top of me. It's not one big weight, but a landslide. I sort through the wreckage, trying to find something to grab onto, something that will help. I think of driving around until we see something that looks like the building where I think they have Rez, calling the police, or waking up Andi to see if she can do anything.

I almost hesitate to say it. "I think … I think I have an idea."

Zeke and Harvey freeze in place and hold their breaths while I explain my plan. When I'm finished, Zeke turns it over in his head. He begins to nod.

"Yeah," he says. "Yeah. Okay. This might work."

It's a terrible idea, and Harvey knows it. He's looking at the art on the walls like he's really interested, pretending that he's not at all involved in our conversation. Son of a bitch might as well be whistling.

"You're staying here," I say.

"Hmm? Oh. Yeah. Totally. I'll wait for you guys. And when you get back, I can help with the …" He motions to me, up and down. "With this."

Zeke is halfway out the door, keys in hand. I follow him but turn to look back at Harvey. He's gone right back to being engrossed in the pictures on the wall, the kind of monoculture art you buy because it matches your new sectional. When he finally looks over at me, I look him in the eye, and we both understand. He's leaving the second we're around the corner.

Good.

\*\*\*

Zeke drives like he's expecting an ambush. With every block, he slows down and scans the street. He checks behind parked cars and trees, gripping the wheel as tight as a throat.

"You sure she's gonna be cool with this?" Zeke asks.

"Oh no. She was definitely trying to kill me. Turn here," I say while I look at the map we printed at Rez's place.

"What about you? You cool?"

"I'm hanging in there. I think maybe …"

"Maybe what?" he asks.

"Maybe I should move or something."

"Like we get a different place to live? New apartment?"

"Like … a different state. A different country. Austin is getting too weird. Somewhere quiet. Wyoming or something."

Zeke nods, digesting it.

"You want to run."

"Yeah. I mean, after we help Rez, but … I'm thinking maybe I'm not cut out for this."

"Hmm," he says.

"That's all you've got? Hmm? Take this next right."

Zeke turns and keeps nodding. Finally, he says, "You're full of shit."

"What?"

"You don't want to run. This is the thing you've been chasing. Maybe your whole life."

"Hell no. I didn't want this."

"Yeah. You did."

"What are you talking about? All of this is insane. It's *in-fucking-sane*."

"Yup. And you love it."

"It's horrible. I just want to go home and play video games."

"No. I don't think so," he says. "You know, I watch these TV shows about people getting abducted by aliens or finding out their house is haunted or whatever. Now usually, these are just crazy white people. It's always crazy white people. But if they really think they saw something? Or they experienced something? Why aren't they out there chasing it? Why aren't they turning over rocks and reading books and trying to figure out just what in the hell happened to them? Why aren't they raising hell? I mean, you got pulled up into a UFO and probed or whatever and the best you can do with your life is appear on a TV show on the History Channel? *Yup. The aliens put things in my butt and had sex with my wife. Ain't that crazy? Oh, well. Back to work at the fucking auto shop!* Hell no, man! Hell no!"

He bangs on the wheel with the fervor of a street preacher. "So, you want to be one of them? Yeah, this shit is scary. Yeah, it might get us killed. But man, we've been blessed by this. *Blessed!* If I was just shown the true nature of the universe, you think I could just shrug it off and go back to work the next day? Have kids? Go to soccer practice? No. The game has been changed. Forever. And if you can go back to that—if you *want* to go back to that—then I don't know what to say to you. I guess I don't understand you at all."

I sink into my seat and bow my head. "I know. You're right. I just didn't think there would be so many nightmares."

And Alan. I never knew I'd damn my friends to the void.

"Yeah, brother. I feel you there." He extends his fist out to bump mine. "That's why you don't fly solo."

We bump fists, and I feel like my dad just told me he still loved me, right after chewing my ass for failing algebra.

"Besides," Zeke says, "the Lazlos are still up to no good. Bad people getting away with bad shit. I can't let that slide."

Zeke turns into a grimy and dark apartment complex. Village Oak. I've never been to Village Oak, not really, but it looks much like it did when I was a ghost. We steer the unmarked Cavendish van into a parking lot full of old trucks and cars held together with duct tape and paracord. Many of the vehicles have halos of dead leaves and dirt around their wheels. They've been here a while. It's not raining, but the brown, wooden walls of every dark building look soft and wet. What lights still work, illuminating the parking lot or the paths that curl around each building, are faint. The night is heavy here. It looms close to every window, every door.

"You think you can find her?" Zeke says as he kills the engine.

Looking down the paths that wind through dark courtyards, I'm wary of mewling faces emerging from the shadows. It all looks familiar, like I'm finally watching the movie of a trailer I once saw.

"Yeah," I tell Zeke. "But there may be some floaty things that try to eat us."

"See, I'm not in the mood for floaty things. Not tonight," Zeke says and climbs out of the van.

We match the silence of the complex with our soft footsteps. This place slumbers. No one is out walking their dog or having a smoke on their balcony. If we raise our voices too loud, all of its invisible inhabitants might stir. After our adventure at the King's Crown Motor Inn, I get the feeling we don't want to engage with any of them.

We walk through a few corridors, bugs making kamikaze divebombs at our heads from the dirty lights embedded in the low, sagging ceilings. Everything has the same shade of rotten claustrophobia, and every turn makes us stop and question if we've gone in a circle. Zeke is getting antsy. He tosses Mina from hand to hand, not even bothering to keep the knife sheathed. I can tell he wants to say something to me, to ask if we're close, but he bites his lip and stays at my side.

Then I see the mask. Its vivid yellow stripes stand out against the damp earth tones of Village Oak. We stop at the end of the corridor, and I regard the mask for a second, unsure if it's going to sense me and spring to life.

Zeke just walks up to it. "Is this one of them?" he says, looking at me like he doesn't believe it.

"Yeah. That's the place. That's not —"

Zeke springs forward and kicks. The mask shatters under his boot. The door flies open with a gunshot.

"Oh shit!" I say.

Zeke strides into the apartment.

"Zeke! Dude!" I yell as I chase him.

When I get inside, Bela Koth is standing on her couch, holding a tall boy of Coors Light. Furious, her milky eyes gleam in the reflection of the television that plays some reality show about car chases. She shifts her weight right and left, and I'm reminded of a cobra swaying in the air.

"So ..." I say, glancing at the television. "You're blind, right? And you're just sitting here getting drunk, *listening* to car chases on television? That's new."

She starts with a guttural hiss. "How dare you come up in here and —"

With one hand, Zeke grabs the edge of the couch and flips it. Bela tumbles to the floor. Beer sprays.

"I ain't fucking with you right now! You hear me?" Zeke yells, and his voice is enough to blot out the stars.

Defiant, Bela's face twists into a snarl. "Oh, you got the bull by the horns now."

Zeke crouches down next to her and lowers his voice. "You know who I am," he says.

Bela's prostrate on the floor but doesn't try to stand or crawl away.

"I ain't scared of the likes of you," she says.

"How many of your friends have I killed?" Zeke asks, as if it's the most natural question in the world.

Zeke throws a glance up at me, and I try not to react. I don't know how successful I am. My best friend just casually mentioned murdering a bunch of people. This is news. This is not something I knew about him, but the mention of it puts a leash on Bela. She cows, her face souring even more.

"How many?" Zeke asks.

"Plenty."

"You're goddamn right," Zeke says, his voice soft as a velvet razor. "That ain't how I do things anymore, not unless I have to. Some old witch comes at my friend with that foolishness and tries to take his soul? Well, then I feel like I *have* to kill somebody. Know what I'm saying? Somebody hurts my family, I come at 'em, you see. I put 'em in the dirt. I'm a reasonable man dealing with an unreasonable world right now, and I'll be honest with you, I'm hanging by a thread … a fucking thread."

Bela swallows. "What do y'all want?"

"We want to make things right," I tell her.

"You want to pull my baby—my RV—out of the damned lake. They said it was ruint! Totaled!" she says, her voice breaking.

Zeke drops the keys to the Cavendish van on the carpet next to her. She looks in the direction of the sound but doesn't reach to pick them up.

"Here," Zeke says. "New wheels. Just for you."

"What are you talking about?" she asks.

"We're giving you a van," Zeke says. "Now I know it's not the cozy little crack-den on wheels that now rests at the bottom of Lake Travis, but … it's better than a kick in the teeth, as my grandmother used to tell me."

Bela's lips tighten into a thin curl of distrust. Before seeing her laying there on the floor, I was more than a little frightened of her. Even without witchcraft, Bela feels like some rare breed of other, the kind of cutthroat junkie you read about on the news. The paths of most decent people don't intersect with Bela's. Letting someone like her into your world opens you up to *hers.* It starts with getting help from her. You come to her and ask for a fix, some strange drug you encountered when you were vacationing in Thailand. She'll sell it to you, but it's going to be hard, she'll say. It's hard to get. Dangerous. There could be trouble with the police. But she does it for *you.* Just this once. Next time, it's a little more expensive. You've got a relationship with Bela. That's what she wants. You're not just a customer, though. Sure, you pay for your transaction in cash, but then she starts to show up asking you for things, favors you can't say "no" to. She needs a ride. She needs you to help bail her friend out of jail. Then you've got her cousin sleeping on your couch "just for a few days" and your laptop is missing.

Now all her bluster and threats wither on the floor at Zeke's feet. I know she's saving them, though, taking all those injustices and sharpening them into knives to use on us later.

"That ain't enough to make us square. Not by a damned sight," she says.

"I'm sorry," Zeke says. "Did I sound like I was here to negotiate with you? 'Cause I promise you, I ain't here for that."

"What the hell do you want, then? To kill me? Go ahead and do it! I ain't scared of that. Look at me and tell me otherwise," she says.

"You sent a bunch of floating faces to eat me while I was astral projecting on drugs," I say, and it sounds even stranger out loud.

In the kitchen, I can still see the remains of the ritual. The sloppy protective circle is still there on the floor, with pieces of dry rice scattered all over the linoleum. Right next to the circle, displayed for the conjurer to focus on, are the masks. Here in the living world, they look like a kid's arts and crafts project. The papier-mâché is lumpy and mottled, beneath the painted-on skin and the demonic sigils. In the dim candlelight of the apartment, the stringy hair glued to them looks real.

"I did," Bela says with a laugh. "You were just wandering around like a little lamb lost in the storm, weren't you? You just came right to me. Couldn't believe my luck. You could've knocked me over with a feather."

She claps and rolls over onto her back, making a show of how amused she is. I can only look at her gnarly teeth. Zeke glowers at her. He stands, walks over to the masks on the floor, and picks one up, the mask of the man.

"Hmm," he says, fingering the dry, brown hair glued around the scalp.

"That's right. My babies," Bela says and turns her attention to me. "They'll getcha. One of these days, boy, you're gonna fall asleep and they'll be right there waiting."

Zeke holds the mask over a candle. Immediately, the flames lick at the paper, devouring it. The hair goes up in a sizzle. The heavy paint on across the face blackens and curls. Smoke snakes away as the mask burns.

Bela's smile fades. She sits up. "What are you doing? No. Don't do that! Don't do that! You son of a —"

The mask erupts into a short, ragged scream. The face peels open, dumping out fingernail clippings and a wedding ring. The ring clatters to the floor among the rice.

"Damn it all," she says. "Damn the both of you!"

"That's one," Zeke says, and lights the next one, the mask of the boy.

This one goes faster. Once the flames tear through the first few layers, it frees whatever magical payload Bela had buried inside. With this mask, it's a shoelace and a faded picture of a boy in a baseball cap. The boy in the cap faintly resembles the mask. My stomach turns as the flames eat the hairs. The lips open to yell, but only gasp before the entire thing collapses to ash in Zeke's hands. He tosses the smoldering ruins into the sink and looks at Bela.

Bela is still on the floor, squirming. Her lips knot as she prepares a string of profanities, or maybe an incantation. She and I both know that Zeke can cover the gap between them in a few quick steps. If she utters anything resembling a spell, I don't think I can move fast enough to save her. She chokes down whatever invective she was preparing.

Zeke grabs the third mask, the woman, and is about to hold it to the flame. Bela grimaces, unable to bear it, but certain of what's about to happen. "Hold up," I tell him.

Now it's my turn to crouch next to Bela. "Bela," I say, "When you sent those things after me, you could see me, right? You could see through them? Through their eyes?"

"They're my eyes in this world and the world beyond. They're gonna be watching you, boy. The next time you lay your head down, you —"

Zeke strides across the room and kicks over the glass-topped coffee table. "Threaten him again and see what happens! One more goddamn time!"

Bela's face goes slack. The sun-scorched leather of her skin turns ashen in the flickering light. I jump out of the way as Zeke looms over her. She scoots across the floor, away from his booming voice.

"Dude," I say and motion for him to relax. "Just … give me a second."

Her hands shaking, Bela fishes a pack of smokes and a lighter from her dress pocket. She flicks the lighter a few times before it sparks. The trembling lessens, if only a little, as she takes a drag from the long, filterless cigarette.

"I'd be doing you a favor if I claimed your soul, boy. What's coming for you ain't pretty."

"What the hell's that supposed to mean?" Zeke asks.

"This one," she says, nodding to me, "he's gonna open the door wide for the Weeping King. And that big ol' storm is gonna blow on through."

"Whatever. It takes more than a little cryptic spooky talk to scare me, lady," Zeke says.

He doesn't see me shiver at her words. He can't feel the chill of sweat dripping down my spine.

"So, Bela," I say, quieter this time, "You could see me through that mask. I heard your voice coming through it."

"Yeah."

"The place I went after I came here, it was like a call center or something. Do you know where it was?"

She draws on the cigarette again and blows the smoke in my face. "Don't reckon I do."

"You don't start being more helpful," Zeke says, "This whole conversation is going to get a lot more interesting. Know what I'm saying?"

Bela springs to her feet, pointing and spitting in Zeke's direction. "If you're feeling froggy, then leap, son! If you think I'm gonna sit here and let you level your threats at me, then you damn sure —"

"Enough!" I yell, loud enough that even Zeke raises an eyebrow. "Can you give us a minute?" I ask him.

"For real?" he says.

"Just a second. Just like … wait outside. I'll be fine."

Zeke looks at me like I've lost my mind. Finally, he shakes his head and mutters as he drops the mask on the floor and goes to stand outside. The door doesn't close, not after he kicked it, so I have the comfort of seeing him linger in the corridor. Bela stands and draws on her cigarette. The cataract-whites of her eyes bore into me, and I wonder if her blindness is just a ruse.

"You're watching your ass around him. That's good. Smart boy," she says.

"What? Zeke? Whatever. I'm not in the mood for your head games."

She laughs and shrugs. "Ain't no thing to me. Just something I noticed."

"This call center you chased me to, you don't know where it is?" I ask again.

"No. Never seen it. Don't much care."

"We need to find it. Fast."

"Well, you can need in one hand and shit in the other. See which one fills up faster," she says and chuckles.

"You're the only one that can help us. My friend ... and I know you have no reason to care about this ... but my friend is going to die tonight if we don't find where they're keeping her. I think she's there with them at that party or whatever the hell it was. Is there any way you can help us?"

"Oh, there's a way. But you ain't even tried to sweet-talk me yet."

"You can keep the van. It's yours and —"

"You think that makes us square, do you?"

"No," I say. "Probably not. But it's a start."

"You ain't got nothing else I need."

I take a deep breath. I can feel her softening, even as she postures. "Maybe not. But over the last year or so, I've seen some pretty weird shit, Bela. I've been rubbing elbows will all sorts of interesting people."

She laughs again. "You ain't got no friends! You're just two dipshits pretending to be ghost chasers. Don't try to impress me by telling me how important you are, 'cause you ain't pulling none of that bullshit on me. All you've got is trouble coming your way. You stink of it."

"No, we're not important. But we do have access. To the Lazlos. Occultex Incorporated has access to Candle House, Bela," I tell her and let that sit for a minute.

I watch her face to see if she's buying it and I can see her do the math. The corners of her mouth turn up in something that's almost like a smile.

"Oh," she says. "Is that right?"

"It is. We've been working exclusively with the Lazlos on their new project. And it's big. I can't tell you much about it right now—they'll kill me—but I promise you, Bela, it's going to change everything."

"You still ain't said nothing that means nothing to me," she says, and her words slither from between yellow teeth. "Ain't said nothing that changes a thing."

"I'll owe you, Bela. You will have me in your pocket."

I have to force the words out. Zeke must not be able to hear. If he could, he would have already burst back through the door and slapped both of us. He'd be right to, but the clock is ticking and I'm out of ideas.

Bela lets the cigarette smoke slide from her lips and veil her face. Finally, she smiles. "Hoo boy, now there's an offer that might be more trouble than it's worth. I've seen a little bit of what's coming down the road for you, son, and it sure is ugly."

"What does that mean?"

"Get mama her mask, you pale, bald sonofabitch," she says. "Let's go for a ride."

\*\*\*

# CHAPTER FIFTEEN

We drive in silence. I'm behind the wheel. Bela is next to me, smoking with one hand hanging out the window, feeling the breeze. Zeke sits in the back. He's been quiet since Bela's apartment, watching me through the open window that separates the cab from the cargo area of the van. I know what he's thinking. I keep catching his gaze in the rearview, a penetrating stare that tells me he knows something is up. He knows I made a deal. I'm not happy about it either and I'm especially unhappy about having to hear about it from him later.

"You're sure it's this way?" I ask Bela.

"Yup," she says and offers nothing else. In her lap is the mask. I know she needs it to find where this little soiree is, but I don't know what that means. I'm half-expecting it to spring to life and fly out the window. I can just see us hauling ass down the quiet streets, trying to keep up with this thing. Then we get pulled over. There's gonna be a whole lot of questions that I don't have good answers to, like why my dead body is in the back of the stolen van.

"Do you think I'm rotting back there? In that body bag? I mean, I've been dead for a few hours now. That can't be good, right?" I ask him.

"It doesn't work like that," Zeke says.

"How do you know?" I ask. "Oh wait. I guess there's a lot of things about you I don't know."

Zeke frowns but dodges the implication. He's not the only one who gets to ask pointed questions later.

He says, "There's a sect of Russian monks known to meditate into a state of expanded awareness, where they claim to leave their bodies to explore the cosmos for weeks at a time. This is like that."

"Yeah, but I'm not breathing. I'm dead. You know how I know? 'Cause that's me in that goddamn body bag!"

"It doesn't work like that," Bela says.

Zeke nods at her. "See?"

"You got time," she says. "Probably."

"Probably?" I ask.

She shrugs. "Yeah. Probably. I mean ... shit happens."

"Shit happens? This is my soul we're talking about and you're saying *shit happens*?" I ask.

Zeke sighs and sits back. "I'm gonna meditate."

He puts on his headphones, closes his eyes, and presses play on the Walkman strapped to his side. A staccato blast of punk music takes him the rest of the way.

Bela sits upright and holds up her hand as we rest at a stop sign. "Hang on now."

"Are we close?" I ask.

"Shh," she says and holds the mask up to her face.

When she draws her hand away, I realize that the paper mask clings to her, like it belongs there. The shape of the mask itself bends and melds to match her features. It's subtle. It still looks like something an eight-year-old would make if he were into Satan. Bela's milky white irises make the hollow eyeholes all the more unsettling.

"Left," she says, and points.

I turn at the light. We're just off the interstate in North Austin, where the strip malls full of cash-advance businesses and nail salons give way to office parks of tech and shipping companies. Bela sits with her hands in her lap, staring straight ahead. Whenever we come to a turn she likes, she raises a single bony finger and gives a direction with a flat croak. I follow her instructions and don't speak, worried I might interrupt the spell.

The neighborhood we find ourselves in isn't unlike Cavendish. It's row after row of small, unmarked professional buildings. All brown brick and greenery arranged with precise geometry so that you're fooled into thinking these are anything other than lifeless husks. With the sodium glow of the streetlights, everything blends into one long, muddy blob interrupted only by empty roads.

When we pull up to our target, I recognize it not by sight, but by the sinking feeling in the pit of my stomach. Bela points, but I don't need it. I can see the lobby and the two Helpers standing still by the front doors. The lot is full, mostly with cars I will never be able to afford. As I imagine what's going on inside, the hair on my neck stands on end.

"This is it," Bela says and turns to me. "I hope you're still around to honor your end of the deal, Vandermeer."

"Yeah, me too," I say and climb out of the van.

Zeke crawls out of the back and begins to stretch. "So, tell me," he says.

"Tell you what?"

"What'd you promise that old bag?"

I sigh. "Are we doing this now?"

"Mm-hmm," he says, and bends to press his palms flat to the ground.

"I owe her."

"You *owe* her?"

"Yeah."

"Great. Like a favor?"

"Something like that," I tell him.

I poke my head around the van and watch the two Helpers by the door. We're too far away to show up on their radar, and they're too stupid to care. Unless we're an immediate physical concern, they're going to follow the last order they were given and just stand by the door. I wonder if that's my future if I don't get this fixed. I worry that before long, my words won't come. My brain will soften into something that can only respond to simple commands, and I'll only be able to make Muppet noises. I take the stun baton and slide it into my coveralls. If it sparks my testicles and turns me into soup, that would be the perfect punctuation at the end of this shitty day.

"Something like that," Zeke says, leveling his gaze at me. "You're in her pocket now."

"Dude," I tell him, throwing a glance at the building to remind him of what's coming, "I didn't have a lot of choice."

He nods. "Yeah. I know. But still … I don't like being under the thumb of someone like her."

"I left you out of it. It's me. I owe her."

"Don't be like that," he says.

"Like what?"

"You know damn well what. If somebody comes at you, they come at me."

"I appreciate that, brother. I do."

"So, when you sign a goddang pact with a goddang witch, that puts me in that mess, too," he says, throwing his arms in the air.

"I didn't sign anything! No blood was drawn. We didn't even shake on it!"

He shakes his head and clicks his tongue. "Yeah, that don't matter. Deal's a deal."

"You gonna kill her?" I ask, and I'm only kind of kidding.

He looks at her as she sits in the passenger seat, her bare feet propped up on the dash. She takes the mask off, drops it in her lap, and lights another smoke.

"Probably not tonight," Zeke says, "but I see now why she and Harvey are friends."

"Yeah," I say. "I don't want to hang out with these assholes anymore."

"This is the job, my man," Zeke says. "But do you know what time it is?"

"Is it game time?" I say, a smile on my face.

"Damn right. It's game time, son."

We cross the parking lot, past the Lexuses and the Cadillacs, and for the first time today, I feel like this is what we're supposed to be doing. Zeke's enthusiasm, his love of the fight, surges inside me.

"Is it a bad idea to leave my body back there with a necromancer?" I ask.

"Oh. Definitely."

"Cool."

The moment we step out of the car, I almost pull my leg back in. A cat darts out from under a shiny new Mercedes. Two more follow. They're everywhere. Under cars. Sitting on cars. Loitering around the steps. Stray cats, all rheumy-eyed and lanky. I wonder if any of them remember what happened to Alan and my friends. I choke down the bolus of panic lodged in my throat and wade through the cats as they slink around the parking lot.

Matching blank smiles greet us as we approach the doors. The Helpers furrow their brows, hands poised over the door, as they do the math.

"He's with me," I tell them, and open the doors myself.

"It ooh?" one of them asks.

"Yeah," I tell him and lead Zeke through.

They close the glass doors behind us. Zeke and I keep moving. I try not to look over at the Lighthouse logo on the wall. I know the eye will be staring back at me.

"I thought we were going to have to throw down," Zeke says, keeping his voice down.

"You punched one of their friends until he turned to melted marshmallows. Word gets around."

"And this is the place?"

"Yeah," I say as we pass the cubicle farm. The ambient sounds of office life still play on loop.

I lead Zeke into the back hallways, the facsimile of corporate America. Zeke peeks into offices as we pass, his face curling with growing unease.

"What is this place? It looks ..."

"Familiar?" I ask. "It's a Lighthouse. At least, that's what I call it."

"Like the shit at the school?"

"Just like that."

This is the third one I've been inside, all of them in the Austin area. Real estate is pricey here, and maintaining a business that effectively does nothing can't be cheap. There are resources at work, spent on setting up these facilities all across the globe.

*Tanzania*

*Siberia*

*The South Pacific*

The stack of tapes. There were dozens of them. The enormity of their endeavor is something that looms on the edge of my awareness, like an unpaid bill or a voicemail from my mother. I've tried to ignore it. If I look directly at it, it might swallow me whole.

After several twists and turns, including having to double back more than once, we come to the basement. The other two Helpers are still there, flanking the door. My heart races as we walk up, and an insane pop of laughter threatens to escape my lips as I realize how happy I am that this body even has a heart. If this form is held together by a bundle of writhing, albino earthworms, I wouldn't be surprised. Feeling my blood run cold is for once reassuring.

"Eh-ell," the left Helper says, eyeing Zeke.

We just walk past them.

They step aside with nothing but curious glances. As we descend the steps into the basement, chamber music plays from an old phonograph. It's a dungeon cosplaying as a fancy dinner party. Posh rugs, vases spilling over with flowers, and hand-carved tables can't hide the barren concrete. One of the Helpers inside flips the record and nods to us, as if he's giving us an entrance. The eyes of the room are drawn to us. The audience squirms. They exchange glances. It's not me they're looking at. It's Zeke. I'm just another Helper. Zeke is a muscle-bound man with a mohawk and shredded surgical scrubs with little kitties on them. The look on his face tells people they're right to be worried. They stop chewing their fancy canapes and smooth their expensive dresses. Someone clears their throat. At the back of the room, Rupert and Kitty Lazlo realize what's happening. Rupert raises up from his seat, mouth open to speak, but he can't find the words.

"Sorry we're late," I say.

The entire audience flinches. They gasp. Rupert steadies himself, clutching the edge of the chair.

"What's up, asshole?" I say with a big grin and wave to him. "Oh! And we forgot your necromancer. That's on me. My bad. But I can go pick up some chips and queso or something if you guys are running low."

I snatch a snack from the tray of a passing Helper and pop the whole thing in my mouth. A wildfire of whispers spreads across the crowd. Zeke postures in front of them, cracking his neck like a challenge.

"What exactly is going on here?" Rupert asks.

Before I can come up with a smart-ass answer, I see Dr. Void. She's still sitting there in her high-backed chair. Now she watches me, head tilted as if she's curious how this will play out. I can't see through the lenses of her gas mask, but it seems like she recognizes me. Even in this pallid, lanky form, she knows it's me, the roaming spirit from earlier.

"Mr. Silver, this is very unacceptable behavior," Kitty says and looks around the room for help.

The whispers in the crowd turn to murmurs. Two of the guests, an older couple dressed like they could be heads of state, quietly excuse themselves. They offer prim smiles to everyone as they sneak up the stairs. A few more guests follow. We let them go.

"Now y'all," Rupert says as he scurries through the crowd toward us, "this is just a minor interruption. We'll get this resolved lickety-split now."

He licks his bright red lips as he approaches, his eyes flirting with panic. I cross my arms to greet him, but Zeke is distracted. Something else has his attention. He's dumbstruck as the wind is sucked out of him. He's looking into the locked chamber at the front of the room. All the chairs are arranged to peer through the Plexiglas window to watch what's going on inside, but we have front row seats.

Rez is in there. She's strapped to a medical table with an array of microphones suspended overhead. Dozens of them hang above, as if they're preparing to drop and skewer her. The nest of wires snake along the walls and floor to a large console where a reel-to-reel slowly spins. A single light on the ceiling pulses in the center of the microphones. Rez's eyes, all vacant and glossy, are fixed on it as it strobes with a slow rhythm. Her lips move, twisting and curling around sounds no man was meant to hear. The rest of her body is limp as the Voice of the Storm speaks through her.

We should've dragged Harvey here, kicking and screaming. This is the fate he was dodging, one he probably deserved.

"Oh, hell no," Zeke says and strides around to the side of the chamber.

When he reaches for the door, Rupert's face goes electric with fear.

"No. Wait!" I yell, but Zeke throws open the door.

It hits us all at once. The soundproof door cracks and unleashes the howls from within, howls coming from Rez's mouth. It floods the room. Immediately, guests clutch at their ears and pitch over out of their chairs. Rupert falls to his knees, frothy spittle erupting from his lips.

It starts in the center of my forehead, a cold, lancing pain that goes right through my skull, skewers my brain, and rips down my spine. It radiates outward, and my breath locks up in my chest. The wave of agony is only an instant, tearing through every cell in this pale body. Just before I go blind, I look at my slender hand. The skin liquefies, exposing bone and muscle in a split second before that, too, melts into thick fluid that spatters on the rug.

*** 

I can't breathe. The darkness isn't just all around me, it's close. It envelops me, and I can feel it wrapping around my legs, my torso, and my head.

I can't breathe. I'm choking. As my body breaks down, my own lungs dissolve, and I start to drown. I thrash against it.

I kick, pushing and gasping for breath. A tiny spark of light glimmers. I reach for it, trying to claw my way out of the black. Cold air blasts in through the tear as it widens. It's heavy with the scent of nicotine and the sounds of ...

Alice Cooper? *No More Mr. Nice Guy* plays on a tinny car radio. I sit up, heaving for air. A scream rips out of my throat as I reach to grab something to keep from drowning.

Bela shrieks. She's standing over me, loading up the back of the van with malt liquor and bags of chips. I look up into her cloudy eyes. She's watching me through the misshapen sockets of the paper mask. I scream, too. A sixer of cheap shit smashes onto the pavement.

I look at my hand. It's normal. It's not pale as melting ice cream or dripping off my bones. I flex the fingers and laugh to myself.

"What in the nine hells!?" Bela yells as she scrambles out of the vehicle.

It's me. It's *me* me. I wiggle everything, unsure if it's all going to work like it's supposed to. I'm back. I'm whole.

I kick loose from the body bag and escape out the back doors. I stumble, spinning around and trying to get my bearings. The basement and its gaggle of weirdos are all gone. Fluorescent lights flicker overhead. People, walking through a parking lot. Cars at the pumps. We're at a convenience store.

Someone rolls down a window to ask if we're alright, but I ignore them. Bela is capering about, barefoot on the sidewalk. She clutches her chest with one hand and holds a cigarette with the other.

"It's you!" Bela says.

"You were supposed to wait for us! Where the hell are we? I've got to get back."

"But you ... you left the keys ..."

"But you're fucking blind!" I yell as I brush past her.

"I was doing all right," she says, wounded.

I jump behind the wheel of the van, start it, and throw it into reverse. We're less than a mile away. I can make it. Hopefully, Zeke's brains won't be liquid shit by the time I get there.

Loose bottles of Mickey's fly out of the back and shatter in the parking lot. Bela capers out of the way as the doors swing.

"Wait. Where in the —" Bela starts to say.

I slam the pedal down and tear out of the parking lot. The wheel jerks as I clip the curb and struggle to keep from smashing into cars parked along the opposite side of the street. A pedestrian walking his Basset Hound pulls out his phone to film my escape. In the distance, a police siren.

"That's my van!" Bela screams. "You son of a bitch, that's my van!"

I watch her in the side mirror as she stomps around the sidewalk in her black dress and papier-mâché mask, waving her hands and ranting at me as I pull away. I really hope that's not a spell she's casting.

*Jason Murphy*

\*\*\*

# CHAPTER SIXTEEN

Guests are vomiting in the parking lot. Half-digested *hors d'ouevres* cake to their fancy suits and dresses. There are only a handful out here, sitting on the curb with their heads in their hands. They use their ties to wipe away the blood from their noses and ears. "What happened?" they ask. "What was that?"

A black sedan pulls away as I steer into the lot, but it's the only one. The lot is still full. The escaping car rolls down the road, weaving from lane to lane. I park the van in the fire zone just as another couple comes fleeing through the front doors of the call center. The Helpers watch them. They hold the doors open and smile, oblivious to the sobbing and howling.

Engine running, I sit behind the wheel and look up at the building. I don't have a play. If I walk in there, I'm going to be attacked by the same sounds. Right now, dozens of guests—and Zeke— are lying on the floor as the Voice of the Storm crawls from Rez's lips and takes root in their brains. I look around the van for something to help. Bela's cigarette butts litter the floorboard. A few pocks in the dash still smolder from where she stubbed them out. In the console are crumpled receipts for gas and a fast-food joint. Loose change. An empty pack of cigarettes. A pack of gum. I grab the gum and pull out a few sticks. With shaking fingers, I roll the sticks into tiny wads and cram them in my ears.

In the floorboard, rolling loose, is one of the shock batons. You're damn right I grab that thing.

When I climb out of the van, a middle-aged man sitting on the curb looks up at me. His wife, her makeup running down her face, gently pets the back of his head. "I saw him," the man says, his voice quavering.

"What?" I ask.

"I saw the king. I saw his face," he says.

Two cats lap at the puddle of orange puke at his feet. I step over them and keep moving.

At the top of the steps, one of the Helpers by the door holds his hand out to stop me. Without slowing, I jab the business end of the baton into his open palm.

SPLAT!

A gout of goo explodes in every direction. I pause, letting the remains of the Helper slide down my face. The second Helper looks at me, eyes wide. He steps aside.

Inside, the lights are flickering in the call center. They're dimmer now, as if the noises from the ritual have drained everything in the building. The gum in my ears muffles the artificial sounds of the office. It's working well enough. I hope it will shield me from the Voice of the Storm. I try to ignore the molten, sick feeling festering in the pit of my stomach and focus on making my way back to the basement. It doesn't take long. The makeshift lobby at the door is a soggy disaster. White goo clings to the ceiling, dripping from the tiles to collect in thick puddles where the Helpers once stood. Their shoes are filled with bubbling sludge. Shreds of their clothes stick to the wall where the fluid congeals in streaking splotches. They didn't just melt. They exploded. I slip in the slime as I run past and grab the door frame to keep from pitching headlong down the stone stairs.

Below, the basement floor is crowded with toppled-over chairs and writhing guests. Some gnash their teeth and tear at their clothes. Their eyes roll back in the sockets, and I'm grateful I can't hear the torment that escapes their lips. Others lay still. They stare off into space and let the cacophony of screams and metal and buzzing insects run riot all over them. I can faintly hear it through the gum. It's familiar, the broken and inhuman noises. On the tapes, the sound was horror captured on cassette. It was barely contained, something too vast and awful to be held by magnetic memory. Now, as the madness erupts raw and unrefined from Rez's throat, it's a force of nature. It is the Storm. With my ears stuffed, I only catch hints of it.

On his hands and knees near the open door to the chamber, I see Zeke. Blood pours freely from his nose, running onto the floor. He doesn't weep or contort with agony. He's trying to stand. Next to him are the remains of my Helper body. I just exploded where I stood, with enough force to rip apart my coveralls. Great, sticky gobs of Helper-goo cling to chairs and drip from the horn of the phonograph.

I rush over and close the door. When it seals with a soft click, the lights surge again, glowing at full strength. It feels like a window was shut against a violent squall. The people on the floor begin to move again. They stretch through their agony and vomit some more. The smell mingles with the sharp odors of pissed pants and flop sweat. Somewhere in the tangle of bodies, a woman begins to sob.

Through the window in the door, I watch Rez's lips continue to move, shaping screams and utterances that couldn't possibly come from her body. Her vacant stare is lost in the pulsing light overhead. I put a calming hand on Zeke's back. Clutching his headphones in one hand, he growls at me and doesn't look up. I pull the gum from my ears.

"You just straight-up exploded," he says.

"It's cool. I'm back. I'm here," I say.

With the back of his hand, he wipes away blood and looks up at me with watery eyes. His voice gravelly, resistant, he says, "*Perdurabo.*"

"Huh?"

He's smiling through gritted teeth, a smile that makes me slowly pull my hand away.

"I endure," he says.

When he stands and sees Rez still in there in the grip of the Voice, his face hardens. A few feet from us, Rupert Lazlo is in the fetal position on the floor. His eyes are squeezed shut, and his ragged nails have dug deep furrows through the makeup and into the flesh of his cheeks as he clawed at his face. His own lips move in a silent, rapid-fire prayer. Zeke grabs him by the lapels and yanks him to his feet. Rupert is still praying when Zeke slams his face against the Plexiglas.

Rupert whimpers. He sprays spittle across the glass, intensifying his pleas. "Be our light across the Sea of Mon. Let your wind be my breath and your thunder, my voice. We raise our voices up and shout at the three moons of —"

Zeke pulls his head back and again smacks it against the glass. "Enough of that shit. You want to pray? Pray that my friend in there is going to be okay. 'Cause if she isn't? Your ass ain't leaving this room."

Rupert stutters, a car-salesman smile spreading across his face. "Now son, what you have to understand is what an honor this is for Marianne. You see, those words will rewrite the known universe. That wisdom is spoken from the heart of everything and it is the end of all human suffering. It is the spawning ground of all knowledge, all that is, not this profane façade of highways and all-night pharmacies and soda in a can, no. *Vocea Fortunii* is the gospel of the howling core of forever. It is a fountain of things forgotten by man, hidden not at the end of all things, but at its beginning. His suffering is our suffering, and only when he is without pain can the world be at peace. It is the truth, and Marianne is the burning bush. She has been elevated."

"Keep this up, and I start breaking things inside you," Zeke says.

Rupert shuts up. Across the room, Kitty is there in her motorized cart. Her face is buried in her hands as she weeps quietly. Most of the party is sitting where they fell, trying to collect themselves. The room is quiet but for the sniffling and shaking breaths, only occasionally interrupted by a choking sob.

"I'm gonna go wake her up," I say and move for the door.

"No!" Rupert says, his hands flying up to his ears.

Across the room, others scurry away from the chamber. They crawl away from it, trying to cover their heads with their hands or their coats.

"Oh God, no!" they scream.

"Wait. Wait. No!"

Rupert slides back down onto the floor. Zeke lets him.

"What's the plan?" Zeke asks.

150

I look through the window at Rez. "I don't know. I'm going to go in and wake her up, see if I can get her to stop. Then we take her to Andi. Maybe she can help."

I reach for the door again, and a gloved hand falls on my forearm. Dr. Void stands there, using the phonograph table for support. The record is skipping, playing the same few crackling notes of chamber music over and over.

"Wait," Dr. Void says, her voice sounds robotic, coming through a speaker clipped to her belt. There's a trace of a woman in there, but it's modulated with clicks and whirs. The respirator on her belt pushes air from the box up into her gas mask. It's working hard now, lights blinking and cycling across its panel. From it, I recognize the familiar scent of tangerines and sawdust.

"No," Zeke says, shaking his finger at her. "I don't think we need to hear from any Star Wars bounty hunters right now. Sit your weird ass down."

"If you try to wake her," Dr. Void says, wheezing, "she'll be lucky if it kills her. To pull her out of the process at this point will surely break her mind."

As Dr. Void stares at me, I can only see the comic books of my youth, come to life. The Specter Society, traveling the globe to examine the unknown and protect the world against the forces of darkness! Those images of Dr. Void coming to the rescue by building some wild device are crystal-clear. Mysterious and inscrutable, she would save the day by revealing a quantum harmonic contraption to turn away the undead, a radio signal to confuse the murderous golem of Ostrava, or a spray that made ghosts visible to the naked eye. Now she's here, standing next to me, and I can't make sense of it. It's like someone walking up and telling you Superman is real.

"This is you," I say to her. "You built this."

She nods, leaning on the chair. "So I did. And you've heard the Voice before. You were here earlier, traveling. I saw you."

"So how do we help her?" I ask.

"She is in a speaking cycle. The Storm is using her, but it will ebb in a moment. When it recedes, only then can you retrieve her."

Zeke says, "Wait. Why are we listening to Dollar Store Darth Vader?"

"She's going to stop with all of that noise in a second and then I can go in and grab her?" I ask.

Dr. Void shakes her head. "Not quite, I'm afraid. As you were earlier, your friend is travelling. She has projected herself across a great distance, one that you can barely fathom. Simply waking her would cause her great harm."

"Tell us now to fix it," Zeke says. "How many times do I have to say that?"

She points a finger at me. "You must go and get her. It's possible to slowly bring her out of this state, with the proper medications and hypnotic stimulus, but that takes time. She will be riven by the time she surfaces."

"Riven?" Zeke asks.

"Ruined," Dr. Void says.

"Go get her," I say. "You mean astral-project. You want me to go under. I have to go in there and find her."

Dr. Void nods. "Precisely. It's the only way to rescue her, truly. During her next ebb, I will gladly escort you into the chamber and guide you into the meditative state so that you can follow her."

"Yeah, that sounds like a trap," Zeke says.

"How much time does she have?" I ask.

Dr. Void shrugs. "There is no way of knowing what she's seen while she's traveling, what she's experienced. Her mind may have already been splintered."

"How long does it take to get me under?" I ask.

"Dude," Zeke says, "No. No, you are not going in there, too. Hell no."

"The process is delicate. It takes approximately an hour, depending on your … resilience," Dr. Void says.

I watch Rez through the glass. Her lips are slowing, no longer twisting into the great, exaggerated shapes to birth those sounds into the world. Fresh tears stream down her cheeks, but she doesn't blink. The ebb is coming.

"See?" Dr. Void says, stepping forward. "You see? The Storm recedes for the moment, but it will return soon. We can make sure you enter at the next cycle."

I open the door. The crowd lets out a collective gasp, but Rez is only whispering. Her voice is raspy and shattered. I bite my lip as rage swells. Zeke and I exchange glances, and I know he's ready to pull the trigger, ready to unleash ten different kinds of hurt onto these privileged sacks of shit.

"If you'd like to sit in one of those chairs," Dr. Void says, gesturing to a chair inside the austere chamber, "we can begin the process. Even now, I must confess, it is unlikely you can help her in time."

"Grab her," I tell Zeke.

Zeke grabs Dr. Void by the hose and pulls her into the chamber. Her voice box emits a strange yelp-like sound. Her arms flail as Zeke pulls her along. He dumps her into the chair with enough force to nearly tip her over backward.

"Oh! What?! What is this?" She asks.

"We're not doing it that way," I tell her.

"Close the door?" Zeke asks, standing by the open chamber door.

"No. They get to listen. Get me another chair," I tell him and stand over Dr. Void.

Through the glass, I watch the crowd in the basement start to stir. They're finding their feet and looking to each other for cues. Some of them start to gather their things.

Zeke steps out, "Nuh-uh. Ladies and gentlemen, please return to your seats. The show's not over."

They stand there, frozen in place, many of them in mid-flight to the stairs.

"I'm serious," Zeke says. "If any of you try to leave, I will chase you. If you think you can outrun me, I promise you, you are wrong. So, sit your asses down. Now."

The audience, faces etched with fear, exchange uncertain glances before finally returning to their seats. Rupert stands and smooths out his suit. I can't hear him, but he's going guest to guest, reassuring them with glowing platitudes and a grandfatherly pat on the arm. No one is buying it, but he goes over to the phonograph, wipes away some of the goo from my mishap, and flips the record.

Zeke returns with the high-backed, hand carved chair Dr. Void was sitting in. It looks like an ancient throne when compared to the medical minimalism of the chamber. He places it beside Rez's bed. Next to her are medical accoutrements all laid out on a tray—syringes, latex gloves, and various vials of medicine. The light overhead keeps up its rhythmic pulse.

I sit in the chair and take a deep breath, thinking through the steps. I could grill Dr. Void for answers, make her walk me through everything I'm about to experience, but we don't have time. The Storm has receded. I can feel it in the room. The lights burn brighter, and the air is crisp.

"What? What is the meaning of this?" Dr. Void asks.

"I'm going in," I tell Zeke.

He nods. "Let's do it. I'll get another chair."

"No. Just me. I need you here."

Zeke stops. "What? I don't want you going in there solo."

"I can do this. But I need you out here to watch these jerks, okay?"

"Yeah," he says, but I can see him deflate. "Okay."

"If anything goes wrong—" I start to say.

"If anything goes wrong, I'm burning this place down."

"Good. Do that. If I die, I want you to go on a bloody rampage of revenge. I'm serious. I want some real *Man on Fire* shit."

He fist-bumps me. "I got you. Now go get our sister back."

"Okay then," I say, looking over at Dr. Void. "I guess it's game time."

I grab Dr. Void's respirator hose and jerk it loose from the mask. Dr. Void thrashes. With gloved hands, she fumbles for her mask and tries to cover the hole. It hisses as yellowish mist spews into the room. The gas carries the aroma of old wood and citrus. Zeke steps back.

"This is cairn root, right?" I say, showing the hose to Dr. Void. "That's how you could see me? A low dose that lets you keep a foot in both worlds?"

Panicked, she nods as she grabs for it, but I pull it out of reach. Her belt speaker screeches with feedback. "Give ... please ... must ..." she says.

I wrap my lips around the hose and take a big hit.

This time I can feel it. Reality shifts underneath me, around me. The universe itself becomes unscrewed, and I can feel the emptiness behind it all. Sounds are merely vibrations floating in the nothing, and my surroundings are nothing more than two-dimensional paintings propped up so that I don't have to look at the endlessness beyond.

As my body slumps into the chair, Dr. Void grabs the hose and quickly reattaches it to her mask. The click and hiss tell her its done. The angry beeping from the console on her belt calms down. She adjusts dials and checks readings before she relaxes again. Zeke is watching her closely as she studies my still form. I've slumped back into the chair, looking like I'm taking a little drunk nap. In the medical bed to my right, Rez doesn't fight against her restraints. Glassy-eyed, she stares up into the gently pulsing strobe, but it's clear that she's not really looking at it. She's elsewhere, her lips twitching without sound.

After staring at my physical form, Dr. Void turns just a few inches to the right and looks right at me, at my astral form. "There..." she says to Zeke.

Zeke steps forward, and when he speaks to me, it's with the just-over-my-shoulder gaze of someone who can't see. I'm reminded of Bela, spitting invectives in my general direction.

"You alright, bro?" Zeke asks.

"This is our plan? I think maybe I should have workshopped this a bit," I say, looking down at my body in the chair.

"He can't hear you," Dr. Void says, coughing.

"I know. Where's Rez?"

Dr. Void makes a few more adjustments to the device at her belt, a little black box that clicks and whirs. The lights flash, and it beeps as she delicately turns the knobs. When one of the lights turns green, she looks around the room, and points beneath Rez's bed. There's a door. It's set into the floor, just a little hatch with a metal ring handle. It wasn't there before.

"You must hurry," Dr. Void says and points at the door. "The Storm approaches." Dr. Void looks right at me when she speaks. Zeke follows her gaze.

"Well, you're being awfully helpful," I tell her.

"Of course," she says. "I'm a scientist. I want to see what happens. Quickly now."

She shoos me along, so I crouch and grab the metal ring attached to the door. It opens with little effort, revealing a staircase so small I need to crawl down in on my hands and knees.

I take a long look, trying to see what waits down the steps.

"Is there another way?" I ask her. "Like maybe one of those little scooters I can take? Or ... you know ... a normal door?"

"You must take the way that's presented to you."

"Yeah, but ... I had a bunch of tacos this morning and between you and me, I'm a few pounds over my ideal weight right now..."

Above me, Rez squirms beneath the restraints. A faint moan escapes her lips. She's in the clutches of the Storm. As I stare into the passage, I think of the crimson tarot card displayed by the Wanderer at Third Moon. It was only earlier today, but it feels like forever.

The Storm Beyond is chaos. It is madness. It is the purest state of the uber-verse before it was birthed with song. It is the unformed, raw and hungry, sitting at the edge of everything.

I still don't know what any of that means, but it's a reasonably good description of today—blood-red storm clouds rolling into my life and ruining everything. Great metaphor. Those clouds are probably waiting to rain down metaphorical shit. Or with my luck, *literal* shit. It's waiting at the end of this hole. Rez is going to owe me big time. I crawl inside.

"You sit down," I hear Zeke tell Dr. Void as I disappear into the portal. "You move, and I hurt you. Either of them dies, then you die next."

***

# CHAPTER SEVENTEEN

I don't know how long I'm in there. Thirty seconds crawling through a space this tight makes every passing moment seem like an eternity. Every breath seems constricted. Every time my shoulders scrape the sides, panic surges, and I think I'm stuck. A halo of light glimmers at the end of the tunnel, and I realize that the sides are smooth and white now. The stairs I crawled down are gone, and I'm working my way through a slick, plastic tube. As I draw closer, a sputtering, coughing sound, like a lawn mower, gets louder.

I push the trap door ahead of me and spill out onto a metal floor. An ice chest. The trap door was just the lid to an ice chest that I emerged from. It's tipped on its side, the top hanging open. The insides are filthy with furry mold, but past that, where the tunnel I came from should be, is only the dirty bottom of the ice chest. I kick the chest over to see if there's some trap door hiding beneath it, but there is only floor. The room I'm in now, all four walls, is corrugated metal, all rust-red and illuminated by a work light hanging from the low ceiling. Crowded around me are cardboard boxes veiled with thick clots of dust and cobwebs. Stray wires dangle, poking out of the containers. Microphones hang from some of the wires or sit unused next to a boxy, metal-plated tape recorder from the 70s. Other devices are stacked haphazardly, monitoring equipment with gauges and foggy green tubes for screens. Unused cassette tapes still wrapped in a bundle. Stacks and stacks of printouts. Partially obscured by the boxes is an image I know too well. The golden eye of the Lighthouse. I stare at the logo and it at me. The blazing yellow eye above the blue pyramid seems unreal here, and more a direct threat than before. To keep it from watching me, I nudge another box in front of it.

An errant spray paint can falls and rolls to a stop on the floor next to a cracked-open door. Sprayed in sloppy, fading blue paint is a message across the metal wall.

I SAW HIS FACE.

I read the writing over and over, trying to make sense of it, but not wanting to let it inside. It's a bit of truth. It's madness. It's the bad news that I can't deal with right now.

*His. Him.* The Weeping King. He suffers the Storm and within it sleeps his court, the Court of Eight.

I don't know and I don't care. I shake off the memory of the broken man lying on the couch at Candle House and push the door open. The noise of the engine gets louder, and as the door opens, I step out of a large shipping container situated on a concrete slab in the middle of a vast darkness. I'm really sick of darkness and all of the vastness. Another shipping container, this one also the color of dried blood, sits some thirty feet away. They're the kind you see on cargo ships, bulky and unadorned, but repurposed to serve as shelters out here in the empty. In between the two is a lawn chair laying on its side with its seat rotted out. Next to that is an old generator, the kind with two wheels and a handle to cart it around. Its red sheen has faded, covered up by a thick coat of dust that's collected in the oily grime. It chugs along, its struggling sounds swallowed up by the impenetrable black all around.

"Rez?" I call out, but my words seem to disintegrate just past my lips.

Another light, this one an industrial lamp, pulses like a beacon, casting its illumination across the makeshift camp. Situated on a pole next to the generator, its brightness ebbs and flows in a soothing, irregular pattern, the exact soft pattern of the hypnotic light suspended over Rez. Long shadows surge across the concrete to flirt with the true darkness before retreating to the abandoned island. This was an outpost, some sort of observatory long since abandoned. I have no idea how in the hell they got this crap out here. I don't even know where *here* is. The astral plane? The moon?

The second shipping container is equally squalid. An extension cord from the generator connects to another work light clamped to the ceiling of the box. A sweat-stained cot is cast aside in the corner. Beneath it, on top of it, and all around are more stacks of printouts and old photographs. They plaster the walls and dangle from masking tape that's lost its hold. Star charts. Maps of the planets. Elaborate mandalas. My mind spins as I try to make sense of it, to wrestle some meaning out of it, but the numbers won't hold together. The equations, writ in tiny, precise script in the borders and margins, have variables and symbols mingling with hieroglyphs and other crude sigils of the occult. They float disorganized across the surface of the paper, like dead leaves in rain water.

*A* over the square root of *theta* equals the astrological symbol for Jupiter.

Even if I *could* get a good look, they wouldn't make sense.

A phantom wind picks up and rustles the papers on the wall. One thick sheet of star charts pulls loose and collapses onto the floor. As it peels away, it reveals a padlocked door. My heart stutters, and my breath is sucked out. The door is wooden. It looks flimsy, hanging there in the center of the immovable metal wall. Barely visible in the feeble glow of the work light is a chalk symbol drawn onto the door. I can't quite make it out, but I don't have to. I see enough of the curves and sharp points to recognize the style. Each of these shapes isn't some sigil representing a demon or some arcane belief system. They're spells. This one, drawn on a door, is meant to open that door. Where it leads, I have no idea. I stand there looking at it for a moment, but don't want to get too close. The lock is rusted and small, just a fig leaf to give the illusion of modesty. When the Storm comes, I wonder if the howled incantations will be enough to open it. I don't plan on being around long enough to find out.

Thunder peals. It's far away, but even with the roar of the generator, I can make it out. At the opposite end of the container is another door, this one without any of the familiar runes. It's cracked open, letting through a growing breeze that stirs the stray papers and dust bunnies into a lazy dance.

"Rez?" I ask, louder this time.

On the other side of the door is a landing. The space is small, extending almost like a patio from the shipping container. It's covered by a tattered pop-up tent. The ragged edges of the holes in the canvas flutter in the breeze. The area is littered with abandoned gear—broken tripods, mangled fold-out chairs, and an old VHS camera. At the edge, overlooking a black gulf, sits Rez. She's in a chair, perched on the lip of nothingness, a balcony over the abyss. In front of her, beneath, above, and to all sides, is infinite gloom. When I approach, she doesn't acknowledge me. Her lips slightly parted, she stares out into the darkness with the same glassy eyes she had in the waking world. In her lap, her hands are crossed. The backs of them are riddled with thin gouges where she's scratched away the flesh in long strips.

My touch on her shoulder causes her to stir, surfacing from a dream. She looks up at me and her eyes swim into focus. I don't say anything as she stares, but I can see her trying to piece together who I am. There's a spark of me somewhere in there that keeps slipping through her fingers. She opens her mouth, trying to find words, and I realize that if she starts speaking in Witch Tongue, I won't know what to do. The incantations will spill from her lips and I won't know how to help her. Everything else threatens to topple down onto my head. The Storm is coming. Rez is broken. I don't know how to get us out of here.

"What the hell do you want, Clark?" she asks.

My knees nearly buckle with relief. I throw my arms around her. "Oh, thank Christ," I say.

"Okay," she says, patting me on the back. "Hugs are good. I like hugs."

"Alright. Let's go," I say and start to make my way back to the container.

"Wait. What? Where are we going?"

Another clap of thunder. This one is closer.

"Rez, we gotta go. Seriously. Get up."

"But …" she says and looks back out into the darkness. "But the Storm is coming …"

The wind kicks up, and now I can hear it. The disembodied howl carries with it strangled voices. I follow Rez's gaze out into the darkness. With nothing to measure against, it's impossible to tell how far, but from out of that perfectly opaque sheet of black, a plume of red cloud roils. It flickers with lightning as it grows, edging closer.

"Maybe this time, we can see his face," she says, and gets comfortable in her seat.

"Rez…"

"The Storm is the true nature of the universe. It's the chaos that birthed it all and soon it will return to chaos. It's so pure," she says, and her voice melts into the torpid drawl of an opium trip.

I grab her by the arm. "I'm real tempted to slap you right now. It might be my only opportunity. But seriously. Get up. Now."

Rez stands. The look on her face tells me that she doesn't understand why we would want to be anywhere else. In the struggle to get her to her feet, the fold-out chair slips off the edge. I watch it fall end-over-end. It's a tiny dot below us before the shadows swallow it.

Another clap of thunder, this one close enough to feel. Both of us jump and look out at the horizon as the tent's canvas pops in the growing gale. The wind threatens to tear it from the landing. Papers from the storage container get caught, thrown into small whirlwinds, then cast out into the void. What was one plume in the distance is now a vermillion monolith. The massive thunderhead rolls forward, black lightning arcing through its belly.

Not waiting for her to agree, I drag Rez away from the landing. More thunder chases us. The wind shrieks, tearing through the camp as though the storm doesn't want us to leave. We take shelter in the nearest container. More maps, photographs, and sheaths of madly jotted notes are pulled from the walls. They tear free in the wind and whirl around us. A black-and-white photograph does drunken spirals at my feet. There in the muddy blacks is a blurred, pale face staring up at me, smiling. The smile cuts through everything. The cacophony of the approaching storm, the suffocating darkness, the chaos of today … all of it flits away on the wind. The only thing in my world is the face in that photo. It's Alan. He's out of focus, his face floating in the gloom like one of Bela's masks. He's looking over his shoulder at the camera and I can make out other vague shapes walking with him. DJ? Travis? There's nothing around them to indicate what's happening or where they are, but it's my friends, walking through the endless darkness that surrounds us. And Alan is smiling a smile that is not his own. It's a powerful smile, a sly one, the kind of smile that a bumbling dork like Alan couldn't summon on his best day. As the photo spins there at my feet, it's like he's acknowledging me, looking up at me through his Coke-bottle glasses with a look that says *I see you.* And then the wind takes him away. The photograph leaps back into the air and is whisked out into the darkness.

The thunder is constant now. Volleys launch back and forth all around, a violent conversation. We can barely hear it over the wind. Within it, and growing louder, I catch snippets of words. *Witch Tongue.* The words are not spoken. They're screamed not into the void, but *from* it. Barely resembling human sounds, just nightmares trying to take shape. The words hook into my mind like branches catching on clothes.

Vusha rot … charguttama … salazak

When I look over at Rez, she's gazing out the door back at the landing, and her lips move softly with the poison words carried on the wind. I grab her by the arm and pull her from the container. She stumbles along behind me. Her feet move, but her face is slack again. When we emerge into the courtyard, the flashing light on the pole is oscillating with a different rhythm. Outside, I imagine it doing the same thing over Rez, keeping her submerged in this state. Behind us, I glimpse the storm looming over everything. Like a roiling wall of blood, it blots out the darkness of the sky. It's not just the biggest storm I've seen, it's the largest thing I can imagine, like the sun itself coming to devour all life. Its arms stretch around the sides of this island in the darkness. To the right and left, the churning red pillars threaten to engulf all of it.

Rez is looking at me. She's back. "What now?"

"I gotta be honest with you. I didn't think this one all the way through."

"Of course you didn't. Can we leave? I feel like maybe we should leave."

"How? Do you remember how you got here? Did you have to crawl out of an ice chest, too?"

She looks at me like I'm crazy. "What? No. I …" She drifts as she tries to piece it together, then shakes her head. "No," she says. "I don't know. I don't know how I got here. There were these people in my house, I think? But … I'm not sure if it was a dream. Is this … is this a dream?"

The wind roars in response. The other old lawn chair skips end-over-end across the bare concrete before tumbling over the edge.

"I wish."

The Storm is everything now. I can't see the top of it, but I don't look at it too long. The voices—still vague utterances and broken phrases—are growing louder. They ride on claps of thunder and cling to torrents of wind. Every flash of black lightning within the storm's guts reveals hints of other things lurking there.

Great clouds of insects.

Stretching and thrashing limbs tipped with barbs.

Faces.

I tear my eyes away, knowing that if I stare at it too long, it will have me.

"Alright, Rez," I say. "Truth time. If Dr. Void explained how to get you out of here, I wasn't paying attention."

Rez scowls. "Your friends are assholes, dude."

"Yeah …"

Beneath all the thunder and the wailing of the wind is another sound. It comes at us in threes, fast and insistent. It's a knocking sound, and at first, I think some board has been pulled loose and is banging against the side of one of the container habitats. But then it comes again, this time faster. Rez and I exchange curious looks. When it comes again, it's louder, coming from the shipping container we were just in. I turn and look back inside.

Boom-boom-boom!

The door with the sigil written on it. With each knock, it rattles against the flimsy lock holding it in place.

"What is that?" Rez asks over the noise.

We run inside. A column of dot matrix printer paper extends from the stack on the floor and out into the red sky, dancing like a streamer, and reaching for the heart of the storm. Rez and I stand in front of the old door and I stare at the symbol, waiting for it to spark or to glow with some arcane magic. But it's just faded chalk.

The door rattles again. A voice yells at us from the other side. It's muffled, but the urgency is sharp and clear. Outside, other voices come into focus. The words of the ancient tongue grow louder. Each syllable becomes a tangible thing. It's the voice of machines screeching in agony. It's a chorus of insects with human faces.

Tug'at. Mugrub azzitharux.

It slides beneath my skin and wraps around my bones. I can feel it prickling in the back of my brain. Rez steadies herself with a hand on the wall. The blood drains from her face.

I pull at the padlock on the door. Rusty as it is, it won't give. Through the tempest of papers, I search around for something—a hammer, a fire extinguisher, a rock—anything to break the lock. I make do with the stray leg of a tripod, wedging it between the lock's shanks and putting my weight into it. The lock warps and finally gives under force. It clatters to the ground, and I step back.

Zeke will be there with his knife and a steely-eyed *Let's get out of here* look.

Alan will be on the other side, but it won't be Alan.

The Lazlos, clapping and grinning.

Rez's nails dig into my arm. The door flies open.

Harvey is standing there, face white with fear.

"Harvey?" I ask. "What are you doing here?"

"Something goddamn stupid. Why the hell are you just standing there? We've got to go!" he yells.

161

\*\*\*

# CHAPTER EIGHTEEN

I wake up to screaming. I can't move my arms. I can't breathe. The light hurts my eyes as shapes move in and out of focus. Finally, breath comes in great, strangled gasps. Feeling the Storm's embrace, I try to kick free of it. The grip on my arms squeezes tighter.

"I got you, bro. We're good. We're all good," Zeke says into my ear, holding me down.

The pressure around my arms loosens, and I'm able to move again. I taste copper dripping down my lips and onto my tongue, a fresh nosebleed. Zeke lets go of me but keeps a warm hand on my shoulder as he steps around so I can see him.

"Sorry. You started to fight," he says as he removes his headphones. "You okay?"

I nod and realize I'm digging my nails into the arm rests of the chair. When I release, my knuckles ache. Next to me, Rez quivers beneath the straps. The light above her pulses with a relentless strobe. I swat it aside. The armature swings wide and smacks against the wall, but the disco flashes continue. Rez blinks away tears as I undo her restraints.

"Dr. Void?" I ask Zeke.

He looks around and shakes his head. "She ran. It got pretty intense while you were taking a nap."

He nods to the Plexiglas of the protective chamber. It's webbed with cracks. Beyond it, the crowd of people squirm among pools of vomit and toppled-over chairs. Some stagger to their feet, covering their eyes and sobbing quietly. The room is heavy with the silence of the aftermath. Sitting in the front row is a charred corpse. Every inch of flesh and clothing is blackened, and as I try to understand what I'm seeing the odor of cooked meat fills my nostrils.

"Yeah," Zeke says. "Dude straight up just caught on fire."

"I was going to ask if you wanted to get barbecue after this, but now I'm thinking I'll just have a salad."

"Word."

We help Rez off the bed. She wipes away streaks of mascara as she tries to find her footing.

"We got you. Slow now," Zeke says. "Slow."

"I'm fine," she says, her voice sharpening at the end.

We let her go. When we step out of the listening chamber and into the basement, it's like climbing out of a fallout shelter. The odors of piss and puke compete with the charred meat of the man sitting placidly in his seat. His program is still in his hand, unburnt. On the wall, a pipe has ruptured. Its side burst open, and a steady trickle of wriggling grub worms spills out onto the woman beneath. As the grubs rain down into her hair and decorate her clothes, she walks face first into the brick wall, over and over. She doesn't say a word. Each time she hits the wall, the bloody smear left by her ruined face gets a little wider.

Among the traumatized audience, more sobs break out, mingled with raspy, haggard wails. Some guests try to get to their feet. Others just sit on their knees, their eyes glossy and unfocused. Maybe they see the gathering Storm. Lying on his side in the back of the room, Rupert Lazlo paws at the floor. His tongue lolls out of his mouth as he tries to dig through the concrete with his fingertips. I can't make out his mumbling.

"Yeah. Y'all did this," Zeke says.

"What do you mean?" I ask.

"Both of you were quiet. Then you started to mumble. I thought that would be a great time to listen to some Thunder Hag. Glad I did, 'cause when you two got to screaming, that's when shit got real," Zeke says.

"Where's Harvey?" I ask.

"Harvey? Harvey ain't here."

I take another look around the room for him, but I know I won't see him. He was never here. Not really. Rez lays eyes on Kitty Lazlo. Kitty is across the room in her motorized cart, parked next to Rupert. She reaches down and tugs at his shirt, but he's focused on digging a hole in the floor. His fingers are starting to leave thin streaks of blood on the concrete. Kitty looks up at us, and lines of hate are carved into her face. With her bouffant wig askew on her head and her heavy mascara streaking down her aged cheeks, she looks like a Muppet from hell.

"You fat-headed dummies!" she says to us, hissing.

She fumbles with the controls on her chair and navigates the sprawled bodies all around.

"You poop-faced wieners!" she says, rolling right up to us.

"Umm. Excuse me?" Zeke asks.

"You don't understand what you've done! You've gotten in the way of science, of discovery. Of bringing peace to the world! We only want to end all this pain! I thought better of the two of you, Clark. This is important work, and you nincompoops come in here and make a mess of things. I'm so mad I could spit! Brother and I spent so much time and money and you just—"

Rez lashes out and nails Kitty in the jaw. The old woman's head snaps back. Her wig falls to the floor, revealing a patchy and scabrous scalp. Her eyes roll back in her head as she tries to recover, and a tendril of blood spills over her bottom lip.

"Nice right!" Zeke says to Rez and examines her form. "Use your hips next time. Put some force behind it and you can take this old bitch's jaw clean off."

"He's right," I say. "I've seen him do it."

He gets next to Rez and widens his stance, pivoting at the waist to demonstrate. Rez just watches Kitty's head roll on her shoulders as the old woman's fingers fumble across the reddening bruise on her chin.

"My friends did a job for you today," Rez says. "Pay them."

"I ..." Kitty starts, wheezing. "The heck I will. They're not getting a —"

Rez parts her feet and puts her weight into another blow, just like Zeke showed her. This one lands across Kitty's cheek with a sharp *crack!* Kitty's head whips to the side. She yowls with pain as her hand flies up to cover the blow. Rez shakes her hand and kisses the knuckles as she winces.

"Good!" Zeke says and claps. "Ordinarily I wouldn't encourage violence against the disabled, but you're already showing improvement. Beast mode!"

Kitty, still upright in her wheelchair, is speechless and glassy-eyed. Rez may have knocked something loose.

She leans in close to Kitty and barely raises her voice above a whisper. "You owe Occultex Incorporated money for services rendered. I'll have an invoice to you tomorrow afternoon. Pay up. Or I'm going to come knocking on your door. You hear me?"

Rez turns and heads for the stairs. She doesn't look back. As Zeke and I follow, Zeke calls back to Kitty, "She ain't playin'! Y'all don't make me send her after you. I'm gonna teach her how to kick just so she can put that foot up your old ass. You just wait."

Outside, the parking lot isn't much better. A few cars have left, but others are sitting with their engines running. The driver of a BMW is leaning her head out of an open window, dry heaving. A few other guests wander around the parking lot. It's not a big area, but they're lost, weeping and staring off into space. The cats prance around them, curious and ignored.

"Fuck 'em," Zeke says as we step out into the night.

Rez looks down at her clothes. She's wearing stretchy pants and a baggy t-shirt from a local coffee joint. She's not even wearing shoes.

"You good, girl?" Zeke says.

Rez doesn't look up. She just stares down at the shirt before finally throwing her hands in the air. "I left the house like this?"

The tears come. Rez slumps down to the curb. We slide our arms under hers and let her down gently as she breaks into pieces. She cries into her hands. Zeke sits next to her and throws an arm over her shoulder.

"I didn't think anyone was coming for me," she says, and it's all I can do not to walk back inside and punch Kitty myself.

Zeke pulls a knife from the sheath around his ankle. It's Mina. He flips it around and presents Rez with the handle. "You want to go back in there? I won't stop you, sister."

She laughs and sniffs away the tears. "No. I think I just want to go home."

"I changed my mind," I say as I fish the keys from my pocket. "I think I do want barbeque."

\*\*\*

# EPILOGUE

They paid us. It wasn't a penny more than we agreed, but I'm surprised we saw any of it. I guess the Lazlos really didn't want Rez paying them a visit. I can say with certainty that it was the right call. Rez invites us over a lot more than she used to. Her life is a mystery to us. I know she has other friends—people from work or yoga buddies—but they never come around. Every day, on her lunch break, I get a text from her. Usually she's complaining, bitching at me about little things. I'm always late. She's hungover. Zeke ate all her plantain chips. Any excuse to make sure we're still out there. At first, she made excuses to hang out with us. She worked up a business plan for Occultex or she needs help cleaning the white goo out of her townhouse. Zeke and I don't say anything about it, to her or each other. We know the score. The first few nights, we slept on the couches in her living room. She was upstairs by the time I drifted off, but when I awoke, she was down there with us, curled up in an armchair and wrapped in a blanket. After that, she'd find some reason to call. She never asked for help, never admitted that she would dream about the Storm and whatever came with it. But I see it. Every day. Every conversation. Her eyes glaze, and she's back there on that concrete pad, surrounded by shipping containers. The Storm keeps getting closer.

Tonight, it's 3:00 a.m., and she's rearranging furniture while I play video games. I shift and lean, trying to see around her as she compares different paint swatches to her furniture.

"Do you think Clay Pot?" she says, holding a rust-colored sample next to her rug. Before I can answer, she switches it out. "Or Charcoal? I'm kind of drifting back to Charcoal."

"I wish I gave enough of a shit to bother answering you," I tell her.

"Dude, don't be a dick. Just help me."

"Charcoal."

"Hmm," she says and scrunches up her face. "I don't know."

I pause the game and put down the controller. "Are you okay?"

"Huh?" she says and turns to me.

"Are you okay? I know we haven't talked about this and believe me, I'm really not sure if I want to, but … are you okay?"

She's back on her hands and knees before I finish, scrubbing at the baseboards with a rag. "Yeah, I'm good," she says. "But this white shit will *not* come out. I think I might send those assholes a bill for having my floors redone."

She gives the wall a vigorous scrub, pauses to inspect her progress, then scrubs again at some spot on the wall that I'm not sure is really there. I just watch her, all too aware that she's avoiding looking at me. Before I can un-pause my game, there's a knock at the door. My heart leaps into my throat. I never know what to expect with unannounced guests. A visit from the UPS guy makes me grab something to defend myself and hide behind the couch.

Rez jumps up with manic energy. "Got it! Got it! Got it!"

She opens the door, but I can't hear the exchange with the person on the other side. When Rez turns to face me, the mania of fixing her house is gone. In its place is a dour look, one I haven't seen since she punched Kitty Lazlo.

"There's a weird old lady on my front steps. She wants to talk to you," she says, and tosses her cleaning rag onto the floor. "I'm tired of you two bringing creepy old people into my life. For real."

I'm on my feet before I know it. This was what I was waiting for, the kind of thing that keeps me up at night. Outside, I picture a Cavendish van waiting for me or a carload full of Helpers. Something in the back of my mind warned me that the bill for that day was going to come due, but I let myself buy into Rez's salve of domesticity. I kind of believed that if she picked the right shade of paint, we could just put all of this behind us.

And there *is* a white van waiting outside. Perched halfway on the sidewalk, the engine ticks hot. Sitting on Rez's steps, barefoot and smoking a cigarette, is Bela Koth.

She doesn't say anything. I look back over my shoulder and shout back into Rez's house. "Hey, Zeke? Bela's here!"

Zeke comes barreling down the stairs in a bath towel, his eyes blazing. He also has a sword.

"Why do you have a sword?" I ask him as he joins me in the doorway.

He nods to Bela. "Why do you not?"

She takes a languorous drag on her cigarette and basks in the plumes of smoke from her cracked lips. In her hand is her remaining mask. I guess she used it to drive over here.

She doesn't look at me when she says, "You owe me a favor."

"Yeah."

"Yeah," she says and takes another drag. "You said the Lazlos are writin' themselves that book of spells, the Voice of the Storm?"

"That's right."

"And those spells are all on cassette tapes."

"They are."

"I got me a cassette player."

"Ok, but—"

"You said you got access to the Lazlos. Well … I want them tapes."

"Bela ..." I start to say.

"You owe me. I reckon I saved your bacon, ain't that right?"

"Yeah. I guess it is."

"I guess it is," she says. "Well, you're gonna march into Candle House and steal them tapes for me. Ever last one of them."

I look over to my friends. Zeke raises his eyebrows at me and lowers his massive sword. Rez grins. I can't help but smile back.

"So ..." I say to them both. "You guys want to pull a heist on a haunted house?"

## THE END

# AFTERWORD

Want to read the next adventures of The Occult Technologies, Incorporated gang? Look for Occultex Book Three; *Robbing A Haunted House.*

# ABOUT THE AUTHOR

Jason Murphy lives in Texas and spends most of his time writing novels, screenplays, video games, narrative podcasts, and comics. When not researching or writing about tradecraft, the occult, or the fantastic, he can be found spending time with his family, reading, or watching movies. He collects records, PEZ dispensers, Star Wars stuff, and Conan comics. He can occasionally be lured out of his lair with the promise of barbecue/tacos and good conversation.

Made in the USA
Las Vegas, NV
02 March 2024

86623965R00098